CHARLIE DICKENS'

DOCUMENTS

MERCEDES MYSTERIES #2

Peg Herring

ISBN: 9781944502225

CHAPTER ONE

CREWE HALL, CHESHIRE, 1819

Charles loved hide and seek at Grandmother's. Crewe Hall, the great mansion where she served as housekeeper, was huge, with a long, tiled gallery lined with arched doorways and rooms along the way filled with dark hulks of furniture perfect for concealing a boy somewhat small for his age. Their space was limited to the servants' area when the family was in residence, but Charles liked it best when they were in London and he could hide anywhere he liked: in the great hall with its high windows, intricate ceiling, and massive fireplace, in the library lined with shelf after shelf of books, or in one of the many bedrooms upstairs with canopied beds and wide, airy windows. Fanny was older and better at the game, knowing her little brother's favorite places. Today Charles was determined to remain hidden till dark and give his sister a terrible fright.

Moving on tiptoe, the boy climbed the latticed stairway and crouch-walked along the railing until he came to the entryway to the upper story. Here were huge, overhanging beams and odd sized doorways, some taller than Grandfather, some shorter, and some slightly out of square. Charles had never ventured higher than the servants' quarters before today, and he noted the inward slant of walls directly under the roof. At one window he peered out at a stretch of garden below. Petrie the gardener was there, on hands and knees as he pulled weeds from a bed of pinks. Charles felt suddenly powerful. He who was so small, so weak, looked down on them all from his lofty viewpoint.

A sudden pinch at his shoulder made the boy turn, and his eyes widened at the sight of the creature that held him in her grasp. Panic surged through him. He should call for help; he should run back to Fanny; he should visit the water closet. In the end he only stared. The lurid tales Grandmother told at bedtime often left him cringing in the dark of night. Charles prayed he'd awake and find himself in his room any second now, the figure before him only a bad dream.

The woman's musty smell convinced Charles she was not a dream. Her hair was white and thin, wisping about her head however it would. The face so close to his own was lined with years and, it seemed, care. Her clothing, of another age, showed wear at the elbows and wrists. The hem was tattered where it trailed the floor, as if the gown had once been worn by someone taller.

He'd seen old women before, of course, so it was not this one's age that made him so fearful. Something told him she was mad, and not with the serene madness of his neighbor Mrs. Millicent, who forgot her children's names and put her hat on backward. This woman's eyes shone with an anger that terrified him as her gnarled fingers dug painfully into his shoulder.

"Where is the head?" she demanded. She spoke in English, but her accent was thick with the rolled *r*'s and distorted vowels of the French. Her stale breath caused him to pull back, shuddering, but the crone took no notice. "Is it done?"

Charles remembered his manners. They were servants at the hall, at least Grandmother was, and he'd been schooled to be at his most polite. "I-I can't say, ma'am," he stammered.

"They've hung it on the gates by now." The anger in her face died, and the voice took on a keening tone. "Ah, *ma pauvre*, to have died so!"

He didn't contradict the madwoman, didn't explain there'd been no recent deaths by beheading in Cheshire or anywhere else he knew of. To pacify her he said, "Such a thing would be very sad."

"Sad?" The crone's face changed again, and her voice rose. "Not sad, no. It is treason!" Her pale eyes squinted, and her bottom lip tightened, pressing upward almost to her nose. "To kill a king is against the law of God Himself!" Grabbing his other shoulder,

6

she shook the boy as if to jostle understanding into him.

"Yes, ma'am." He felt tears rise as he pictured himself the prisoner of this terrifying person for days, maybe weeks. What if they never found him at all? What if they thought he'd run away?

Just then a voice came from below. "Boy! Come down this instant." Grandmother was angry, but he'd never heard anything as beautiful as the sound of her voice.

The old woman released him, glancing from side to side as if looking for an escape. "I must go," the boy said, trying not to show the relief he felt.

"Come again. Please." Her voice turned pleading. "I mean you no harm. I, I..." She looked around desperately. "I once had a boy of my own."

Suddenly she seemed less frightening, more frightened, and Charles, whose heart was kind, softened toward her. "I will," he promised.

With a sharp nod that said it was a bargain, the woman scuttled down the hallway and disappeared into a room. As a door slammed behind her, the boy hurried to the ladder. "Here I am, Grandmother."

She was frowning. "You should not go exploring without permission."

"I'm sorry," Charles said as he backed down to her level. "But who is that lady? She was frightful at first, but then she seemed very sad."

Grandmother looked up the ladder, putting an arm around his thin frame. "Someday I shall tell you about *Tante* Claudine," she promised, "but it's not a story for ears so young." With that she led him to his sister and to their luncheon of cheese and bread, with freshly picked strawberries to delight them afterward.

Chapter Two

Detroit, Michigan, Today

Mercedes was unlocking the door to her apartment when the phone in her purse signaled a call. The "Scotland the Brave" ringtone she'd chosen for Colm was screechy, and she vowed for the twentieth time to find something less blatant. Setting down the groceries she carried, she dug the phone out of her purse and stopped the clamor. "Mister Kennedy," she said, slightly out of breath. "Greetings from America."

"I didn't think anyone ran for the phone these days, what with the mind-boggling number of communication devices per capita on your side of the pond." The hum of traffic in the background told her Colm was on the highway, or at least near it.

"I was wondering when you'd call."

There was the slightest pause before he answered, but his voice remained light. "The lines—or satellite beams, I suppose—run both ways."

Mercedes began putting items into their correct places. If he'd seen, Colm would have teased her about her need for order. Her answer would have been that it was just as easy to talk and work as it was to simply talk.

"With your crazy schedule and the time difference, I never know if you're sleeping or in the middle of a rehearsal or doing a show," she defended herself. "I, on the other hand, have no life, so you may call at your convenience."

It was a sore spot. After she was swept up in a treasure hunt while on vacation in England, she'd found her life drastically changed, and not all to the good. She'd almost been murdered, but she'd met Colm Kennedy in the process. That was good, at least it had been for a while.

"How was September in beautiful Edinburgh?" she asked.

"Rain so steady the castle would have floated away were it not so high. Two shows in Birmingham ended the tour, and I'm on my way back to London."

"And were the audiences charmed and amazed at your talent?"

"How could they not be?" He used an exaggerated thespian voice, round with deep vowels.

Though talented, Colm didn't see himself as the next John Gielgud. He loved the theater, and in particular Shakespearean comedy. Having seen him as Petruchio in *The Taming of the Shrew* and Robin Goodfellow in *A Midsummer Night's Dream*, Mercedes thought he played them as Shakespeare intended, as individuals full of fun.

"And now you're free of this year's circuit of theatricals?"

"Will be on Thursday, after we debrief and evaluate."

Mercedes paused. "And then?"

Colm's voice betrayed the grin she couldn't see. "I thought I might come a-visiting Detroit, if you haven't anything else in the works."

Her pulse quickened at the suggestion, apparently casual but heavy with possibilities. So much had been left unsaid between them over the last six months, things better discussed and decided in person than on the phone. "I'd love to have a visitor from Scotland, but only if he brings shortbread."

Colm sighed dramatically. "I might have known you were

only having me on all this time. And to think it was me biscuits that caught your fancy."

"That and your stunning resemblance to a Greek god."

"Don't you mean a Scottish leprechaun?" Picturing his pleasant face and the lock of light brown hair that often fell onto his forehead, Mercedes admitted he was a little of both.

"Leprechaun or not, just hurry and get here."

"You could have come to Scotland."

The question of where they might be together stood between them like the Atlantic itself. Did Colm want her to move to Scotland permanently? Would he give up his growing popularity in Britain to live with her in the States? They had no answers to those questions, because neither had the nerve to ask them.

Early on in their relationship, Mercedes had feared they'd been drawn to each other only by the danger they shared. Now she recognized that on her part at least, it was more than that. She wanted to be where Colm was, wanted to be with him, whatever it took to make that happen. But Colm avoided talking about what they were to each other or what they might become in the long term. Once he'd brushed the subject aside a few times, pride kept Mercedes from bringing it up again. She would not be the type of woman lampooned on sitcoms, demanding, "We need to talk about our future."

Keeping her voice light she answered, "Only ask, O Master of My Desire, and I will come to you!" As she said it, she recalled the nights they'd spent together. Her words were true, though spoken fancifully. In a different tone she added, "But I can't come today. I have a dental appointment."

"Then I'll have to come to you, but not today. I too have an appointment."

"A pretty lassie with a lust for Scottish actors?"

"Those the doorman lines up by the back entrance, and I send down me sweaty hankies." When she snorted he went on, "This appointment is with a funny little man by the name of Dickens."

"As in Charles?"

"A distant relative, he claims. I'm to call him Charlie for the sake of clarity."

"Hmm. Charlie Dickens sounds like a bratty schoolboy."

"Oh, no, Charlie's prim and very proper."

"And is he a moneyed gentleman who might back a new production?"

"Afraid not. If Charlie's an example, *Hard Times* isn't merely a book. It's the story of the family fortunes since the famous Dickens died. Lots of pride and no means."

"From what I've read there was a general inability in the family to live within their means." She began shifting eggs from carton to refrigerator. "What brought you and this little Dickens together?"

"You did, indirectly. Mr. Dickens had a job he wanted done, and your pal Lonnie told him you were just the one to do it. Since you're all the way across the blue Atlantic, Lonnie gave my name as his second choice."

"Lonnie?" Blue-haired with lots of body art, Lonnie had been at first a conspirator and later a helper as Colm and Mercedes searched the answers to a Shakespearean puzzle.

"His hair is a shrieking white now, or was when last I saw him."

"I suppose this Dickens has a sure-fire scheme for quadrupling the money I got for the letter." After solving "The Riddle of Shakespeare's Blood," as the newspapers dubbed it, Mercedes had been given a letter in Shakespeare's own handwriting. Since then she'd been bombarded with offers, pleas, and scams designed to separate her from the money she'd received from its sale to a museum. Though she'd insisted Colm deserved a share of the sale, he'd refused to take a cent.

"Nothing to do with the Bard," Colm replied to her comment. "Dickens wanted advice about some mysterious papers of his own."

"Ah, mysterious papers!"

Colm chuckled at her doubtful tone. "I felt I owed him a hearing, since Lonnie had built us up so grandly. His papers also pertain to a literary lion."

"Which?"

Colm's tone turned chiding. "I've said his name is Dickens, haven't I? Charlie makes a meager living as a souvenir vendor, and he keeps what he calls his 'Dickens Documents' in a display case as a way of garnering interest in his shop. Not one of the items is in Dickens' handwriting. In fact, they predate anything he might have written, but the great man did once own them, and they are old. Charlie does with what he has."

"Is it family stuff?"

"I didn't see a connection. Anyhow, Charlie wants to sell the papers. He'd put up an advert, but Lonnie convinced him it would be wise to do some research before going further with the deal."

"Lonnie's become an expert on antique documents?"

"Apparently he thinks so. He sold Charlie on the idea either you or I could—and would—look into the papers and assess their value."

"So you took the case?"

Colm hesitated before answering, and Mercedes realized too late he'd taken it as a criticism that she hadn't been consulted. Those proud Scots!

"Dickens wanted someone to go to Scotland, and I was headed there anyway. I told him if he didn't mind settling for second best, I'd look into it."

There was a ring of hurt in the words, and Mercedes wondered again if there was hope for them as a couple. Colm was uncomfortable with her new-found wealth, but what was she supposed to do if he wouldn't take a share?

"Though Charlie sees me as Robin to your Batman or Tonto to your Lone Ranger, he agreed to let me look into the matter." Colm's tone was amused but a bit aggrieved as well. Media reports had all but omitted mention of Colm or Mercedes' other companion, David Cutler. Papers sold better when the headlines trumpeted: *Lone Woman Tourist Foils Killer, Finds Shakespeare's Secrets.*

"You'll be more help than I'd have been." She lightened the mood with a teasing complaint. "Then you'll be seeing Charlie before you see me?"

The tension in his voice relaxed a little. "Don't be jealous, but yes. I'm to meet him this evening to give a full report."

"You found something?"

"It's a bit of a jumble right now, but it's an intriguing mystery. I have one more stop to make on my way south."

"Then the papers are valuable, even if they don't relate to Dickens?"

"No buried treasure maps or secret messages, but the story is compelling. By the time I get there, I should have it all figured out."

"Sounds intriguing. Another reason for me to be eager for your visit."

Colm chuckled, a sound Mercedes loved. "Since I'm free between now and Thursday, I plan to drive to Salisbury and see what your other boyfriend can make of what I've learned. He's a fount of information on many topics."

"David will get a kick out of the Dickens connection."

"I'm not sure of that," Colm commented. "The French Revolution is modern history to that old reprobate."

"Point taken." David Cutler centered his scholarly studies on the Renaissance and saw little of interest in the world since the 1600s.

"Still," Colm said," I thought I'd see if he's willing to take a look."

"Be sure to give him my love."

"I will."

"And don't miss your flight to the States," she warned in closing. "It's nice that you're interested in Dickens, but our tale of two cities had better end in Detroit or I'll come to London myself!"

***

LONDON

Charlie Dickens was unpacking figurines from a box when a visitor came into the shop, causing a small silver bell mounted above the door to tinkle discreetly. Pausing with a Miss Havisham in one hand and a Jarvis Lorry in the other, Dickens looked up, irritated by the distraction.

What he saw caused him to set the figures down, draw himself more erect, and adjust the front of his frock coat with one hand while he pulled off the half-glasses resting at the end of his nose with the other. Laying the glasses aside, he put a pleasant expression on his pinched face.

The woman who approached the sales counter was attractive, to say the least. Long, dark-red hair fell around her face and brushed her shoulders. She wore a trench coat appropriate for a damp, cool afternoon, dark trousers, and low-heeled shoes. After she fought the breeze to close the shop door with a prolonged scrape, she pushed swept a hand through her heavy mane from brow to nape. The waves settled nicely into place, framing an intelligent face.

"May I be of assistance?" Dickens' tilted his head to one side, an unconscious habit.

"I hope so." Her voice was as impressive as her appearance. "Are you Mr. Charles Dickens?"

"I am." He made a courtly little bow, adding, "Usually called Charlie, to distinguish myself from the more eminent Charles."

The woman smiled at his little joke, but he noticed her eyes didn't warm. "I understand you have papers that once belonged to him."

Dickens' expression tightened. "That's true, but I'm afraid the situation has changed since I placed the advertisement on-line. The papers are not for sale at this time."

Her smooth brow furrowed briefly and her right shoulder shifted under the coat. "Then I've come a long way for nothing."

"I'm sorry." Dickens was relieved to see she wasn't going to make a fuss. "I hired a man to evaluate their worth, and he called just this afternoon to advise me to hold onto them a bit longer."

The redhead leaned closer, and Charlie caught the scent of expensive perfume. "The advert said 'Miscellaneous documents from the late 1700s to the early 1800s, some in French, belonging to Dickens but not pertaining to him.' Why did that require further evaluation?"

Charlie shrugged, unsure of the answer to that. The papers had been in his family for generations, and no one had ever cared much. "When he burned the rest of his papers in 1860, Charles kept these for some reason. My researcher says they might be historically important, though he doubts they shed new light on my ancestor."

She looked at him as if trying to decide something. "And this man convinced you not to sell."

Dickens hesitated, confused. It had been only a few hours since Kennedy called, almost ordering him not to sell the papers. He was driving down from the north, he'd said. "If you need money so badly, I'll give you a fair price for the papers myself when I get there."

Still, Charlie was dubious about turning down the living, breathing prospect before him. His shop was badly in need of an influx of cash, and he'd been willing to take almost any amount for the Dickens documents. Kennedy insisted he'd explain when he got there, but here she stood, warming his blood with the heat of her gaze. No one had cared about his cache of papers for two hundred years, and now two offers in one afternoon. Of course, he knew and trusted Colm Kennedy to offer a fair price. He didn't know this woman.

Seemingly able to read his mind, she gave him a slow smile

that made sweat pop out on his brow. "I'm willing to offer cash, Mr. Dickens."

He licked his lips. "Mr. Kennedy said I shouldn't."

She raised an eyebrow. "What could he possibly have found in those papers that no one's known all this time?"

He couldn't resist sharing a little of what Colm had told him. "We think Mr. Dickens used the information in those pages for the writing of perhaps his greatest work, *A Tale of Two Cities*. Colm says there might be interest in what the three different sources as a whole reveal about the French Revolution."

Her eyes hardened a little. "This man who advised you to keep the papers is an expert on that time period?"

"No." Charlie folded his hands on the counter. "Mr. Kennedy is an actor, but he has some experience with such matters. Once I speak with him I'll decide whether to sell or not and what the price will be." His gaze went to the display case between them, where the papers lay scattered attractively on a bright blue cloth.

The woman stepped back to look. Charlie had placed brightly-painted figurines along the edges: David Copperfield, Smike, Little Nell, and other characters from Dickens' stories. "Very nice," she said.

Charlie smiled professionally. "It's what I do, you see, give folks a bit of a feel for the man and his works."

She was examining the papers. "You gave this Mr. Kennedy copies?"

"Yes." He brushed the black coat he wore with a white shirt and black silk tie. He even affected the great man's beard, though his was somewhat sparse. "I suppose if he's correct and the papers really are of value, I'll have to put them somewhere more secure." He glanced at the clock on the wall. "Why don't you leave me your telephone number? I'd be happy to call you if I decide to sell after all."

She didn't move. "I think I'll wait with you until your man arrives."

"Oh, I didn't mean to—" It was all Charlie Dickens managed to say before the woman raised the gun she'd been holding in her pocket and shot him in the forehead.

Forty-two minutes later, the shop door opened. The man who entered was of medium height and squarely-built, with tawny, overlong hair and green eyes. When he saw the woman standing behind the counter, he paused for a moment in the doorway.

"Charlie Dickens is no longer available, Colm," she said softly. "Now you and I have all the time in the world to discuss what we should do with the Dickens Documents."

CHAPTER THREE

CREWE HALL, CHESHIRE, JULY, 1824

The boy walked the estate, picking up items of interest: stones with eye-catching hues and leaves of kinds he hadn't seen before. The day was mild, and the sun on his shoulders soothing, so he didn't notice how far he'd come until he stopped and looked around. Trees blocked his view of the huge, redbrick house with its high windows. He couldn't see even one of the numerous chimneys, the finials that spiked its roof, or the single tower that pointed to the sky. Charles didn't mind. He felt at home at Crewe and knew the grounds as well as he knew the house.

Suddenly a figure separated from the grove ahead of him. "You, there! Boy!" The man was a sailor, judging by his loose clothing, pigtail, and bare feet. Since his father clerked for the navy, Charles had seen many sailing men. This one's hands were not as rough as they'd have been had he handled heavy ropes. His feet were pale, meaning he usually wore shoes and stockings. Still, he moved like a seasoned tar. His voice had the rasp of orders shouted above wind and water, and the skin of his face was weathered to the color of old cowhide.

Approaching, the man took Charles by the shoulders. "Do you come from Crewe Hall?"

"Yes, sir." He gestured backward clumsily. "My grandmother is housekeeper there."

His eyes narrowed as he looked in the direction indicated. "And who is in the house today?"

"Just us, sir. His lordship took the family to London. He said Fanny and I might stay."

"Who is in the house?" The repetition was impatient.

Charles tried to think, but it was difficult, since the man gripped him tightly. He seemed unaware of it, so intent was he on his questions. He was agitated, both eager and cautious at once.

"Fanny and Grandmother are there," Charles told him. "Mr. Billups and his wife. Three maids—Edith, Kitty, and Beth, and two grooms, Peter and William."

"And who else?"

"No one—" Charles' lips trembled. Tante and her maid were at home, but he'd been ordered not to talk about her.

The man knelt to look into his eyes. "You did not mention the old woman."

Relieved that the man already knew, Charles nodded. "Yes, sir. Tante Claudine is there, with Meg."

"Ah!" The sailor released him so quickly Charles had to step backward to keep his balance. He wanted to rub his shoulders where the man's fingers had dug in, but he didn't.

"What does she look like, this Claudine? Like this?" The sailor pulled a miniature from his pocket and held it out to the boy, the gesture abrupt, as if the portrait were a weapon. The boy shied a little but regarded the picture carefully, unsure whether an affirmative or a negative reply would win his release from the uncomfortable interview.

"Not like that, sir, no. She is very old." The man's brows dipped and the boy searched for something encouraging. "But the frame is very like one she wears around her neck, very like it indeed."

"The frame?"

"Yes, sir, but that portrait is not of a woman. It is a boy, her little boy. He is dead now. At least that's what she says." Not everything Tante Claudine said was true, but as mournful as she was when she spoke of her son, she was probably right about his being dead.

"It is not true." The sailor's tone was surprisingly gentle.

Like Tante herself, the sailor seemed suddenly less frightening and more tragic, as if life had not turned out the way he'd imagined it. After a moment though, his peremptory manner returned and he grabbed Charles' shoulder again. "Can you visit Tante Claudine?"

"Yes, sir, sometimes I do, on her better days."

The man brought his face so close that the boy recoiled in fear once more. "Can you speak to her alone, give a message no one else hears?"

Charles thought about that. Since the day he met Claudine while playing hide-and-seek, he'd come to know her fairly well. Though he pitied her, he couldn't say he enjoyed her company. Tante made sense only occasionally and, like this man, held onto a person when she wanted his attention.

Afraid to disappoint the hard-looking sailor he said solemnly, "I might be able to, when Meg is at some chore."

He looked away for a moment. "Can she come here to meet with me?"

"She's crippled, sir. She never leaves the attic."

"Crippled, is she?"

"Yes, sir, an accident. I think a shipwreck."

The graying head dropped. "Shipwrecked. No wonder, then."

"Sir?"

"Nothing. Return here tomorrow at the same time. Bring me something to eat and to drink, as much as you can manage." He held out a coin, as if payment would make the task easy.

Charles was thunderstruck. How was he to explain to Grandmother that he needed food to give to a vagrant? She would never agree. "I—sir, I—"

"Tell no one I am here." Releasing the boy's arm and ignoring his helpless expression, the man stalked off into the woods.

Charles stumbled away in the opposite direction, afraid to look back. The demands laid upon him were frightening, and the questions about this meeting were confusing. Who was this man, and why did he want to see Tante Claudine? She was only a crazy old woman Lord Crewe had taken pity on when she fled France during the Terror. Charles knew it had been dreadful, with people killed in the most horrible ways for no good reason. Though it happened long ago, Grandmother said it was because the French were all civility on the outside and wild beasts on the inside.

Tante Claudine's mind had been ruined by what she lived through. She grieved the loss of her family, particularly her son, which was why she so enjoyed Charles' visits. Still, he didn't like the fusty smell of the old dress she always wore. He felt cramped in her tiny sitting room, which she insisted be kept a certain way, with a collection of forlorn, mismatched items she considered suitable: a silk-upholstered chair with three legs, a mahogany table with a deep scratch across the top, and other items once grand but now disowned by the lord of Crewe Hall.

The old lady would not allow items in her rooms to be moved, so when Charles visited he had to step very carefully and sit on the narrowest edge of a wobbly chair that also held a painting of a very grand lady. He patiently endured questions about his education and lectures on deportment. Tante called him the wrong name half the time and insisted he must "take his place in the world" when the time came. Being a polite child, he always agreed with her and pretended to eat the sweets she provided, though he was too afraid of her to trust her gifts.

Sometimes hatred boiled out of Tante Claudine, and she seemed to feel the world owed her a debt that could never be repaid. On those days, Grandmother would lead Charles away, leaving the old lady spitting angry words in French.

Why did the man want to see Claudine? Grandmother said she hadn't left Crewe Hall in thirty-five years. The sailor would have been a boy like Charles when last she was part of the world. What could the two of them have to say to one another?

***

DETROIT, TODAY

Colm didn't answer the phone all day Wednesday or the next morning, though Mercedes left several messages. A niggling fear grew each time she got no response. *He's found someone else. He's decided it won't work. He was never as interested in me as I was in him.*

The phone jarred her from her dull reverie, but caller ID said *Unknown*. She almost ignored it but on the fifth ring picked up with an abrupt movement that almost set her glass of water toppling. "Hello?"

"Mercedes, it's Colm Kennedy." His tone was formal.

"Colm, what—"

"I need you to do something for me, and it's very important."

"Of course, but—"

"Listen, Mercedes!" Was he angry with her? "You are going to receive a packet in the mail from me. I need you to return it without opening it."

"If that's what you want, but"

"It's what I want. Sorry to bother you at home on your day off, but it's rather important."

Her day off? "Don't worry. I'll send it back."

"Unopened. That's essential."

"All right, Colm." Mercedes felt resentful that he felt he had to repeat the instruction.

"Good, then. Remember what I've said."

"Colm," she felt like a fool but had to ask. "Are you still coming here?"

In the moment it took for his answer, dread settled in.

Mercedes knew she was about to be brushed off. Finally he said, "I'll be as honest with you as I was that first night we met. I don't want to see you again." The call ended, and he was gone.

She looked accusingly at the phone for a moment, as if it had somehow colluded with her arrogant lover. *Former lover*, she corrected. Colm had changed his mind about them working together on Dickens' papers and also about his trip to Detroit. His heart had apparently turned away from all things where she was concerned.

How hard would it be now to turn her own heart in a new direction, to evict from it the love she felt for Colm Kennedy, with his crooked smile and his charming manner? Neither of them had been very good at expressing their feelings, and she'd obviously misjudged his attachment to her. For pride's sake, Mercedes hoped he'd underestimated how much their time together meant to her.

***

Somewhere Outside London

Colm handed the phone to the woman who sat beside him on the bed. "You did well, lover."

He didn't answer, and she ran a hand along his jaw-line teasingly. "Was it hard to give up your little American girlfriend?"

"She's nothing to me," Colm replied. "Chance threw us together, but things didn't work out."

"That's good," she said with a smile, pushing her hair back from her face with a practiced hand. "It would be a shame if we had to hurt her."

CHAPTER FOUR

CREWE HALL, JULY 1824

Charles crept out the kitchen door, a loaf of bread under one arm and his pockets stuffed with whatever had met his low line of sight: a hunk of cheese, a leftover tart, and a cucumber from a basket gathered for pickling. He made his way to the buttery, making sure no one was inside then slipping in to grab the first bottle he found. He darted past the shed and through the garden, so intent on keeping his load balanced and his feet under him that he didn't see Grandmother until he almost ran into her. She stood, arms akimbo and face like a stone.

"Where are you going with all that, boy?"

Exaggeration Charles could manage, but he had no talent for real deception. And a face-to-face lie to his beloved grandmother? Impossible. He tried evasion instead.

"I need it, Grandmother, really I do."

"Need it! No boy needs that much! And stealing my wine as well? You wicked thing!"

Seeing the look that came over the boy's face, her manner changed. "What's wrong, Charles?" She knelt down, and sympathy did what anger had not. The boy flung himself at her, the wine bottle clutched in his hand making an awkward bump against her shoulder.

"He says I must bring him food!" the boy sobbed. "He's frightful, Grandmother!"

"Who?" she demanded. "Who threatened you?"

"A man in the wood, a sailor, I think. He wanted to know about Tante Claudine."

She pulled back to look him in the eye. "Claudine!"

"He wanted her to meet him, but I said she never leaves the attic because of her back."

"Is he a Frenchman?"

"I'm not sure." Charles sniffled. "He knew Tante was here. I didn't tell."

Grandmother stood and paced a few steps. "Lord Crewe is in London. I don't know what's to be done."

"He said he would have a plan when I came."

"A plan? He can plan all he likes. The old woman died this morning."

Charles looked up in shock. Claudine had been part of Crewe Hall since before he was born. It was odd to think of her gone and distressing to think of the sailor's reaction when he learned of it. Charles sensed he'd come a long way to find her, and now his search was fruitless.

Grandmother gently disentangled herself from Charles and took the food and wine from him. "Go into the house and tell Meg to bring Tante Claudine's wooden box down to me. I will speak with the sailor, and he will not trouble you again."

***

DETROIT, TODAY

When the package came, it was too large for her mailbox, and Mercedes had to go to the post office counter to collect it. The sturdy container was shoebox-sized, and she wondered what Colm had sent that he now wanted back.

Her fingers itched to tear off the brown paper wrapping and look inside. He'd said she shouldn't, but their brief conversation bothered her. Colm had mentioned her day off, knowing very well she had no job. The notoriety of her adventure in England and the wealth it had provided made taking a job in her chosen field of teaching elementary school both unnecessary and problematic. It was bad enough that she got calls daily from people insisting they should help her invest her money, increase her money, or spend her money. Like a smart lottery winner, she'd hired a reputable firm to manage her new-found wealth, taken an apartment in a gated community in Farmington Hills that kept her safe from most tipsters and frauds, and invested in some pretty sophisticated technology to put layers between herself and scammers and thieves. It wasn't the way she wanted to live, but her advisor said people have short memories, and her adventures would soon be old news.

Setting the box on the visitors' counter, Mercedes considered it somewhat spitefully. What was so important about it? Did Colm even have the right to ask her to return it? It was addressed to her, so legally, she had the right to open it. With sudden decision she attacked the wrapping. He might be able to tell she'd looked, but so what? He'd just ended their relationship, coldly and without explanation.

Removing the cardboard lid, she set it aside. Inside the box was a lovely woolen scarf in autumn colors with a note that said, *To keep you warm when I'm far away.* Feeling its softness, Mercedes warmed toward Colm. It was a lovely gift. Then she remembered. She was supposed to send it back.

Under the scarf was a stack of paper, perhaps forty sheets, held in place by a large rubber band. Removing the elastic, she glanced through the top few pages. From the look of them, they were copies of old documents. Missing edges, grainy writing, and lines where creases had obliterated the message all showed with the faithful representation modern machines make of ancient pages. Some of the pages had dated entries: journals of two different people, judging by the handwriting and the different paper sizes. Last were two letters written in French in a casual manner different from the others. It must be the papers Colm had told her about, the ones assembled and saved by the more famous Charles Dickens.

On the top was a sheet of notebook paper, folded into precise thirds. The letterhead contained a Victorian skyline and the address and contact information for the What-The-Dickens Curiosity Shop. The precise schoolbook writing was as neat as she'd seen anywhere.

Dear Mr. Kennedy:

After our discussion of the enclosed documents, I am prepared to place complete trust in your integrity. Once you have perused the copies, please see what you can learn in Scotland about events mentioned therein. You may contact me at the number printed above with any information you discover. I am very hopeful you can shed new light on my ancestor's papers in a way that will benefit me financially. I will happily provide a ten percent share if the information results in a profitable sale.

Sincerely,

Charles W. Dickens

Mercedes' first reaction was amusement at the tone of the note. Following that came doubt. Colm had sent copies of what Dickens had given him, but now he wanted them back. Why? And what should she do about it?

A copy machine stood nearby, its cover yawning open. It was a good one, the kind that accepted a stack of sheets, pulled them in one by one, and spit the copies out the side. On impulse, Mercedes set the sheaf of papers into the machine and pressed *Start*. When the job was done, she folded the copies she'd made and put them into her oversized bag.

Next she put the rubber band back in place, laid the papers in the bottom of the box, and set the scarf atop them. At the counter she bought a roll of packing tape to seal the box back up. Putting a new label over the original one, she addressed it to Colm's London apartment and filled out the documents necessary to mail it overseas. Finished, she paid for the copies, postage, and tape. She felt oddly reluctant to let it go, wishing she could hand it to Colm herself and ask him what was going on.

CHAPTER FIVE

DETROIT

Carrie watched the Maxwell woman enter the post office, which was the old-fashioned brick kind, raised and closed to view from outside. She considered following her in but decided against it lest she call attention to herself. She could see both exits from her rental car, so she waited.

It took longer than expected, but a steady stream of customers came and went, so she guessed the pace inside was slow. Carrie almost fell asleep, being jet-lagged and in need of a shower, but Scylla had insisted she make sure Maxwell returned the package. She left her rental car running, letting the heater warm the biting air. Detroit was prettier than she'd expected, but she found the freeways confusing and the roads appalling. Didn't the Americans ever repair them?

Carrie tapped the steering wheel impatiently. Where was she? She hoped she hadn't missed her exit somehow. Just as she stepped out of the car to go in and see for herself, Maxwell left the post office. Her hands were empty, and the purse slung over her shoulder wasn't big enough to hide the box Colm had described. Still, she wanted to be thorough. Taking out her cell, Carrie looked up the number and made a call using her best American accent.

"This is Mercedes Maxwell. Sorry to be a pain, but I just mailed a package to England, and I feel like I might have forgotten to add my return address. Could you check? It's only been a minute, and it's important." She waited a few seconds. "I did? That takes a load off my mind. Thank you so much." Carrie stored her phone in her purse. Maxwell had done as ordered.

Back at home, Mercedes hung up her jacket then tried Colm's phone again. There was no answer, not even a prompt for voice mail. Digging the papers out of her purse, she sat down at her desk and began reading. The two letters in French were indecipherable, though she could pick out words here and there: *soeur*, which she recalled from high school was "sister;" *majeste,* which had to be something like "majesty;" and *fille*, which she thought was a female child. Other than that, she had no idea what they said.

A dozen sheets that had been clipped together in the original packet showed several months of a ship's log with dates, locations in latitude and longitude, and notations that made little sense to one with no knowledge of sailing in an earlier era. Mercedes scanned them quickly, noting some entries were about ship's business and others more personal. The latter were interesting but would take time and study to decipher, written in spiky, cramped handwriting.

Other pages, much more readable, were a physician's notes concerning a patient who, she learned from the first page, was both crippled and mad. The account began in 1793 and ended in 1824. The doctor must have been a young man when he took the case, and his notes spanned almost thirty years. They ended with the madwoman's death due to advanced age.

Doctor Jacob Hill's notes were abbreviated but written in a clear hand, and Mercedes got the impression of a caring professional charged with a difficult task. The patient had been in her thirties when he was first called to treat her. She was badly injured, and for the first few months Dr. Hill feared she would die. Over time it became clear that her body would live on, but her mind was permanently damaged. She had delusions, fits of weeping, and days of deep, black melancholy. Her condition was exacerbated by constant pain. The doctor did what he could, and it was clear from his notes that he pitied the woman he referred to as "the Invalid."

Nowhere did Mercedes find the name *Dickens*.

The journal was interesting, but between deciphering the old-fashioned terms and the blurred pages filled with handwritten script, Mercedes found it difficult going. She tried to remember what Colm had said about the papers. Charles Dickens—the eminent one—had collected them and kept them for some reason he'd never divulged to anyone. Colm had agreed to investigate the events described on these pages. He'd begun in Scotland, though she didn't find it mentioned anywhere in Doctor Hill's notes. The doctor was English, and the letters came from France.

She turned back to the captain's log. The ship he owned was called the *Thistle,* and since it was the symbol of Scotland and his name was MacPherson, she guessed both ship and captain were Scots. In terse form he described his latest voyage to France, where he was asked to wait at a certain spot for two passengers. It sounded like he'd made such trips before, and he was careful not to identify his precise destination or who'd paid for his services. People were dying at Madame Guillotine, and Mercedes guessed that in a small but courageous way, Captain MacPherson had worked to lessen the number.

> The passengers were late but I waited, wanting to give them as much time as possible. In the end we heard a horse's hooves beating on the dirt path. A man sat on its back, hunched in obvious pain. With him was a boy whose condition was dire. When my men helped them aboard, I saw that the man had been shot. The boy seemed malnourished and dazed. We laid them on the deck, covered them with a canvas, and shoved off.
>
> That first night, the man died. Knowing not what to do with the boy, we have kept him with us. He is more healthful day by day, and I find him a good lad.

Mysterious passengers. An orphaned boy. This is what had sent Colm to Scotland to investigate his "intriguing mystery." He'd seemed enthusiastic and eager to tell her about it at first. Why had he turned so cold and demanding?

Though she knew she was grasping at straws, Mercedes decided to call Colm again. She wasn't being clingy; she had to tell him she'd mailed the package back. Yesterday's call hadn't come from his cell, and hitting *Reply* resulted in nothing. She tried his usual number again: no answer.

The name of the theater company whose tour he'd just completed wouldn't come to her. Perhaps his uncle, who taught at Glasgow University, would know where Colm was. Though she was reluctant to have the deceptively cherubic old man think she was chasing his nephew, Allen Rankin was the kind of person who'd understand.

After quickly estimating the time change, Mercedes made the call. Unfortunately, the department secretary informed her, Professor Rankin had taken a leave this term to oversee a Stone Age excavation in Morocco. "He might call in," the woman offered. "I could pass your message on."

Thanking her, Mercedes said she'd call back if her question wasn't answered elsewhere. She didn't want to wait, and if Rankin was deep into study he'd probably paid scant attention to Colm's itinerary anyway.

After pacing her living room for a few minutes, Mercedes turned to her computer and opened the mailbox. Consulting the *Deleted Items"* section, she scrolled through dozens of old messages. Sometimes it's a good thing to empty a file so seldom, she told herself, because in July's trash she found the message Colm had sent from her apartment to his agent in Edinburgh. In a few minutes she'd Googled the agency and gotten a phone number.

"Markham and MacDonald, how may I help you?"

"My name is Mercedes Maxwell. I'm a friend of Colm Kennedy's." Suddenly this didn't seem like such a good idea. How many people called saying they were friends of actors represented by the agency? "I know you can't tell me where he is, but I'm concerned." She paused, and the woman at the other end said nothing. "He called me, but he seemed nervous, different somehow. Not himself."

It wasn't convincing, and the secretary said, "You understand we can't give out personal information—"

"May I speak with Colm's agent—" She hesitated until the name came to mind, "—Vivian?"

The woman paused. "I'll see if she's in her office." Which meant, of course, that she'd ask Vivian if she wanted to speak to one of Colm Kennedy's groupies. Mercedes waited impatiently, trying to decide whether to hang up now or wait for the inevitable, *I'm sorry; she's on another line.*

There was a click, and a new voice spoke. "Miss Maxwell? It's Vivian MacDonald." The voice was rich, precise, and warm, and could have done well reading advertisements for investments in gold coins or retirement properties. "Colm's told me about you."

"Really?"

The agent chuckled. "Nothing too personal, but I can tell he's smitten. Frankly, I'm afraid he'll run off permanently to America if you require it. It's maddening at this stage, when his career is taking off, but it's also charming. I'd never thought him such a romantic."

Mercedes felt her face flush, both at the idea of a stranger knowing about her love life and at the thought Colm really cared for her. Remembering the reason for the call she said, "That's just it, Ms. MacDonald. I thought Colm was coming here, and then he called to say that—" She paused, unwilling to speak the words. "—that I won't be seeing him again."

"Had you had some sort of disagreement?" Vivian MacDonald was nothing if not forthright. "He can be impossible if his pride's stepped on."

"No, nothing." Mercedes winced inwardly at the memory of

Colm's references to her higher status, teasing though they'd appeared to be. He wasn't a man who'd want to be seen as a fortune hunter.

"Perhaps he's going to surprise you. I shouldn't ruin it for him, but I don't want you to worry needlessly. I think he's on the way there."

"Here?"

"He emailed a few days ago, said he'd be off to Detroit after the end-of-season evaluation. I'm not sure where that is, but it's in the States, right?"

"Yes, barely. Across the lake from Windsor, Ontario."

"Then there's hope you could become a proper Brit." Vivian became serious again. "I'm only telling you that to put your mind at ease. Colm must have been playing some sort of joke. He should arrive any day now."

"Thank you. You've been very kind." Mercedes ended the call, but her mind wasn't relieved. The scenario Vivian envisioned would be nice, but if Colm had planned to surprise her, he should have arrived by now. Plus there was the packet he wanted back. And on the phone he hadn't sounded at all like he was joking.

Something was wrong. The only question was whether it was a problem between her and Colm, or something else, something she didn't understand.

Chapter Six

Dickens left the lecture hall pleased with the evening's performance. The audience had been particularly appreciative, and his voice had held up well. It was not easy to make oneself heard and achieve the nuances of meaning from the written word in a large hall with coughs, shuffling feet, and creaking chairs for accompaniment.

As he set his silk hat on his unruly hair, a voice called out to him. "Master Charles, is it?"

He turned to find a woman of small stature, older than he by about ten years, and vaguely familiar in the way of people one knew in the past who've aged beyond immediate recognition. "Your servant, madam."

"I'm Meg. I worked for your grand-mum at Crewe Hall."

Memories flooded his mind: the huge old hall with its vaulted ceilings and dark passages. He'd been so young then. And Meg—which one of the servants was she? Oh, yes, the girl who'd cared for the crone in the attic.

"How pleasant to see you again, Meg. Are you well?"

"Yes, sir, very well. I did so enjoy your talk. Very smart, you are. 'Course we knew when you was young you'd be someone. Everyone said so."

He doubted that. "Puny and shy," they'd probably said with rueful shakes of their heads. Still, he'd made something of himself, and it was partly because of Grandmother and her stories. She'd inspired him to write his own, and he'd found he had a gift for weaving realistic characters into fictional situations. It had brought him a satisfying sense of success.

"What brings you to London, Meg?"

"I live here now. My daughter married a man who works in a factory." Meg spoke slowly, and he suspected she was checking her grammar before each phrase so as not to embarrass herself.

The word *factory* brought a frown to Dickens' face. His own time in a factory, though short compared to what others experienced, had scarred him for life. He hated the thoughtless cruelty of life there, the brutish selfishness of those in control, and the crushing indignity of mindless physical labor. He'd never forgotten the humiliation of being too poor to escape it.

Still, those years had provided a rich background for his novels, characters both kind and evil, and settings that wrung tears from the Victorian upper class, feeding the fires of social reform. The pitiful children in his stories represented in various ways the young Charles Dickens. Assailed by the evils of life in society, they eventually overcame them with their own inherent goodness and the assistance of those who chose to do good.

"Do you remember Tante Claudine?"

Meg smiled. "I watched over her for five years, until she died."

"You were very good to the poor old thing, mad as she was."

Meg became animated, pleased to be holding a real conversation with the author who'd grown so popular of late. "Tante was your grand-mum's charge when she first married your granddad and came to Crewe. Later, when she got the job of housekeeper, I did for the old lady."

"She always frightened me, yet I felt sorry for her too," he murmured. In truth, he had in mind a character very like Tante for a future novel, a woman twisted by events in her life into a bitter shell, unable to leave the past behind. He would use Tante's insistence that things be left a certain way, her unwillingness to change her clothing, and her wild soliloquies on the cruelty of life. "She lost everything when she left France: her home, her son, even her reason."

Meg rolled her eyes. "More than that, to hear her tell the tale."

"What do you mean?"

"Did you never hear her go on about being French royalty? Tante claimed to be the queen's great friend. Said she saved Marie Antoinette's life."

***

DETROIT, TODAY

When she woke Saturday morning, Mercedes was still convinced she needed to speak with Colm. She tried calling the building where he lived, but the manager informed her it was not his job to watch over actors and drug addicts. It was clear he put both in the same category.

Finally she thought of David Cutler. Colm had mentioned visiting the old scholar in Salisbury, and if he had, she'd at least know he was all right. There was no answer at David's house, though she tried several times. That was odd. He wasn't one to leave home, and even if he was away, his taciturn housekeeper Mrs. Peterson should have been there to answer during the day.

Her inability to reach both men made Mercedes even more nervous. Colm didn't seem to want her around. Now David was off on some strange errand. She paced the floor, trying to talk herself out of worrying, but she lost the argument. The solution came with sudden clarity. In England she could answer all her questions at once. She'd assure herself the Colm was all right, discuss their future face-to-face, then rent a car and drive up to see David. At least then she'd know instead of trying to guess what this phrase or that tone had meant.

Within two hours the arrangements had been made. The good side of having money was that Mercedes could call someone, in this case a travel agent, and say, "I want this," and it was done. The fastest route to Heathrow included a layover in Montreal, which brought to mind her Canadian cousin, Eleanor Millwick. Retired from nursing, Eleanor kept busy with dozens of projects and a lively interest in everything around her. At seventy, she was a better companion than most people Mercedes' age, despite her slightly too fervent insistence that women were downtrodden and in need of liberation. Mercedes had never considered her sex a disadvantage, but she supposed it must have been in Eleanor's time. She pictured her cousin rapping on closed doors with bony, no-nonsense knuckles, demanding she be given an equal chance with the men around her.

Eleanor's fluent command of two languages brought Mercedes to a second decision. She intended to study the Dickens documents on the way to England, and she needed a translator for the letters written in French. Perhaps Ellie would meet her at the airport and do that on the layover.

"Better yet, why don't I come with you?" Eleanor said briskly when Mercedes called. "London in autumn is truly something to experience."

Though it didn't seem to occur to the older woman that she hadn't been asked, Mercedes didn't mind. Traveling alone was always dreary, and the very independent Eleanor would be no hindrance. While Mercedes followed the plan she was still devising, Ellie could see London, one of her favorite cities.

And what was her plan, Mercedes asked herself. First she'd face Colm, who should be back at his apartment by the time she reached England. If her suspicions were correct and she was now his ex-girlfriend, Ellie would help her get through it. Being rejected would be terrible, but having someone with her whose company she liked might take away some of the hurt.

She also wanted to meet Charlie Dickens. Colm might have solved the question of what his papers were worth, but if not, the challenge of finishing the puzzle might help Mercedes throw off the listlessness she'd been feeling for months.

The short drive to Salisbury would answer the question of David's absence from home. She wouldn't take Ellie there; in fact, she winced at the thought of David and Eleanor in the same room. Her friend saw women of his own age as predatory, and her cousin saw men in general as chauvinistic, either by overt assumption of superiority or well-meant condescension. One would undoubtedly say something that upset the other. Better if they never met.

"How long will we be gone?" Eleanor asked.

"You can return any time you like. I plan to keep my options open."

"A man, is it?" Eleanor was nothing if not perceptive. "The same one?"

"It's complicated. I'll explain when I see you." Suddenly she felt better about the trip. "I'm glad you're coming along."

"Who could turn down a few days in London?" Eleanor's voice turned serious. "Of course I will pay half."

She'd expected this. "My proposal. You'll go as my guest."

"I can afford my own holiday, Mercedes. Make me a reservation and tell me what it costs."

"All right." Mercedes immediately began figuring how much she could shave from the actual cost without her cousin becoming suspicious. "But I'll pay for hotels. After all, I need a bed, too."

"Fair enough. Email me the particulars and I'll start packing."

***

LONDON

The delivery man knocked at the door of the shop several times, blowing on his fingers to reverse the wind's bite as he waited. No one came to answer.

"It's been closed up for several days," said a young woman who was passing. "He must have gone away."

"It's not like him," the driver complained. "He knows I deliver on Mondays."

The girl's grin revealed a small gem in her tooth. "We all need to break free from time to time, don't we?"

The driver grunted, glaring at the shop door for a few seconds longer. There was nothing to do but return tomorrow. Dickens had better be back by then, or he'd get an earful when next they met.

***

DETROIT

As she was closing her suitcase, Mercedes' cell chirped its annoying tone. Distracted by a latch that didn't want to close, she answered with ill-concealed impatience.

"Miss Maxwell, please? Mercedes Maxwell?"

"This is she." She simply couldn't make herself say "It's me." Too many past English teachers had condemned it.

"It's the post office, about the package you sent on Friday. We—um, had an incident, and the box is still here."

As is often the case with tasks we think of as completed, it took Mercedes a minute to comprehend the message. "An incident?"

"We think it fell out of the bin, which was full, and then someone must have kicked it accidentally. It went under a shelf, and no one saw it until the cleaners came in over the weekend." He hurried on, perhaps trying to forestall a scolding. "The package is intact, but the address got ruined. They were mopping, you see, and... Anyway, we have to ask you to come down and repair it. Of course we'll provide any supplies you need free of charge. We're terribly sorry." The man stopped, ready for the angry response he no doubt expected.

"Don't worry about it," she told him. "I'm on my way out of town, but I'll stop and take care of it before I go."

When she got to the post office, the harried clerk handed her the box and the items needed to readdress the package. She took it to the visitor's work area, blinking in the bright sunlight that streamed in through the window. She was on her way to England.

Why mail the box? With any luck at all, she could demand Colm explain himself before she set it in his hands.

Turning, she looked at the mailing counter. She wasn't sure of the legality of taking a package back after placing it in federal custody, but the workers were all busy with customers. Returning the supplies to the counter, she set the box under her arm and slipped out. Wouldn't Colm be surprised when she delivered his copies of the Dickens documents in person!

It was a gorgeous day for flying, and Mercedes watched Detroit disappear beneath her between little clouds so puffy they looked like cartoon images. The trees had turned gorgeous colors, and she thought, as she always did, how tidy things look from far above the earth.

No one unacquainted with Eleanor could have discerned how excited she was when she joined Mercedes at the stop in Montreal. Tall, with a swan-like droop to her elegant, silver-crowned head, Ellie looked more like royalty returning home to Windsor Castle than an American tourist. Dressed simply in navy pants and a colorful blouse, she carried a small suitcase and a large tote bag.

Mercedes guessed her cousin's outfits would revolve around navy pants. She'd chosen black, with a second pair of the same color and a variety of tops. Along with two pairs of comfortable shoes, they each had a fresh look daily with only light luggage to haul around airports and hotels.

Settling into the seat beside Mercedes, Ellie squeezed the younger woman's hand affectionately. "I'm so glad you thought of me. It's been years since I've seen England, and there's no excuse for it. I just get inertia in that old barn of a house."

Ellie was the least inert person Mercedes knew, but she understood. A widow with no children, Ellie had contacted Mercedes several years earlier as part of her genealogical research. It turned out Mercedes was the last of a branch of the family that left Canada for Michigan in the late 1880s.

As a result of phone conversations and letters, they had struck up a friendship, and eventually Mercedes had driven to Montreal to meet her cousin in person. There had been an immediate connection between the two, despite the difference in age and the distance between them.

It was time to fully explain their reason for the trip. "I hope you don't mind, Ellie, but I might be on a fool's errand." Mercedes related the events of the last few days, ending with the bitter truth: "It's possible Colm wants to dump me and has dropped out of sight until I give up."

"I don't know the young man, of course, but he doesn't sound like the cowardly type to me." Ellie folded her hands on her lap. "If he'd met someone new, he would tell you." She fiddled with the gold chain around her neck. "Though I'm not sure what else it might be."

Mercedes admitted to her own uncertainty. "I've had a sense for months that Colm wasn't saying what he was thinking." Rubbing her hands together, a substitute for her usual habit of pacing as she thought, she went on. "Maybe he doesn't want an attachment at this point in his life. His career is taking off, and we live on opposite sides of an ocean. It's too inconvenient, I suppose."

"If two people care enough about each other, inconvenience isn't an issue." Ellie sighed. "I'm sometimes sorry for young people, in spite of the fact that our society appears to worship youth. Maturity gives one something in exchange for the loss of youth, a sort of confidence that comes from knowing one's time on earth is limited."

"What do you mean?"

Ellie frowned. "It's hard to explain to those who aren't there yet, but you come to a point where you don't make excuses anymore. You accept yourself and expect others to do the same."

"But Ellie, you're always nice."

"Oh, I don't mean a person has to become ornery in old age, though some do. I mean you have the confidence to say, 'I don't want to do that,' or 'I want that,' without feeling guilty. For example, a couple of my age in your situation would have been honest with each other from day one, saying outright whether they wanted a long-term relationship or just recreational sex."

Mercedes tried to keep her shock at the bald statement from showing. Still, it would have helped if she and Colm had been more honest with each other. Was that what this was about now? Was he trying to tell her the interlude was over and he'd never intended for it to be more?

"It's harder when you're young," Ellie went on. "You haven't learned to take that sort of risk, to cultivate the attitude that too much time is wasted with emotional hesitancy. In my last post as a private nurse I met a man—" She stopped herself. "Never mind that. What must we do to find out the truth?"

"I need to see Colm," Mercedes said. "But there are also these papers. I'm not sure why he sent them to me in the first place or why he wants them back now. If Dickens didn't know he was going to do that, he might have demanded Colm get them back."

Eleanor frowned in thought, then asked gently, "Might Mr. Kennedy be trying to pull some trick on Dickens? Maybe he found something that made him want to keep the documents for himself."

"Colm isn't dishonest," Mercedes assured her. "He wouldn't take a cent of the money from the Shakespeare letter, even though he saved my life."

"I understand." Ellie's tone hinted she wasn't fully convinced, and Mercedes didn't allow herself to dwell on her cousin's hint that this time Colm wanted the prize all for himself. If she'd met him, she'd know that was impossible.

But then, how long had she known Colm? How many days had she actually spent with him? A handful, if she was honest. Two weeks the first time. After that, a week here, another week later on. A month. Was that enough to believe that Colm Kennedy could never be tempted by wealth?

She shook off her doubts and spoke firmly. "I don't see what it will hurt if we read through the papers."

Ellie agreed. "We can always drop the subject if Dickens wants us to."

"Then here's where you can help." Mercedes took out the box she'd retrieved from the post office. "Two items are in French, which I've mostly forgotten."

"So that's why I'm allowed to come along?"

She put a hand on Ellie's arm. "I'm thrilled you're here, you know that."

"It's good of you to say so. And I'm more than willing to translate."

Mercedes sifted through and found the letters. "Here you are."

Ellie sniffed. "Looks like a child wrote it." Taking a pair of black-rimmed glasses from her purse, she put them on. "The letters are from someone named Louise."

Pointing at the signature, Mercedes snickered. "I figured that much out!"

Ignoring the sarcasm, Ellie scanned the first one. "Bad handwriting, old wording, and terrible copy quality. This will take some study."

Mercedes reached up and clicked on the overhead light. "A little better," Eleanor murmured. "Let's see. The year is 1787. Louise writes to her sister in Cannes." She paused, scanning the text. "She comments on the weather, her daughter's progress—the child is a budding genius according to her mother—and the Queen's wardrobe."

"The queen. That would be Marie Antoinette. Interesting."

"There isn't much here. Louise has a new dress, modeled after

45

one the queen has, and she's very proud of it. 'It pleases Her Majesty when ladies copy her dresses, for she likes to make a pretty scene.'"

"I've read that about her."

Ellie read on. "Apparently it delighted Her Highness that one of her ladies, Marie Claudine, was often mistaken for her. The two women played amusing tricks on lesser members of the Court."

"Marie Antoinette should have paid attention to the rumblings of the people," Mercedes commented. "Maybe she'd have kept her head."

"I suppose they were products of their environment and simply couldn't see the danger ahead."

"But I've read about Marie. Her family, her friends, officials of the state, lots of people tried to tell her to conduct herself with more decorum and spend less money."

"And those in government today are much wiser, right?" Ellie asked with an impish grin. "No one these days is ever caught in a scandalous affair or found with a hand in the public cookie jar."

"You're right," Mercedes admitted. "Louis and Marie had, or thought they had, absolute power. That probably made them feel invulnerable."

Now Ellie took the other side. "They had to ignore a lot to feel that way. Only a short time before, America's experiment with democracy won a war against the British monarchy."

"The French people must have watched that and decided power to the people was a good idea." Mercedes leaned over and squinted at the page in Ellie's hand. "So that letter was written two years before the revolution began. I wonder who Louise was exactly. One of Marie's ladies, but what else?"

"The second letter answers that," Ellie murmured as she scanned it. "Her husband is the Comte de Jarjayes."

"Doesn't help me much," Mercedes muttered, but she dug her

tablet out and booted it up. In a few seconds she was scanning material on the French Revolution. "Here he is. The Comte de Jarjayes was one of several ardent royalists who worked to protect Louis and his family. They tried several times to smuggle them out of France but always failed."

"I recall they disguised themselves and Louis dressed as a lady's maid. Their coach was stopped at the border and the ruse discovered."

"Right. It always seemed to me that the plots were poorly planned. If new information on the last days of Louis and his queen is in those letters, they might be worth something."

Ellie shook her head. "Revolution was unheard of when these were written." Reading on she said, "Louise is jealous that the queen finds this Marie Claudine so amusing. It says here, 'Her Majesty allowed her to order the rest of us about all day today, as if she were queen!'"

"She loved her little games. Playing at being a milkmaid herself, letting a friend pretend to be queen. Not much reality in Marie Antoinette's world."

Ellie set the letters on her lap. "Nothing here relates to Charles Dickens."

"Then they contain information Dickens was interested in."

"We know he was intrigued by the French Revolution. Some of his best characters come from *A Tale of Two Cities*."

"I love Madame La Farge and Sidney Carton. But he dealt with individuals swept up in the struggle between classes, not real history."

"So why keep a few letters containing gossip about Marie Antoinette?"

"I don't know." Dishes rattled behind them as the flight attendants approached with the meal cart, and Ellie tucked the papers into the pocket of the seat before her. "It's a long flight.

After we eat, we'll split the packet and each read half. If there's time after that, we'll switch. Once we know what we have, we can discuss why Dickens might have kept them."

When the meal trays were picked up, the cabin lights dimmed. "A little nap before we go to work?" Mercedes suggested.

Ellie nodded. "Good idea. The time change always hits me hard."

Mercedes thought she'd only doze for a while, but after a few minutes the drone of the plane's engines lulled her into real sleep. When she woke, her eyelids felt as if they were lined with pebbles, and she experienced the momentary confusion common to travelers. Where was she? When she remembered, she glanced beside her. Ellie slept peacefully, her head against the window in a position likely to cause a sore neck. Twisting her shoulders to loosen her own stiffness, Mercedes blinked in surprise. The papers were gone.

Ellie opened her eyes and looked around, orienting herself to the situation. "What?" she asked when she saw Mercedes' look of concern.

"Where are the papers?"

First they searched their belongings. Then they tried to concoct an explanation. The stewardess hadn't tucked them away for safe-keeping, they weren't scattered on the floor, and neither of them had stowed them in the overhead compartment and forgotten. Someone had waited until they were asleep and taken them.

Mercedes stood to look at the dozens of faces framed by blue tweed seats. Most were asleep, some listened to earphones, and others were busy with their laptops or a book. No one paid any attention to her. She sat back down again.

"Shall we tell someone?"

"Tell them what? That we want everyone on the plane searched for some loose sheets of worthless copy paper?"

"But we need those sheets to figure out Dickens' secret."

Mercedes leaned in to speak quietly. "I have a second set in my carry-on. They're even less clear, but now that we've seen the others, we'll be okay."

"Good." Eleanor frowned. "But why would someone steal copies of old documents?"

"There's something in them. We just don't know what."

"Shall we read them now?"

She looked around. "Not here. Let's let whoever took them think he's succeeded. In our room this evening we can go over them word by word."

Ellie considered. "But you're going to be busy. You want to find Colm, you want to see your friend..."

"David," Mercedes supplied.

"Yes, David. While you do that, I can research the people mentioned in the documents. Someone there must have caught Dickens' interest."

"Ellie, I can't ask you to spend your vacation in a library."

Her cousin smiled. "But if I want to, are you going to stop me?"

"No," Mercedes said, giving her a hug. "You're too good. I shamelessly drag you off to exploit your talents, and you fall right in with my wild plan."

"When a person hasn't had anything wild in her life for a decade or so, it becomes a very attractive prospect." The *Fasten Seat Belts* light came on with a chime, and they buckled up and began gathering their belongings for arrival at Heathrow.

CHAPTER SEVEN

MID-FLIGHT

Carrie was pleased with herself. No one had seen through her little ruse, in which she appeared to knock something off the Maxwell woman's lap, pick it up, and softly return it to its place without waking her. Of course what she'd actually done was grab the stacks of loose paper from the two women's seat pockets. She'd stuffed them into her jacket and moved to the bathroom, where she concealed them more completely in her tights. It made sitting uncomfortable, but the chance her theft would be discovered was minimized.

In the airport restroom she removed the papers and transferred them to her briefcase, buried between sheets of boring tractor company sales figures. Customs officials took little interest in the tall, dark-haired businesswoman from Montreal. One seemed aware she was attractive; the others were interested only in the fact that she had nothing to declare.

Outside the restroom a man waited. Taking her carry-on, he led the way to a waiting car. "You were successful, I take it?" They'd traveled separately, though he'd been close enough to assist if she'd been caught in the theft.

"Of course." She climbed into the car as he held the door. "Where's Robert?"

"Still in Mexico, but he plans to come to London in a day or two." Flashing a sassy grin he added, "In the meantime, Beautiful, I'm yours to command."

Her eyes lit with anger. "You'd better hope Robert doesn't hear you've been flirting with me, Lover. The last guy who tried that got a one-way trip into the Sonoran Desert."

Though no weakling and not a coward, he took a step backward. "Sorry." Going around to the front, he got into the driver's seat. "It's hard not to appreciate a woman who looks like you."

As he started the car Carrie chuckled. "I'm not insulted by the admiration, Sweet. I just felt I had to give you fair warning."

***

LONDON

The city was as beautiful as Mercedes remembered. The hotel shuttle took them over leaf-strewn streets, past multi-colored trees. Though it was her third visit, it was still hard for her to believe she was in the land of William Shakespeare and Winston Churchill. The city moved as cities do, the inhabitants unaware of the history around them. But for a girl from Detroit, ancient buildings, double-deck busses, and the sense of history was magical.

Upon reaching their hotel, Mercedes called both Colm's cell and home phone numbers again. Still no answer. Despite wondering what in the world she was doing, she was determined to see it through. She asked the concierge to make arrangements for a rental car for the next few days. Whether her visit with Colm turned out ill or well, she meant to drive to Salisbury and see David before returning home.

She tried again to call and tell David she was coming, but there was still no answer there either. Was he ill? She felt a little silly for crossing an ocean because two friends weren't answering their phones, but it felt like the right thing to do. With luck she'd see each of them for herself tomorrow.

After the preparations were made, she planned to sleep for a few hours. It would take several days to feel fully recovered from jet lag, but a nap on the first afternoon was almost essential. Eleanor was already stretched out on the other bed, her shoes on the floor beside it.

When they woke it was almost six. "I'm going to put these in the hotel safe until we get back," she told Ellie as she picked up the documents. "It might be overly cautious, but I don't want to lose our last copies."

"Tomorrow I'll make several more sets. We can leave one in the safe, you can take one to your friend, and we can each take notes on our own."

While Ellie freshened up, Mercedes went downstairs to secure the papers. As she stood at the desk, a man stood by, knocking his knuckles softly on the countertop as he waited. The quintessential American tourist, he wore white tennis shoes, baggy jeans with a T-shirt, and a baseball cap. Around his waist was a fanny pack, though he was at least three decades too young for it.

He glanced at Mercedes once, then again. "Are you Nancy? Nancy Coe?"

"No."

"Oh. Sorry." He glanced over again. "But you're American, right?"

"Yes."

"Me too!" He pointed at his chest. "Madison, Wisconsin." When she merely smiled in response the man went silent and returned to tapping on the desktop. The clerk turned from the safe and looked at him questioningly. "I'm Tim Carnes. Is there a message here for me?"

The clerk moved to her desk, and Mercedes started for the elevators to wait for Ellie. "No, sir," she heard her say. "No messages."

The evening was mild and dry, so they decided to walk until they found a likely place to eat. Mercedes was pleased that Ellie preferred "pub grub" to formal dining, as she did, and they chose a basement public house with low ceilings and a shape best suited for a bowling alley. Mercedes ordered for them at the impressive bar, shepherd's pie for both with Guinness for Ellie and a gin and tonic for the less adventurous Mercedes. As a lively game of dominoes took place on the other side of the room, Ellie sipped creamy stout. "I got directions to the nearest library at the hotel desk. It's only a short walk."

"Are you sure you wouldn't rather enjoy your time in London, Ellie? I'll feel terrible if you spend half the trip shut up inside."

"It's October," Ellie said with a smile. "Do you think it might rain? Besides, I'm willing to bet you'll be visiting a hospital, which isn't a great holiday activity either." They'd decided the reason for David's absence from home was most likely illness, given his age and dislike of travel.

She chuckled "David would under no circumstances be a good patient." She wouldn't let herself think about the possibility of a serious illness.

"There are some things I want to clarify at the library." Ellie frowned at her lack of forethought. "I should have brought my laptop, but it's old and it weighs a ton, so I'll work there. For example, the captain's log in those papers. I have no knowledge of nautical measurements, but the first entry was made at five degrees longitude and fifty-seven latitude, give or take a few minutes. Any idea where that would put him on a map?"

Mercedes shrugged. "I don't even know where Detroit is in that sort of reckoning."

"You're between the fortieth and forty-fifth parallels; I know that much. Longitude I'm not so certain of. I think London's latitude is in the low fifties, so the captain must have sailed north."

"From where?"

"He doesn't name his point of departure, just chart numbers. He made port in the early morning hours and took on two passengers and some cargo. The date was 1795, during the French Revolution."

Mercedes frowned. "Do you think his purpose might have been

53

taking émigrés to safety in Britain?"

"The nobles would have been desperate to escape by then. Even powerful people didn't know if they'd live from week to week with all the shifting of alliances going on."

"It must have been a nightmare."

Ellie shivered. "Why do you think they call it the Terror?"

"But there was incredible bravery too. People took great risks to save a few poor souls from the guillotine." She shivered. "I read once that the lawyer chosen to defend the queen at her trial did the job so well he was arrested for it. His assistant took up the cause and found himself in the same predicament."

"Yes, revolutionaries are often intolerant of those who speak with the voice of reason."

After the meal they started back to their hotel in Kensington, taking a different route in order to sightsee along the way. They passed Hyde Park, somewhat dimmed by the season, since it was too late for summer blooms and too early for ice skaters. Victoria's statue gazed regally over their heads, close to the palace where she'd been awakened one morning in 1837 and told she was the new queen of England.

Thoughts of Victoria brought to Mercedes' mind the documents Dickens had collected. Allowed time to sift through the information, she hit on a new idea. "She was French."

"Who?"

"The crazy woman the doctor kept notes on. He calls her the Invalid, but at one point he mentions the family called her Tante Claudine. *Tante* is French, right?"

"For aunt."

"So she was someone's aunt, but she came from France. Could your sea captain have brought her?"

"I don't know. When was the doctor first called to Crewe Hall?"

"Seventeen something, I'll look when we get back."

Consulting the pages brought disappointment. The doctor's account began in 1793. "Too early by two years."

"Hey! Remember me?" Turning, Mercedes saw the man from the hotel coming toward them. "Did you guys have dinner yet?"

"Um, yes."

He stopped, and Mercedes felt it would be rude to walk on. "Can you recommend a place?" He smiled disarmingly. "It's my first time in London, and I don't know anything."

Ellie made a sound of dismay. "Are you alone?"

"Yeah." He shrugged. "It seemed like a good idea at the time."

"We ate at a little pub about four blocks down," Ellie told him. "The Dog and Pony. We can recommend it, can't we, Mercedes?"

"Yes." Mercedes gave Ellie a warning glance. Tim—she recalled the name he'd given the hotel clerk—caught it and backed up a step.

"Sorry. I appreciate the help. I won't bother you again."

At the hotel they made copies in the business center then locked one set in the hotel safe again. She and Ellie went up to their room and tried to read, but jet lag and a good meal made them sleepy. "My eyes refuse to stay open," Ellie finally said. "We'll do better with a full night's rest."

The next morning both women woke early, since their internal clocks were still confused. They breakfasted in the hotel, shuffling through the papers as they shoveled in eggs and grilled tomatoes. Mostly they tossed out ideas, some worthwhile, some speculative. They parted when Ellie insisted she wasn't totally senile and didn't need an escort to the library. "If I get lost along the way I'll ask someone," she stated firmly. "You have a long drive, and the worst of it will be getting out of London."

Mercedes admitted she was right. She'd driven very little the "English way," and never in the confusing city of London. Best to get going early and perhaps beat the worst of the traffic.

Her first order of business was a visit to Colm's London apartment. It was possible he was there, comfy and relaxed, and simply not answering her calls. She told herself she owed him an explanation for the loss of the packet, but she knew in her heart it was an excuse to look him in the eye and see for herself what had changed.

Colm's place wasn't far away, and the concierge helped her find the easiest route on the Tube. Meeting the landlord was not a thrilling experience, since he was even more irritating in person than he'd been on the phone.

"Keen on him, are you?" he said with a leer. "I told you I don't watch over him." Jowly cheeks flapped as he spoke, and he needed to shave all of his face, not just the easy parts.

"Is there someone here who might know where he's gone?"

"Ask the birds." He scratched absently at his belly. "There's always birds around asking after 'im, just like you." He watched to see if the American girl got it. "Girls can't resist actors." He sounded more envious than disgusted.

"Don't suppose you'd let me look in his apart—his flat."

One bushy eyebrow rose along with a poorly barbered upper lip. "I don't suppose so, no."

Though it wasn't any worse than she'd imagined, the visit didn't answer any of Mercedes' questions. David was her next hope, so she made her way to the rental company to take possession of the car she'd reserved earlier.

As she exited the building's sheltered porch and headed toward the section where her car was parked, a violent push in the back sent her staggering directly into the path of an oncoming courtesy van. Unable to maintain her balance, she fell forward onto hands and knees. Pain shot through her knees as the van screeched to a halt, inches from hitting her.

"Are you all right, Miss?" A freckle-faced young man jumped out and ran to where she crouched on the pavement, bruised and fuzzy-headed.

"I think so."

"What were you doing anyhow?" A note of irritation crept into his voice. Seeing she was unharmed, he indulged in the luxury of being angry.

"Someone pushed me."

The skinny redhead looked around. "I didn't see anyone."

Mercedes chuckled grimly. "Neither did I."

His expression revealed disbelief, but his lips pulled in as if to block the comment. *American tourist forgets traffic comes from the other way in England. She's embarrassed, so she claims she was pushed.*

"Mercedes? Is that you?" She looked up to see Tim Whoever peering at her from the sidewalk. "What happened?"

"The lady fell." The driver sounded faintly aggrieved now.

"I was pushed."

"Miss—"

Tim looked from the man to Mercedes and frowned. "Listen, buddy, if Mercedes says she was pushed, she was. You'd better start looking at your surveillance tapes and see if you can find the guy."

The driver licked his lips. "We don't have surveillance here, sir."

"No cameras? No way to see who pushed her?"

It was nice to have someone believe she was telling the truth, but the conversation wasn't going anywhere. "Don't worry about it, Tim. It's over."

She could walk, though her right knee was badly scraped. The heels of her hands were raw too, but overall she was lucky. If the driver hadn't been so quick on the brake, she might have been seriously injured.

Tim helped her up and hovered around her like he was afraid she'd go back down any second. Inside the building, she told the story three times and got the same doubtful looks. Tim kept insisting she knew what she was talking about, but in the end Mercedes decided against involving the police. Perhaps someone had jostled her accidentally then hurried on, unaware of the chaos he'd caused. She felt very shaky though, and Tim noticed.

"How about if I get you back to the hotel?" he suggested.

"I was on my way to—somewhere."

"You can start again tomorrow morning, yeah? When you've recovered."

He was right. Driving for the first time in London would be tough enough on a good day. Still, she didn't know this guy from a plant stand. She shouldn't go anywhere with him.

She didn't get much choice. Tim told the people at the rental agency he'd handle everything, and pleased to see the last of a complaining client, they greeted the idea with enthusiasm. Soon they were in the car she'd rented. Though Tim muttered a little about the traffic, he did a surprisingly good job, and soon they were back at the hotel.

"I'll let you off at the door and park the car in the hotel garage," he said, "The ticket and keys will be at the front desk under your name. Can you make it upstairs alone?"

Forcing a smile, she said she could. As she opened the door, Mercedes turned back for a second. Tim was a really nice guy, and while she wasn't interested in getting to know him better, she couldn't just walk away. "Listen, I'm really grateful for the help. You didn't have to do this."

He tilted his head and shrugged. "Hey. Us Yanks have to stick together."

By the time she got to her room, Mercedes' knee was throbbing. She threw away her slacks, torn beyond repair, and washed her hands and the damaged knee carefully, making sure there were no tiny gravel particles embedded in the skin. Putting on a different outfit, she went downstairs and bought antibacterial cream and a box of bandages to replace the ones the car rental clerk had hastily applied. In a hotel boutique she found a new pair of black pants. The price was exorbitant but to save herself steps, she paid it.

Back in the room again she consulted her iPad Pro, researching several areas suggested by the Dickens papers in order to make connections. By the time Ellie arrived to find she hadn't gone to Salisbury after all, Mercedes had some new ideas to try out on her.

Ellie's first concern was the reason for her injury. "Someone pushed you in front of a van?"

"I'm certain of it. The only thing I'm not sure of is why. Was it punks pranking tourists?"

"Some prank! You might have been killed."

"Kids don't think of that, at least not that type of kid." She told her how Tim the Tourist had helped her out. "He was really nice," she finished. "He was the only one who believed I really was pushed."

Ellie raised gray eyebrows. "You don't think it was kids."

There was no sense trying to fool Ellie, and Mercedes shook her head. "No, I don't. Someone doesn't want me here, and it's something to do with these papers. They tried to get me to mail them back—"

"But that was Colm, you said so."

"Yes, but he didn't seem like himself." It sounded lame, but it was true.

"I see."

"And then they stole them on the plane, thinking that would stop us. They couldn't have known we had another set."

"But they do now."

"I suppose when I made arrangements to leave London they assumed I'm going somewhere they don't want me to."

"But we don't know anything," Ellie objected.

"Someone's afraid we'll figure this out before they do, and we'll—we'll—"

"We'll what?"

"I guess they're afraid we'll solve the puzzle."

"This secret has been around for two centuries and all of a sudden it's important enough that someone attacked you to stop you from investigating?"

"I don't know. I just don't know!"

Ellie sighed. "Let's go to dinner. What I learned today might shed light on some of it."

In deference to the injured knee, they dined in the hotel. Though she didn't mention it, Mercedes had begun to worry about Ellie's safety. If someone was out to harm her, she'd been wrong to bring her cousin into it. Staying inside provided the best security she could devise for the present.

"I spent the day on the good ship *Thistle*," Ellie said over sole and fried potatoes. "Though it was a trial to figure it out, I now know that our Captain Andrew MacPherson sailed her from 1775 to 1807."

"Which covers the whole period of the French Revolution."

"One Lewis Charles MacPherson registered as the new captain in 1807. The *Thistle*'s home berth was Coleburgh, Scotland, which is about five degrees longitude and fifty-seven degrees latitude."

Mercedes nodded. "So the father, Andrew MacPherson, kept the log we've got. His son took over the ship when the old man retired or died."

"Except there are no wedding records for Andrew MacPherson and no baptismal or birth records for Lewis Charles MacPherson. He never went to school, never did anything worth official mention in Scotland until he registered the *Thistle* in his name."

Mercedes followed Ellie's thought. "The captain adopted the boy whose father died escaping the French Revolution."

"Being young, the boy might not have known his destination or whom his father intended to contact outside France. I think Andrew kept him on as cabin boy and trained him to take over. Neither of them had anyone else."

"So Lewis was really the son of some French nobleman."

"There are hints that lend credence to the theory. Though MacPherson traded regularly with France up until that time, there's not a single instance of the *Thistle* returning there after the boy came aboard."

"Too dangerous?"

Ellie finished her Cabernet. "It's only speculation, of course."

Mercedes finished her own and rose cautiously to her feet, babying her scabbed knee. "Let's go back upstairs. I want to read the rest for myself."

Chapter Eight

Captain's Log, 1794—MacPherson

I am surprised by the boy's will to live. Despite an emaciated, cough-ridden body and fear of everything and everyone, he clings to life. Dark eyes watch me move about the ship, and no matter how often I vow not to encourage his dependence, I cannot resist a kind word from time to time. My mother raised fowl, and the first thing they saw upon hatching became their focus, their guiding star. Perhaps because I was close when the boy's last link to his old life died, he has fixed his loyalty on me, like the goslings. He says nothing, but his haunted eyes turn bleak whenever I leave his sight.

What to do with him is the question. He cannot return to France, but I suspect there is no welcome for him in England. The man entrusted with the boy's escape is dead, and I have come to believe he was an escort, not a relative. I should turn him over to the authorities, who will put him in an orphanage where he will be fed, clothed, and educated to a degree. Still, I sense that such an existence would condemn him to a slow death, and the lad has already been close enough to death for one so young. He needs more. How will a sickly child fare alone in a country where he does not even speak the language?

***

London

"The boy has to be the son of some nobleman," Mercedes said when Ellie read her the passage as she followed along on her own copy. "But it's time to give our eyes a break." Deciphering the ancient handwriting of the log was a laborious task, figuring out each word and then putting together sentences that made sense. The captain shortened words in an idiosyncratic manner, and the paper itself was blotted with age. Mercedes wished they'd magnified the pages when they copied them. "What else did you learn at the library? Could the boy be the son of the woman who wrote the letters?"

"No. She had only daughters." Ellie took off her glasses and massaged her eyes. "I did some research on Marie Antoinette's ladies, specifically our letter writer, Louise."

"And you found what?"

"I confirmed that her husband was indeed the Comte de Jarjayes, and they were close to the royal family. They made several attempts to get Louis and Marie out of France, but none was successful. After the king was executed, they tried unsuccessfully to help Marie and the children escape."

"In her letters, everything seems so peaceful."

"How little they knew!" Ellie shook her head ruefully. "I found the other name too. Marie Claudine was one of thirteen ladies in Marie's inner circle."

Mercedes chuckled. "Lucky thirteen, huh?"

"Claudine was very loyal. She stayed with Marie until her captors refused to let the queen have any friends with her at all. After that, she disappears from history."

"Do you think she escaped France while she still had her head?"

"That's what the de Jarjayes did when they could do no more for their queen." She shivered. "The times must have been terrifying for those who remained loyal."

"Yet some were devoted to Marie personally, as well as to the idea of divine right to rule."

"Not something we see much today."

"We've had some Presidents who'd like to get the American people to buy into that one," Mercedes remarked.

Ellie chuckled but didn't comment on American politics. "I wondered if Marie-Claudine might be the patient described as the Invalid in the doctor's journal. That would explain why Dickens kept letters that mention her with the doctor's account."

"That's a good theory, but how did she end up in England, and at Crewe of all places? It's not even on the water."

"I worked on that too." She consulted her notes for details. "Crewe Hall was owned at the time by the Member of Parliament for Chester who lived from 1742 to 1829. The hall is a copy of an Inigo Jones mansion and is still a tourist attraction today. The steward of Crewe Hall was—Voila!—William Dickens, who married a servant from the household of the Marquess of Blandford in Grosvenor Square. The new Mrs. Dickens came to Crewe and eventually worked her way up to housekeeper."

"These people were Charles Dickens' relatives?"

"Grandma and Grandpa Dickens." Ellie gave a triumphant smile as the import of her words dawned on Mercedes.

"So Charles might have visited Crewe as a boy."

"Very likely, since his father changed jobs every few years and his mother had one baby after another. Baron Crewe was responsible for getting Charles' father a position with the Navy when he was nineteen."

"So Dickens connects to Crewe Hall near Chester, and the doctor's notes concern a female invalid living there in the early 1800s."

"If he spent time with his grandparents, Charles would have met her."

"And been intrigued by her foreign ways."

"Kids are fascinated by eccentrics."

"If she was Claudine, she'd have been quite old."

"If she was thirty-five when the queen was executed, she'd have been in her sixties." Ellie put on a fake look of outrage. "That is not old."

"I apologize for the insinuation," Mercedes said with a laugh. "When did the doctor's account say she died?"

"In 1820. The servants found her dead one morning when they went to wake her."

"What a life she must have lived, serving the queen in her glory, then watching as Marie's life fell apart, unable to do anything to help. At the last she must have fled on a ship to England. Could it have been the *Thistle*?"

"No, Tante Claudine's ship wrecked along the west coast of England, according to the doctor. She was the only survivor found." Ellie's brow furrowed. "I've neglected the doctor's journal, but I know you read it. I'd like to hear your thoughts."

Mercedes took a moment to gather the story together in her mind. "This doctor, Philip Masters, was called to Crewe Hall when he was a newly-certified physician. Thrilled to have gained the attention of Lord Crewe, he hoped it would be the making of him as a doctor.

"From the outset he was sworn to secrecy. A badly injured woman's life was in danger if she was discovered, Crewe told him, because the French had sent spies out to assassinate members of the French king's inner circle. Claudine was in a terrible state, and Masters doubted at first that she'd survive her injuries. To assure he was never accused of neglecting her care, he kept very careful records."

"Luckily for us."

Mercedes smiled before going on. "The woman had been injured in a shipwreck late in the year when the seas were treacherous. She was found on the shore, unconscious and half-dead. When Crewe heard about the injured émigré, he had her brought to his place in Cheshire. The doctor was never told why the baron did this, but of course there was a great deal of sympathy in England for the royalty of France."

"The upper classes do tend to stick together," Ellie observed drolly.

"They were being killed simply for being born noble," Mercedes objected. "To the revolutionaries, no *aristo* could be innocent."

"Yes, it was horrible," Ellie agreed. "What did the doctor do for her?"

"Masters admits it was probably force of will rather than his skill that brought Tante Claudine through. The Invalid, as he calls her, had a broken back. Baron Crewe let out a rumor that she died, and the story of the survivor was eventually forgotten, except by those who knew differently. The woman suffered constant pain for the rest of her life. She walked in a sideways crawl, and her back was so twisted that her skirts dragged the floor on one side."

"She escaped one Terror to face another."

"The Invalid was never quite sane again, perhaps from constant pain, perhaps from past events. She cried for her children, railed at the rabble of Paris for believing the lies about the aristos, and brooded on the violent deaths of her friends. Some days were better than others, but at the best of times she didn't make much sense. She spoke only French, of course, so the servants couldn't even understand her for some time. When she became able to communicate in English, she spoke of herself as if she were someone else. 'Poor Claudine,' she would say, 'you died because you were loyal!' The doctor thought the Invalid might have had a daughter named Claudine who refused to cooperate with the 'citizens' who ruled France."

"Yes, the same names appear over and over in noble families, as if they can't think of new ones." Ellie grimaced. "If the Invalid saw her daughter guillotined, that could certainly account for madness."

"This part is interesting. Tante Claudine carried a portrait of her son in an oval frame, often speaking to him as if he were there with her." Mercedes looked sideways at Ellie to emphasize her next sentence. "The housekeeper's grandson, who was about eight years old at the time, took her fancy, and she insisted on feeding him sweets, teaching him lessons made of nonsense, and urging him repeatedly to affirm his loyalty to his king. She kept saying he was 'returned to life,' meaning, the doctor thought, that she saw him as her own child given back to her."

"The boy was Charles." Ellie's voice was breathless. "No wonder he took such interest in the doctor's notes."

"I'd say the Invalid became the model for Miss Havisham, but she also kindled an interest in the French Revolution."

"Which he used in *A Tale of Two Cities*."

"My personal favorite. I love how the stories of all the characters: Lucy and her father, Jarvis Lorry, the de Farges, Charles Darnay, Sydney Carton, and even low-life Jerry Cruncher all come together in a wonderfully clever climax."

"In a noble gesture of sacrifice."

"'It is a far, far better thing that I do than I have ever done before,'" Mercedes quoted Sydney Carton. "A person facing something as awful as the guillotine for another is the epitome of drama."

"I should pick up a copy." Ellie began figuring her half of the bill. "I've read everything Boz ever wrote, but it's been a while since I read that one."

They paused, momentarily lost in the 1800s. "We think we know the connection now between Charles Dickens and the Invalid," Mercedes mused, "but we haven't connected the sailor's log to it."

"Perhaps we should turn the matter over to the police," Ellie suggested. Mercedes sensed she'd been looking for a way to say it all evening.

"What would we tell them?"

Her cousin's plain face tightened as she considered the question. "You have a friend who's disappeared. He had papers that suggest…" She stopped.

"What do they suggest? That Charles Dickens knew a French émigré as a child and tried to discover later in life who she was? No crime there."

"But Colm is missing."

"Just because he didn't show up at my door doesn't mean he's missing. If they asked, I'd have to admit he told me he wasn't coming."

Ellie massaged her forearms, thinking. "All right. It isn't something the police would take an interest in. But I consider you a good judge of character. If you don't think your friend would treat you this way, he might well be in trouble." Seeing the look on Mercedes' face, she lightened the subject. "When we find him, if he does indeed want to end your relationship, he can tell you to your face. If you don't slap him for making you run all the way to England, I will."

Appreciative of her cousin's empathy and sense of humor, Mercedes grinned. "All right, then. Onward and upward."

Still jet-lagged, they decided further study should wait until morning. "It will do no good to try to read that horrible writing while our brains are fogged," Ellie suggested. "We'll do better by far with a good night's rest and an early start in the morning."

Ellie wasn't kidding about the early start. She was perusing her copied pages when Mercedes woke at six and mumbled, "Morning."

"Good morning," Ellie replied in a tone that seemed much too cheerful. Of course, her knee probably didn't ache from impact with the street, and her hands, though age-spotted, were not scraped raw from contact with concrete. "I've made coffee." She indicated the small tray on the credenza.

Mercedes headed for the coffee gratefully, adding two sugars and stirring with the annoying little plastic stick that didn't do much of anything.

"I'm almost finished with the captain's log," Ellie said. "Nothing more of interest, except that it's clear he became very fond of the boy, Lewis."

How early did Ellie climb out of bed? Mercedes wondered. And how did she finish the log without switching on the lights?

Ellie seemed to read her mind. "I've been up for an hour or so." She gestured toward a tiny flashlight. "I find these things handy when traveling, especially when it comes to finding the toilet in an unfamiliar room."

Mercedes sipped at her coffee. It wasn't great, but it was brown. Rising, she smoothed the shirt she'd hung over a chair the night before. It didn't look too bad, and she didn't feel like setting up the ironing board. Rummaging through her suitcase, she found socks, underwear, and her kit. "I'm headed for the shower," she announced.

When she emerged ten minutes later, feeling better and fully dressed, Ellie had an idea.

"I know you wanted to speak to Colm before meeting Mr. Dickens, but since he doesn't seem to be around, should we visit the man's shop now and see what he can tell us about the papers?"

"We could. Since David doesn't know I'm coming, a few more hours won't make a difference."

"In person we can better judge whether Charlie Dickens might attempt to perpetrate a forgery using your good name and Colm's good intentions."

Mercedes frowned. "I hadn't thought of that. Maybe it would be wise to meet the man for myself before I spend more time on his documents."

The What-the-Dickens Diorama and Curiosity Shop was a shabby storefront in a block of small businesses with the merest toehold on success. Mercedes and Ellie stopped at the display window, which was all but filled with a large, three-dimensional diorama of Dickens' London complete with Victorian shops, set pieces, and hackney carriages. Outside a bookshop Oliver Twist was enticed by Fagin, menaced by Bill Sikes, and shielded by Nancy. Around a corner Smike lurched along behind Nicolas Nickelby, and down the street came a carriage bringing Jarvis Lorry, Lucy Manette, and her father, recently rescued and "restored to life."

Though a little like Victorian Christmas villages Mercedes had seen, these pieces were much larger, of mixed media, and with incredible detail: fringed scarves for the men, ruffled, bustled skirts for the ladies, and decorative plumes for the horses' harness. The scene was lovely, though a little dusty and faded from years of exposure to sunlight.

"People from the various novels," Ellie remarked.

"Obviously a labor of love."

The two women entered tentatively, since the shop seemed unoccupied and there was no sign to indicate whether it was open or not. Mercedes closed the door, making a scraping sound she guessed would easily become annoying. A clock on the wall chimed as a tiny Queen Victoria figure emerged from double doors over its face, bowing to the first six notes of "God Save the Queen."

"There's a door open back there." Ellie led the way through the maze of shelves, tables, and stands stuffed with goods. There were books in conditions from pristine to downright shabby, hat pins, tie pins, pince-nez, opera glasses, bed-warmers, walking sticks, tobacco cases, pipes, and all manner of other souvenirs reminiscent of the era of the eminent Dickens. One wall had bins full of romanticized prints of Victorian life, many depicting scenes from *Great Expectations*, *Hard Times*, and other stories familiar to those who still read books.

They stopped at a counter set parallel to the wall halfway into the store. Atop it was a hand-kept record book, made out in the same round-lettered writing as the letter Colm had received. Next to it were the remains of someone's afternoon tea, an empty cup and a cardboard box that had once held four cinnamon buns but now held one.

Past the counter on the left was a doorway, and from there came a muffled thud and a disgusted exclamation. Stepping around the counter, Mercedes peered through the open door. On a wooden stepladder a woman of perhaps sixty stood with her back to them. She was counting small boxes on the shelves, pointing her pen at them and holding a clipboard between her arm and her body. When Mercedes coughed to signal her presence the woman started violently, almost falling backward off the ladder.

"I'm terribly sorry." Mercedes hurried forward to steady her. "We didn't mean to frighten you." How had she missed the door chime? Deaf perhaps, or distracted.

The woman came down the rungs carefully, in the way of those with multiple-focus lenses. "You did me no harm," she told them. "I'm a little jumpy with all that's happened."

"We were hoping to see Mr. Dickens," Ellie said.

The woman regarded them critically. "What's your business with him?"

"A friend came here last summer on vacation," Mercedes said smoothly. "He was very impressed with the shop and, knowing that we're both great readers of Dickens' works, encouraged us to visit if we were ever in London."

"Then you haven't heard. Poor Charlie's dead."

"Dead?" They said it together, in the same tone.

"Yes. Murdered, he was. The police were here ever so long, but now they've allowed me to come in and begin putting the place to rights." She tilted her head to one side. "I'm Charlie's cousin, Darcy."

71

The shock evident on the faces of her guests led Darcy Dickens Harris to offer tea. After locking the door, which she confessed she'd forgotten to do earlier, she led the way to a set of rooms above the shop. Charlie Dickens' home was neatly kept and shabbily elegant. A sofa served as both bed and seat, a corner as kitchen. Everything required for simply comfortable living was there, and Charlie had added, probably from things that hadn't sold in the shop, Victorian glass lamps, framed silhouettes, and crocheted doilies.

When they each had a cup of steaming tea and a chocolate mint biscuit, Darcy told Ellie and Mercedes the whole story. "A delivery man alerted us to something wrong," she began. "They called me because no one knew where Charlie might have gone. I had a key, you see, because I sometimes helped in the shop." Her eyes turned sad. "We found him in the storeroom, shot at close range and dragged in there, the police said."

"Was robbery the motive?"

"All I've found missing so far is some papers Charlie had on display." She shrugged helplessly. "They weren't worth anything, but I suppose the thieves thought otherwise. They were old, but they weren't worth kill—" She stopped, unable to finish.

Mercedes glanced at Ellie. By tacit consent, neither acknowledged having copies of the papers. "Why would someone kill Mr. Dickens then?"

"The police are quite puzzled by that," Darcy said, replacing her cup on its delicate, lacy-edged saucer. "Charlie lived very quietly. He seldom left this square, where he'd lived his whole life." Her face changed and she made eye contact to reinforce her next statement. "He didn't have any secret goings-on either. The police asked about that, but Charlie was a good man. No monkey business with women of questionable character—or men either."

"I'm sure you're right," Mercedes said soothingly.

"The police took his appointment book in order to check his

recent contacts. Once they finished with the shop, the inspector said I should begin an inventory, in case things are missing that aren't obvious." Darcy took up the cup again. "Of course I said I'd do as they asked."

"Nothing is missing but the papers?"

She leaned forward, causing a clump of gray hair to catch on her glasses and hang there. "Honestly, I'm having a bit of a problem sorting out the figurines. You see, I've never paid much attention, so I don't know an Oliver Twist from a David Copperfield. I have to pick each one up and look at its bottom for the lettering."

"You never read Dickens?" Mercedes tried to keep her incredulity masked but wasn't sure she succeeded.

Darcy smiled ruefully. "I don't read current novels, much less moldy old ones." She pointed to a bag that sat next to her chair. "If a person's going to sit still, I always say, she should accomplish something. I bring my knitting along wherever I go, so my time is used to good purpose."

Mercedes stifled arguments she might have made in favor of reading, especially reading about the past. It seemed even the great Charles Dickens' descendants could be blind to the benefits.

Ellie's mind went in a more practical direction, and she reached for her purse. "Mrs. Harris, would you mind if we took a few pictures of the shop before we go?"

"Why would you want to do that?"

Eleanor's manner turned vapid, something Mercedes had never seen in her before. "It's interesting, don't you think? The scene of a terrible crime? I'm sure my friends at home would like to see how it was found by the police."

"I see no reason why not." Darcy's tone implied good taste should have prevented her asking, but she wouldn't be equally rude by saying that aloud.

Mercedes tactfully distracted their host by asking about items in the shop while Eleanor took photos with her phone. Darcy had turned cool, and she answered the questions tersely.

"Poor Charles," she said as they made their farewells. "He died for a box of old papers that no one ever made heads or tails of." She sighed. "They wanted money to buy drugs, I suppose. Modern young people, you know. They've got no respect for life."

Outside the shop, gusts of wind blew grit against their legs. Eleanor turned her back to it, shaking her head. "I don't think that man was killed by some crazed drug user."

"I agree. Why did you ask to take photographs of the place?"

"I'm not sure if they'll help or not, but I thought it would be better to have them now than wish we did later after things are moved." Ellie touched Mercedes' arm. "Someone stole those copies you made. Someone tried to push you into traffic yesterday. Someone murdered that poor man."

"If what you say is true, then anyone concerned is in danger," Mercedes said. "You need to get on the next plane for home."

"What about you?"

"I've got to find Colm."

Eleanor's eyebrows rose. "In that case, do you think I'd leave you here alone? You need someone to watch your back."

The thought of a seventy-year-old as backup was both heartening and comic, but Mercedes saw that her cousin was determined. Thinking quickly, she devised a plan. She'd take Ellie with her to Salisbury and find an excuse to leave her at David's house. If she made sure no one followed them from London, Ellie would be safe there. She and David would have to find a way to co-exist.

"Let's get something to eat," she told Ellie. "We're going for a ride."

"What about the police?"

"I don't know what we can tell them at this point," Mercedes answered, but she'd misunderstood.

"I wasn't thinking what we could tell them," Ellie murmured. "I was wondering what they might tell us."

"They won't tell us anything," Mercedes replied, but her cousin was no longer beside her. Two young policeman strolled toward them, and Ellie approached, gesturing at one of them and then toward herself. They seemed unresponsive at first; then the one Ellie had singled out seemed slightly embarrassed. The other seemed amused by the interchange, and they both relaxed. After a few moments they became almost chatty, nodding and gesturing toward Dickens' shop. When Ellie left with a little waggle of her fingers, the cops waved back before continuing their patrol.

"What did you just do?" Mercedes demanded.

"One of those young policemen looked just like my nephew Reggie, who left Canada to study law enforcement in England," Eleanor replied with a twinkle that belied the explanation. "I was so sure he was Reggie that I stopped him to say hello. You see, Reggie looks just like Ben Affleck, and I was certain this young man has been mistaken for that actor many times, since he is also the spitting image." The young policeman had the right coloring for such a comparison but not much else.

"In the course of the conversation, I mentioned I was shocked to hear of a murder recently on this street, very near my hotel. To reassure the dotty American tourist, the young men revealed the basics of the case."

"You are amazing."

Ellie smiled ironically. "Another good thing about being old. One gets away with things."

"What did you find out?"

"Not much more than Darcy told us. The only items taken were papers of no great value. They believe the thief thought the shop was empty when he broke in. He must have been concerned about

Dickens' ability to recognize him and killed him when he interrupted the theft."

"But we know differently."

"They wanted the originals," Ellie said as they walked. "Now they're determined to see that all copies of Dicken's collection are accounted for," "They want no competition for whatever it is they intend to do."

"Why not just take the papers from Charlie?" They'd reached the car, and Mercedes sat for a moment with both hands on the wheel. "They didn't have to kill him."

Eleanor's expression turned grim. "I'm afraid they don't want anyone left alive who's read those documents."

It was a chilling thought. "And they know, or at least suspect, we have. Ellie, it's dangerous for us here."

"Then we should be on our way," she replied breezily. "Who'd ever connect Salisbury with Charles Dickens?"

CHAPTER NINE

SOMEWHERE OUTSIDE LONDON

As Colm slept in the next room, Scylla spoke to her sister on the phone. "Did you get the copies?"

"Of course," Carrie replied. "I do my part. But what about your new boyfriend? Is he doing his part?"

"I've got him researching our next step." Scylla chuckled. "He's leaving his cyber footprints all over the Internet."

"And what is the next step?"

"He hasn't figured it out yet, but he says it might involve leaving England. Is that doable?"

"Of course. Robert will fly us anywhere we need to go."

"Has Robert arrived in England?"

"No, but he's on his way." Carrie's voice lowered. "He says you'd better be ready to pay up."

"If he provides the backup we need, I'll cooperate."

"We already have the help he promised. I've sent Rick to spell you. The Minder is with me, as always. Glen and Carl can be sent to do whatever we need done."

"The Maxwell woman. Where is she now?"

"At her hotel here in London. We're keeping an eye on her."

"How much does Robert know about what we're doing?"

"Only that there's money to be made." Carrie gave an unladylike snort. "I haven't mentioned Dickens, since Robert thinks Tiny Tim is that guy who used to play the ukulele on Johnny Carson."

Scylla knew her sister was no scholar either, being mostly

moved by the desire for wealth and the thrill of launching her own personal crime wave. Carrie had gone all pouty when Scylla revealed she'd shot Charlie Dickens. Murder was something Carrie hadn't tried yet, and for sure she'd be looking for a way to get her own first kill in the next few days. *Sibling rivalry is a bitch.*

Carrie was still thinking of her aging drug lord. "Robert thinks it's cute that you and I have what he calls our 'little project.' He's a jerk about it, but we have money and four men who'll do whatever we tell them to." She giggled. "Of course Robert says we owe him."

"I've said we'd give him a share when we get the prize."

"Robert is interested in something more...I can't think of a word for it."

"Tangible. Immediate. Physical. Those all work." Scylla sighed. "It's not like we haven't done that before."

Carrie chuckled. "What is it about twins that gets a man's fantasies into high gear? I could have asked for a dozen men and he'd have agreed."

"Don't knock it." Glancing in a mirror, Scylla pushed her hair back from her face. "If old Robert's fantasies make us rich and famous, I can't wait for his plane to land. We'll seal our contract with a kiss."

Carrie had to have the last word, as usual. "And more, Sis. And more."

* * *

LONDON

Detective Chief Inspector Blaine reviewed what he knew of his latest case. Evidence had been noted and catalogued, and the scenario was both familiar and disheartening. A shopkeeper senselessly murdered. Charles Lee Dickens had owned nothing that was worth his life, yet that life had been taken.

On the positive side, the chances of catching the killer weren't too bad. There were fingerprints on the glass top of the empty case. The killer must have wanted whatever was inside badly, since he'd neglected to take the simplest of precautions. If they were lucky, the prints would be on file somewhere, and they'd have him. The inspector smiled at the thought. If only all murderers were kind enough to leave behind obvious clues.

***

SALISBURY, ENGLAND

As they drove the ninety miles between Salisbury and London, Mercedes watched the road behind them for signs that someone was following. Traffic was heavy on the M4, but when they exited onto the M25 going south, no one followed. Obeying GPS commands, she took the M3 to the A303 and followed the signs. Each time she turned she checked behind her, but no vehicle trailed them for long. The drivers seemed intent on their own routes, not hers.

The countryside was lovely, with fields of green and gold and wooded areas shedding multi-colored leaves. As they drove Ellie reviewed the notes she'd taken at the library, several legal sheets filled with neat printing. "It isn't obvious how this fits in," she began, "but I found it interesting. Do you know about Count Axel von Fersen?"

"The name sounds familiar, but I can't place him."

"He was a Swedish diplomat, Marie Antoinette's most loyal supporter, and her possible lover. Axel was infatuated with the queen and even sang a song in her praise once at the Opera, to a chorus of boos from the audience.

"When Louis and Marie were imprisoned, von Fersen served as a contact between them and their supporters. He arranged that ill-fated flight to the border."

"Which Marie doomed to failure by insisting the family travel together."

"Yes. Too recognizable as a group, they were captured and returned to Paris. Von Fersen remained devoted to Marie until her death. Afterward he returned to Sweden and lived until 1810, moody and abstracted by all accounts, always wearing the gold ring she'd given him."

"He'd have known Claudine."

"Almost certainly. They'd have worked together on the attempted escapes from the various places Marie and Louis and the children were imprisoned. I gather letters flew thick and fast between the royalists."

"Lots of cloak and dagger."

"Yes. Marie used a simple code to avoid others reading her letters, 1 for *A*, 2 for *B*, that sort of thing."

"That won't stop David for a second, though he likes more challenging ciphers."

"I'll be interested to meet this code-breaking genius," Ellie commented dryly before returning to her notes.

Mercedes hadn't yet told Ellie how difficult David could be, especially with strangers. He claimed to dislike ninety-nine percent of the population and close to one hundred percent of the female side, with Mercedes a notable exception. "Women want to change a man," he often grumbled. "I'm too old to change, and I don't want to anyhow."

"All right, Professor Higgins," Mercedes had teased.

"If I am Higgins," he'd retorted, "I prefer the original one, in *Pygmalion*. The chap in *My Fair Lady* becomes altogether too squishy at the end."

Eleanor was the type of woman David would consider a "women's libber." Sparks would fly when David, the Immovable Object, met Ellie, the Irresistible Force. Mercedes winced at the thought she'd be in the middle.

Focused on her research on Louis XVI's imprisonment, Ellie

went on. "Marie's letters were often written by de Jarjayes so her hand wasn't recognizable. Her friends did their best to protect her, but they also made terrible mistakes. At times their actions read like a Marx Brothers script."

"But Axel von Fersen survived. You said he died in Sweden."

She shook her head regretfully. "He was stoned and kicked to death by a mob of his countrymen."

"Stoned!"

"The superstitious crowd thought von Fersen dabbled in witchcraft. When he was dead they cut off the finger on which he wore Marie's ring and threw it into a river."

"Yuck!"

"Legend has it that the finger and the ring were intact on the corpse at the funeral the next day. Since it supposedly had so much power, the ring was removed and given to von Fersen's family."

Mercedes frowned. "I don't see how that helps us. One gold ring wouldn't be worth all this effort."

"No," Eleanor said. "I've told you the creepy part but not the best part. Quite a few Scots lived in Sweden at that time, their ancestors having left Scotland rather than live under Protestant rule. Many of them served as mercenaries for the Swedish king, and some gained positions of power."

"But that's much too early for our documents. The last Catholic monarch died in the 1600s, long before the French Revolution."

"Yes, but some family names changed over time from Scots to a more Germanic form. If the account I read is true, *von Fersen* was once *MacPherson*." Ellie turned from her notes to look directly at Mercedes. "Axel von Fersen might have been a distant relative of Alex MacPherson, captain of the good ship *Thistle*."

Chapter Ten

Coleburgh, November, 1795

Captain MacPherson looked up from his financial accounts with a distracted air. Numbers relating to money gave him no pleasure. He liked them best when they referred to positions on a navigational chart.

"What is it?" he asked with no bow to propriety.

The young man who stood in the doorway cast shadows around him, like a corpse in one's parlor. He was dressed with plainness designed to provide nothing to catch the eye: loose-fitting brown trousers, a faded brown leather jerkin, and a dirty-white shirt beneath. A brown hat and cloak completed the drab outfit. His face, shaded by the hat brim, held a blank expression that matched the clothing: nothing stood out, not a twitch brought notice. Only after a moment's study did MacPherson catch a feral glint in the eyes that betrayed his dull look. A fanatic. No wonder he kept the hat low.

"For several months I have searched for this ship." The accent was heavily French, the voice toneless.

MacPherson took more interest. "Have you now," he said equably, but a shift of his chin made it somehow stronger.

"I followed you to several ports, always northward."

"This is home," MacPherson said with a broad gesture. "We winter here and trade again in the spring, God willing."

Thin lips tightened briefly at the reference to God, and MacPherson recalled the French were all atheists now, as well as murderers and anarchists.

"I have a question for you." The voice attempted no false friendliness.

"What is it?"

"There is payment attached."

MacPherson frowned. The visitor had mentioned money without taking time to gauge his host's character. MacPherson considered the offer of a bribe an insult, and he met the other's gaze directly. "An honest question requires no pay for its answer."

"You are an honest man." He couldn't let go of his belief men were corruptible it seemed, for he added, "Even so, if you help us there will be payment in British gold." Standing even straighter, he asked formally, "Did you bring a boy across the Channel on the night of June twelfth? Accompanied by a man in a green cloak?"

"I took no passengers to England that night," the captain said succinctly.

"The boy is so high, and sickly. You did not take them to Dover?"

MacPherson was pleased to note the questions were phrased wrongly, so it was easy to avoid lying outright. He would have done so if forced, but his staunchly Catholic soul disliked untruth. Lies gave the Devil the tiny foothold that was all he needed.

"I have told you. I brought no man to England from France that night, and I know no lad with a cough."

At that moment the cabin boy appeared with ale for the captain and his guest. He wore a sailor's coat much too big for him, and his skinny ankles stuck out of baggy pants cut short in the legs and roped around the waist to fit. His silky, light-brown hair had been trimmed to mere fuzz for safety as he moved in and out of the ship's ropes, and his hands were raw and scraped, not yet hardened to a life of harsh winds and abrasive hemp. His face was serious, his eyes without emotion. He said nothing, but stood waiting for instruction, as was expected of him.

"Sir," MacPherson said to his guest, "since I cannot give you the information you seek, may I offer you a glass of peary? My sister makes it from her own pears, and it is quite good."

"And this boy?"

"Named after our own king who lost his head, though with less fuss than you French made of it. Charlie, greet our guest."

"Good day, sir," The words had a round Scot's accent, the *r* softly burred exactly like MacPherson's own. He set the tray on the small table, near the captain's elbow.

"You may go." After he was gone MacPherson said to his guest, "I must admit to pride in the boy."

"A fine lad. Is he a relative, then?"

MacPherson looked the grim stranger in the eye. "He's my son."

The Frenchman's eyes bored into MacPherson's, testing his honesty, but the Captain's gaze didn't flinch. After a moment the man inclined his head slightly to one side, the merest yielding to politeness. "I will trouble you no further. Good day."

"Good day to you as well," MacPherson replied. The man backed from the room, creating the curious sense he was unwilling to turn his back on others. The captain sat motionless until he heard footsteps on the gangplank. After some minutes, he reassured himself by removing a board from the cabin planking and looking inside. The velvet bag was still there. As he'd suspected, its contents spelled danger for the boy. Having no need of the wealth it represented nor any desire for it either, he put the board back and paced the tiny cabin.

The test had come. He hoped they'd passed, he and the boy he'd taken for his own, Louis-Charles, now known as Lewis Charles MacPherson. The necklace would someday be his, but he was too young to be burdened with the knowledge of it now. MacPherson would present it to him as a gift of manhood, as horses and suits of armor had once been given by fathers to sons. But what to do with it in the meantime? MacPherson sipped at his peary as he pondered the question.

***

SALISBURY, TODAY

Approaching the 800-year-old city of Salisbury was a thrill for Mercedes, since the cathedral spire, visible from some distance, was a sight to gladden the heart of any historian. The town that had grown up around the church kept its medieval air, but Ellie suggested Mercedes avoid the High Street, where tourists congregated, and skirt the market area. Since it was almost twelve, they stopped for lunch at a cozy tea room near the motor coach park before continuing to David's home. As they returned from having warm pasties and almost equally warm sodas, Mercedes' phone rang. To shut out the hum of traffic on the street, she climbed into the car and closed the door before answering. Ellie discreetly stayed outside, taking in the charm of her surroundings while allowing her cousin privacy for her conversation.

"Hello?"

"Mercedes Maxwell?" The woman's voice was low and sultry.

"Speaking."

"I'm calling as a friend to suggest you forget Colm Kennedy."

"What have you got to do with Colm and me?" The words were out before she could stop them.

"When Colm told you he doesn't want to see you again, I was there—on the bed beside him."

A wave of anger flashed through her, and Colm's words returned, his trained baritone echoing in her head. "You won't see me again."

Just as quickly the anger passed, and she remembered the oddness of phrasing and the tenseness in Colm's voice. After all they'd been through together, he wouldn't end their relationship so coldly, even if he had found someone else.

Mercedes squeezed the phone as if it were the woman's arm. "Exactly who are you?"

"I'm your replacement, the one who makes Colm's oatmeal in the morning. He knows you're looking for him, but he doesn't want to see you."

Mercedes tensed at the harsh words and cold tone. She'd told herself she could accept it if Colm really had found someone else, but if what this woman said was true, it was worse than she'd thought. She opened her mouth to say something, but there was nothing to say. After a moment she heard a soft chuckle. Then the call ended. As Mercedes stared at the phone numbly, Eleanor got into the car. "Tell me what's happened."

"A woman called to say she's Colm's new girlfriend and I should forget him." Suddenly her expression changed. "But it's a lie!"

Ellie's face revealed doubt, so Mercedes explained. "She said she makes Colm's oatmeal in the morning. I've seen Colm Kennedy polish off a huge breakfast, right down to the black pudding, but the one thing he won't touch is oatmeal. He jokes about being the only Scotsman in the world who hates the stuff. That woman was lying—at least about that part." She heard her voice rise as Ellie's face reflected her own fear.

"What shall we do?"

"I don't know." Mercedes repeated it, her voice breaking. "I don't know."

They were silent for some moments before Ellie said calmly, "We must find your friend David. If Colm's been there, he might know something."

She punched in David's number, listened, and put the phone away. "Still no answer. I hate to show up uninvited but—"

"We must try," Ellie said. "We've come this far."

"You're right." It was better than sitting in a car park trying to keep her heart from shattering into pieces. Forcing her dazed mind into action, Mercedes started the car and obeyed the GPS directions.

***

LONDON

"Sir, there's someone here you should speak with. Says she has information on the Dickens homicide."

Inspector Blaine looked up from a stack of reports. "Show her in, will you, Collins?" He had just enough time to sign his name and slide the stapled sheets into their proper spot before the sergeant returned with a pretty young woman. She had a look about her police professionals quickly learn to recognize. A working girl. Unused to visiting law enforcement hubs voluntarily, she twisted her hands together nervously. The jeans she wore had holes big enough to drive a lorry through, but because of the day's chill, her skimpy top was partially hidden by a white nylon jacket with a fake-fur collar. Despite the weather she wore flip-flop sandals, possibly to show off the screaming orange paint on her toenails.

Blaine was polite. "Please, sit down, Miss—"

"Bagley," she supplied in a slightly defensive tone. "Serena Bagley."

"Miss Bagley, I understand you have information about the death at What-the-Dickens." It was hard to say the shop's silly name with any sort of dignity, but the chief inspector did his best.

Miss Bagley seemed more than ready to talk, being on the right side of the law for once. "I knew Charlie a bit, not in a professional way." She put up a palm to dispel any thought that Dickens had availed himself of her services. "He was always real polite, you know, like an old-fashioned gentleman." She chewed briefly on the wad of gum in her mouth, apparently recalling Dickens' kindness. "Anyway, I saw two people go in there just at closing time."

Blaine leaned forward a little. "Two visitors, you say."

"Yeah, a woman about my age with dark hair. She was pretty,

87

what I could see—well-dressed and all."

"Can you give more detail as to her looks?"

"Not a lot. She wore dark glasses and a green Burberry with the collar pulled up. It had oversized wooden buttons, and the belt buckle was made of the same wood. She had that walk, you know, like a woman who knows everybody's watching her?"

"I see. And the man?"

"Well, that's the interesting part. I'd seen him before somewhere, but I couldn't place him."

"What did he look like?"

The woman reached into her purse and pulled out a flyer from a recent production of *The Taming of the Shrew*. "He looked just like this," she said, laying the flyer in front of Blaine. "The man that went inside with the woman was Colm Kennedy, the actor."

CHAPTER ELEVEN

SALISBURY

Much to Mercedes relief, David's car was parked at the front of his half-timbered Tudor house. As they made their way along the streets of Salisbury through the daily maze of traffic, she'd felt increasing dread. Would she find an empty house and another dead end? The sight of the car pulled close to the front door was encouraging, but the lawn looked untended, the flowers buried in dead leaves. She tried not to let her imagination run ahead. One of her concerns in coming to England would soon be answered.

When she knocked at the door, Mrs. Peterson, David's dour housekeeper, appeared. "Miss Maxwell," she said soberly. "The old lion has had a setback, but he's home now and settling back into his lair. We've only just returned."

"A setback? What sort of—"

"Hospital," Mrs. Peterson said tersely. "I can't say he's in any mood for company, but if he wanted to see anyone, it would be you."

"Mrs. Peterson, this is my cousin, Eleanor Millwick."

She barely nodded before turning to lead them inside the house that was more museum than home. Mercedes sensed Ellie's wonder at the array of artifacts put to everyday use. Antique chairs were draped with coats and sweaters. An ancient china basin sat on a table, half filled with pens, pencils, and odd nails and screws. And everywhere there were books. Every available space had a stack, and many of the walls were lined with shelves of them.

As they followed Mrs. Peterson, they passed a small room where Mercedes noted a modern addition. David had bought a computer. With only a scanner/printer for company, the twenty-first-century device looked lost among older, more beloved things.

They found David paging almost angrily through a book titled *Fifteenth-century Armor and Weaponry*. He looked up, frowning at the interruption until he saw who his visitor was. Much was explained when Mercedes took in his left leg. The pants had been cut away above the knee, which was encased in plaster from halfway down the calf to the ankle. The knee itself was swathed in bandages, leaving an inch or so of flesh visible between the two dressings. The whole leg was extended parallel to the floor by a brace on the wheelchair in which he sat.

"Mercedes! Whatever are you doing here?" David's face showed irritation as he automatically started to rise and realized he couldn't.

"I couldn't get you on the phone. David, what is all this?"

Cutler looked aggrieved. "A rather nasty fall, I'm afraid. I've just returned from a week in hospital. Surgery and pins and all that."

"I'm so sorry. I wish I'd known."

"Why, so you could worry in Detroit?"

"I'd have come, you know that."

"To see an old fool who can't put his feet right? A lot of bother for nothing." He smiled. "It seems you've come anyway, and I must say, it's good to see you."

Mercedes took stock of her friend's condition. He looked fit enough, though lines of tightness around his mouth indicated he was in some pain. "I don't want to jostle you, but give me your hands."

David reached out to her and she squeezed his bony fingers, reassured by the strength in their grip. "I've been calling, and worried when there was no answer." Grinning, she added, "I could have at least given advice like 'Rest and drink plenty of fluids' or some such wisdom."

David raised a bushy eyebrow. "Sounds like everyone else I know, present company included." This was said with a roll of the eyes at Mrs. Peterson, who stood to one side with the air of one poised to physically restrain her employer if he attempted unnecessary movement.

"When a body comes to work and finds her employer at the bottom of the cellar steps, she is justified in recommending a few days in a skilled care facility." She turned to Mercedes. "He's had a bad knee for years. It finally failed in the worst possible place, on the stairs."

"Did our stumbles across the hills of bonny Scotland contribute to this?"

"No, no, dear girl," David replied. "My doctor's been at me for years, claims I walked around on pure English stubbornness."

"And that's the honest truth," Mrs. Peterson put in stoutly. "They put in a new knee but had twice the work, since the ankle's broken as well."

"At any rate, it's over and done," David said gruffly. "Now Mercedes, you've left that poor girl stranded in the doorway." Turning, Mercedes saw the "girl" blushing in a way she'd never seen before.

Surprised by David's gallantry, she made introductions. "Oh, Eleanor, I'm sorry. This is David Cutler. David, my cousin Eleanor Millwick, from Quebec."

Crossing the room as regally as Elizabeth II herself, Ellie put out a graceful hand, though her cheeks remained quite pink. "Mr. Cutler, how nice to finally meet you. If Mercedes' stories are correct, she wouldn't have returned from that last adventure were it not for you."

"Nonsense!" David scoffed, surprising Mercedes still further with a blush of his own. "All I did was drive the car."

"Don't believe him, Ellie." Mercedes again took his hands and squeezed. "David, I've missed you so!"

"And I'm happy to see you, my dear, though I despise this useless state. You'll tire of me in no time at all."

"I have, and it's only half-past one," put in Mrs. Peterson. David answered the comment with a glare, but she left the room with no apparent remorse.

Mercedes had by now satisfied herself that David was himself, which was a great relief. It also appeared he wouldn't misbehave in front of Ellie, at least not at present. That allowed her to approach the second reason for her visit. "Has Colm been here in the past week?"

David shook his head in mock sadness. "I might have known it would be that Scotsman who brought you across the ocean." Glancing at her face, he quickly shifted to concern. "What is it? What's wrong?"

"Maybe nothing," she answered. "Colm said he was coming to Detroit last week. He'd mailed me some papers having to do with Charles Dickens."

"Yes, the Dickens documents."

"So he was here?" Mercedes was somewhat relieved. At least Colm had followed his intended path this far.

"No, he never drove over, but he did call."

"When was that?"

"The same day I took my fall. He asked if he could stop by to show me some old documents and his notes concerning them."

"Did he seem odd at all?"

"I can't say he did." David's tone turned gruff. "He was on about the French Revolution and Dickens." He shook his head as if he'd tasted something bitter. "Never liked the man's writing, all emotion and stereotype. A miser changing into a happy-go-lucky sort overnight—bah!"

Not only did David sound like Ebenezer, he was a bit Scrooge-like himself, a kind heart hidden behind a grumpy exterior as a defense mechanism against the sadness of the world.

"Colm thought there was an important secret hidden in papers Dickens left behind," David went on. "He wanted me to take a look before he flew off to America to see you."

"He sent me copies too, but before they arrived, Colm called and demanded I send the packet back unopened."

David frowned. "That's odd. I recall he said there was a ship's log, and—" He stopped, unable to remember the rest.

"A doctor's journal and two letters in French."

"Right. Colm asked if I'd like a crack at the puzzle." David shifted in the wheelchair, grunting as he did. "I reminded him the era isn't really within my area of expertise." Gesturing at his damaged leg he finished, "I can't say if he ever showed, since I've been dealing with this blasted thing ever since."

"So when he called you, Colm planned to visit me."

David grinned. "I'd say he was looking forward to it." Mercedes blushed, relieved to find evidence Colm hadn't lost interest in her. But what had happened to him? That question caused worry in a different direction.

David noted her concern. "I've been in hospital since Thursday. He might have tried to contact me to cancel but got no answer."

"You were helpless on the cold cellar floor all night?"

"It wasn't that cold, but the leg hurt like the—" He broke off with a dry chuckle. "Never realized how often we involve Charles in daily conversation."

"David, I'm worried about Colm."

"Tell me."

She began with his first mention of Dickens' visit and ended with the call she'd received not an hour before. When she finished, David reached into a stack of unread mail, sorting through several copies of the *London Times* until he found the most recent article on the murder.

"As of yesterday the police had a witness who reported two visitors, one male and one female. They're asking anyone who saw them to call. A relative of the owner says only the papers are missing from the shop."

"Darcy," Mercedes murmured. "We spoke to her." Mercedes looked to Ellie, who took her cue and delivered a succinct report on the shopkeeper's revelation and what she herself had learned from the two young policemen. "I also took photographs of the crime scene, in case it helps somehow."

"That was well done, Miss Millwick." David's brows descended as he thought. "Colm claimed he'd found something of value in Scotland, something that apparently explains why these formerly useless papers are worth something. Colm disappears. The man who asked him for help is murdered. Your copies are stolen, and Mercedes is attacked and almost killed. I'd say the next step is to call the police."

"That's a problem," Mercedes said grimly. "We have no proof that Colm is missing."

"But the police should know what we can contribute to the investigation," Ellie argued.

"You might be correct, but I don't expect them to drop more ordinary explanations for robbery and murder to go looking for secrets of the French Revolution and a Scottish actor who's gone to America, according to what he told his agent."

"They could check flight information easily enough," David suggested. "At least we'd know that much."

Mercedes paced off her frustration. "I've tried his apartment, his agent, everyone I know who might say why Colm changed his plans and where he is now. Who else is there, other than the woman who told me to back off?"

"I can think of one person, though I hesitate to mention the name. Your blue-haired friend formed quite an attachment for Mr. Kennedy, if I remember correctly."

Mercedes' face lit. "Of course! Lonnie introduced Colm to Charlie Dickens in the first place. I'll drive to Birmingham and see if he knows where Colm is."

"You can't just phone him?" Ellie asked, but head shakes from both Mercedes and David stopped her.

"You don't know Lonnie." She turned to David. "If you don't mind hosting Ellie, I can leave now and be back by tomorrow evening. In the meantime you can contact the police."

"Why don't I go with you?" Ellie asked suspiciously.

"Lonnie's a different sort," Mercedes replied. "He lives under the radar, believing that Society in general is a stifling influence on a person."

"Sounds like quite a charmer," Ellie commented.

"He isn't a bad sort," David put in. "He does dislike strangers, but he thinks Mercedes and Colm should be queen and king of England."

Ellie's frown remained, and Mercedes suggested, "While I'm gone, you and David should dig up whatever you can to light our path."

"David can do that himself," Ellie protested. "I don't like to see you go off alone when we don't know what's what."

"Nor do I," David put in.

"No one knows where I am or where I'm headed," Mercedes argued. "You've got the copies and the pictures to analyze." They had looked at the photos on Ellie's phone, but Mercedes saw nothing helpful. The shop was neat and orderly except for several boxed figurines on the counter and the bloodstain on the wooden floor. "David can't reach the higher bookshelves in his state. He'll need help." When neither face changed from its doubtful expression she added, "I know exactly how to find Lonnie, and I'll come straight back afterward."

Colm's descriptions of Lonnie's lifestyle had left her in no doubt that *bohemian* was the kindest term for it. Mercedes was sure she'd be safe, being one of Lonnie's "mates," but she doubted he'd approve of her bringing a second person along.

"You two work on figuring out how the documents fit together. David, you have the resources, and, Ellie, you're a bit of an expert on Dickens."

"Nonsense!" Eleanor sputtered.

"You've read everything he wrote, most more than once." Mercedes shook her head. "This whole thing may be nothing. The Dickens documents might be a hoax, Colm may be in Brighton with some blonde, and Charlie Dickens may have been shot by a jealous husband. But I don't think so."

On one point David was adamant. He wouldn't hear of Mercedes leaving until morning. "It's too dark in autumn to drive unfamiliar roads," he insisted.

In the end she admitted he was right. "Tonight we can go over the information we have. You might notice something in the papers we haven't."

There was still the question of what to tell the police. Believing it was best to tell them some of what they knew, David contacted the office of the police inspector in charge of Dickens' murder. He was unavailable, so he left a message asking him to call.

"It shouldn't be long," he remarked. "In this day and age police officers are seldom out of touch."

"True," Mercedes agreed. "Now let's see if we can find something that narrows our focus. As far as we know right now, Colm may be anywhere in three countries."

CHAPTER TWELVE

SOMEWHERE OUTSIDE LONDON

Scylla put the phone away, a frown puckering her high forehead. "Carrie and her minder lost the two women this morning."

"Her minder?"

"That's what she calls him. My sister's boyfriend isn't one to trust others, so when she's out of his sight she has to have one of his men with her. He calls the man her bodyguard. Carrie calls him her minder."

Colm lay on a bed at the side of the room. "And she lost Mercedes. Guess you people aren't as efficient as you thought."

Scylla came over and sat beside him, pushing the lock of hair that always fell over his forehead back into place. "I really don't see how she can hurt us. With what you've learned we'll get what we want and be gone before she even finds the starting point."

"I certainly hope so," Colm said with some emotion.

Scylla studied his face. "You don't want to see her hurt."

"No."

"We'll have to hurry then. Because if she interferes she'll end up like Charlie Dickens, won't she?"

"No doubt of it." Kennedy's gaze flickered briefly over her face before he turned his eyes to the ceiling. "I have no doubt of that at all."

***

TORONTO, 1842

"A fine turnout, Mr. Dickens," said the stage manager as the author prepared to leave the lecture hall. "I received many positive comments."

"Thank you," the amiable Dickens answered. "It's been a pleasant trip, all in all. I shall never forget the falls at Niagara, and I must tell you, the self-control of the Canadian audiences is a happy change from the ado of those other Americans. What a frenzy they have for news there! Even what I ate for breakfast was published in some newssheet."

The man adopted a sage expression. "A wild lot south of the Lakes. They gave us a bit of trouble in the past, but of late they've settled down to be fairly peaceful neighbors."

As Dickens left the theater, alone for once, a man approached. He was old, probably nearing seventy, but his carriage was upright, as if his back refused to bow to man or to age. Distinguished-looking in a somber way, his face bore the blank expression common to servants. When he entered the lamplight, Dickens saw that his jaw was disfigured, one half scarred and scooped inward, as if a chunk of it had been torn away. When their eyes met, the author saw in the man's gaze intelligence and something else. The word that came to mind was *fanaticism*.

"Excuse me, sir. If I might have a word?" He spoke precisely, a man who thought before each utterance, but Dickens heard a French accent in those few words.

"Of course." Dickens was polite, though he was tired and wanted nothing more than a cigar and then bed.

"My employer would like to meet with you on a matter of some importance to him. He feels it will be of interest to you as well."

"I would be happy to have him visit me tomorrow morning," Dickens began, but the man made a negative gesture.

"He no longer leaves his house, sir, due to ill health. If it is convenient, you might accompany me now. He will not keep you long."

Dickens considered. It wasn't all that late, but he was hesitant to go with the stranger. It was more than likely some tiresome old man anxious to say he'd entertained a famous author. He was about to refuse when the servant, with a gesture obviously planned to intrigue his quarry, withdrew a piece of paper from his coat and offered it. Moving closer to the streetlamp, Dickens read:

Sir:

    We met briefly once many years ago. You were but a boy, walking along the river, and I frightened you badly. My actions that day stemmed from desperation. I am old now, and frightening no longer, but you might find my story interesting. I beg you, accompany Jacques to my home. You will not be disappointed.

Charles Fersen

As memories flooded his mind, Dickens scanned the note again. After a moment he nodded to the manservant, who led the way to a waiting coach in the slow, careful manner of the dignified elderly.

The house where they alighted was brick, solid-looking, and unadorned. The foyer was cold; he supposed it was wasteful to heat unused areas of so large a place. Inside his guide became the butler, taking his coat and hat and hanging them on a wall peg. A single oil lamp burned beside the door, and the servant took it up, holding it to one side he led his guest past an unused staircase and down a dark-paneled hallway. Dickens became progressively more disoriented as they turned corners and crossed intersecting passages.

Finally he saw light ahead, and his guide turned into a room that was noticeably warmer. A fire burned under a white-brick mantle, and gas lights on either side of the room added cheer. The furnishings were expensive but antique in style; many pieces appeared better fit for a museum. They were gently used, but

Dickens, skilled at noticing, saw signs of wear.

My host no longer cares about material things.

In a chair by the fire sat a man of perhaps sixty, stooped so badly that his head came nowhere near the chair back. He leaned his chin on an elegant cane, possibly to ease the strain on his spine. His skin had the look of one who's lived mostly out-of-doors, weathered and permanently brown. What hair remained on his head was white, and his face had a patrician look to it, perhaps owing to the nose, which drooped over the lip, giving a somewhat haughty cast to his expression.

"Your guest, sir. Mr. Dickens." The servant left the room as the host and guest examined each other.

"Forgive me if I do not rise," the host said. "The rheumatism makes it impossible."

"No apology is necessary," Dickens replied. "I am most pleased to make your acquaintance." He smiled as he corrected himself. "Or should I say that I am pleased to meet you a second time?"

The host smiled too, acknowledging their former meeting. "Please, sit down. My name is MacPherson, though here in Canada I am known simply as Fersen. You must call me Charles."

Dickens smiled. "Then you must do the same."

The old man chuckled dryly. "I understand my mother was quite taken with you."

At this point the servant returned, set down an elegant tea set, and quietly took a place behind MacPherson's chair. Dickens glanced at the older man warily. Servants were seldom taken into account, but if confidences were to be exchanged, it was wise to be cautious. "Jacques is a friend as well as an employee," MacPherson said, seeing the question in his guest's eyes. "I have no secrets from him."

Nodding, Dickens returned to the previous statement. "Tante Claudine always said I reminded her of the son she'd lost."

The man's eyes moved to the fire, watching it consume its fuel with crackling lust. "She thought me dead."

Attuned to voices from his work in the theater, Dickens heard the Scots accent. Beneath that was another nuance, pronunciations hinting that English was not the man's original language. French, of course, though he'd left France long ago.

Dickens examined the man before him, an aged version of the sailor who'd frightened him as a boy. That day, despite his own fear, he'd sensed the stranger's desperation. Understanding now what he must have lived through, the author studied MacPherson's face. It reflected serenity and something else: integrity, perhaps. Nobility in the best sense of that word.

"When I heard you'd come to Ontario, I felt the story had come full circle, and now it may be told. I must ask for your discretion, since I prefer it be after my death that the truth is made public. Once I am gone from the world, what I will tell you tonight can harm no one."

Dickens bowed slightly. "I will of course do as you ask, but why have you chosen me?"

"You are a writer, and you are part of the story." He smiled. "In addition, your grandmother was kind to me, so it is fitting that you know all of it."

"And what am I to do with the information?"

MacPherson shifted his shoulders painfully. "When I die, my solicitor will be instructed to notify you. At that time you may publish what you learn tonight, all or any part of it, as you see fit."

Dickens nodded once. "Agreed."

The old man seemed satisfied. After a moment he asked, "You spent that summer at Crewe?"

Dickens nodded. "I was often sick as a child, and my grandmother thought the country air would be good for me."

"I was a sickly child, too," the man said, eyes misting with memory. "Sailing cured me, which is perhaps what made me fall in love with it. When I left Scotland twenty-odd years ago, I looked for a place on the water, like home. I found it at the meeting of the waters, Toronto. Here I prospered a second time, even though I had little desire for wealth."

MacPherson smiled as he interrupted his own narrative. "I met a lovely Irish girl, and we spent many happy years together. It was for her and for our children that I built this house and a fortune." His expression saddened. "They are all gone now. Now I am as you see me, a remnant of my family awaiting death, as I did once before."

"The Revolution separated you from your family?"

The smile that answered the comment was sadly ironic. "My father died in the Terror."

"Then MacPherson was—"

"A sea captain who took pity on an orphan, making me first his cabin boy and later his son."

"You were left in the captain's care?"

"My escort was shot by our pursuers. His last act was to take me to the *Thistle*, which had been hired for our escape." He chuckled grimly. "No one on the ship knew what to do with me. They dared not return me to France, but I had no idea of my destination in England." His eyes, clear despite his body's frailty, clouded briefly. "At the time I was not quite sane. I had suffered much."

Dickens nodded gravely. "It was the worst of times."

Shaking off his reverie, the host continued. "My mother should have died in the Terror, and for years I thought she had. Then I happened to have a passenger aboard ship, a doctor. We struck up an acquaintance, passing the long evenings with wine and conversation. One night he told me of a patient at Crewe Hall who cried daily for her little boy and railed against those who had murdered her husband. The madwoman also wept for someone named Claudine, claiming she'd died in her place, though she herself was called Claudine. The story brought to mind things my escort said on the night I escaped France."

The old man poked his cane at a log that had rolled to one side, trying to push it into the blaze. His arms were too weak to move it, and his face reflected the frustration of one who has been independent and now must depend on others. The guest rose and used the firedog to reposition the log. Sparks showered briefly in a miniature pyrotechnic display. Silence lingered between them. Dickens began to wonder if the man was going to continue, but he waited, letting MacPherson tell his story in his own way.

"In 1795, I had been mistreated for a long time, and I was very sick. One night when my caretakers feared I would die, our servant Rosalie was allowed to stay in my cell in hopes that I would rally with a familiar face for comfort. She seemed tense, and though she nursed me faithfully, it was clear there was something on her mind. They all thought me delirious, and at times I was. But other times I heard the discussion of my fate.

"'He's too weak. He will never survive,' she said once. Another voice replied, 'Then he will die free, Rosalie, for he will surely perish in this place. They've made him mad with their taunting. His only chance is escape.'

"I heard tears in Rosalie's voice. 'I cannot bear to let him go.' The man repeated very softly, 'It's the only chance he has.' I did not know his voice, but moments later I was bundled into a blanket and pushed into a cranny somewhere, perhaps under the bed. I remember Rosalie whispering, 'Be still and very quiet, my darling.'"

MacPherson smiled at Charles. "I was so weak by then that I could hardly move anyway. I heard noises in the room, then silence, then a hurried commotion. A man's voice announced, 'The boy is dead.' They argued briefly about what should happen next, but in the end I heard Citizen Michonis, my jailor, give an order.

'Wrap the body and take it away.'

"Someone objected, saying there should be further confirmation of my death, but Michonis insisted that four of them had seen it and that was enough. 'We have here a doctor who certifies he is dead,' he told them. 'We all know the boy. You, Citizen, can testify that no child entered this cell over the last six hours. Who will disturb Robespierre at this hour to ask him to attest to what is so clear to us?' They were apparently unwilling to do so, and soon the room went quiet again.

"Rosalie pulled me from my hiding place, anxiously checking my forehead. With many kisses and embraces, she prepared me for a journey as best she could with the little we had in the cell. She'd saved some soup, which she forced down my throat, and she stowed a crust of bread in my sleeve, saying I must eat it later to keep up my strength. Finally she knelt before me. 'Louis, you must be brave,' she said. 'A man will come to take you away just before the guard changes at four o'clock. There is a ship waiting to take you to England, where they will make you well and care for you.'

"I began to cry, saying I did not want to leave her, but she insisted. 'Friends of your mother found a very sick boy the same age and size as you. Tonight he died.' Caressing my face she said, 'After the way those horrible men have treated you, my dear, no one but me would be able to tell the difference between you and this poor corpse." Rosalie wiped tears from my face and her own. 'It is the chance we have awaited.'"

MacPherson gazed into the fire for a time. "I won't dwell on that parting, but I knew I would never see those I loved again. The man, when he came, was a giant, well over six feet tall with a broad chest and a beard that hid all of his face except the eyes. They glowed with a fire almost as frightful as those of my jailors, and I knew somehow that he would die for me if it were required.

"My savior was gentle. He had a length of cloth wrapped around his body, and he slung me into it as if I were an infant. Then he covered both of us with a voluminous cloak. Because of his great shoulders and slight middle, Rosalie claimed there was no tell-tale bulge under the fabric. I could hardly breathe, so tightly was I bound, but the ruse worked. The giant walked out of the Temple and into the courtyard unhindered. A horse waited there, and he mounted it as if my weight were nothing." Fersen's thin lips turned down in an ironic smile. "Of course by that time it truly was very little. We were on our way to Calais only moments after Rosalie's tearful farewell."

"What a ride that must have been." Dickens' imagination was fired by the creativity of the plotters. It was worthy of fiction, yet the evidence of their success sat before him. Friends of the nobility had saved this boy, and a kindly Englishman had taken over his care. The world was not such an evil place, he thought, when selfless acts such as these occurred.

Chapter Thirteen

Salisbury

David insisted they should examine the information they'd garnered in an organized manner. Responding to his orders, Ellie and Mercedes dug up note pads, pens, and high-lighters so that each of them began a chart with three headings: *the French Revolution, Charles Dickens*, and *Colm's Movements*.

They started with the documents. Ellie again translated the letters, reading them aloud.

"What are they telling us?" David asked when she finished.

After a few moments' thought, Mercedes said, "Marie Antoinette had loyal friends. That's all I get from it."

"Her women copied her," Ellie added. "One of them took her place sometimes at official events, to save her boredom."

"Where did Dickens get these documents, do you suppose?" David asked.

"He ran an advert," Ellie said. "When he researched *A Tale of Two Cities*, he'd have looked for original documents to use as historical background."

"Very good thinking, Eleanor." David managed not to sound the least bit condescending. "Mercedes, you've concentrated on the captain's journal. Give me a synopsis of its important revelations."

Mercedes complied, adding their suspicion that, though it was never expressly written in the log, MacPherson had adopted the French boy rather than surrender him to a British orphanage.

"Understandable," David agreed.

"The boy, now called Lewis Charles MacPherson, took over the shipping business when he grew up. The *Thistle* sailed under his name until 1824, when it was sold. I found no record of him after Andrew MacPherson died some years later.

Next Mercedes described the doctor's journal and his impressions of the pitiful woman he called the Invalid. "His care for her covered decades, but we have only scattered entries here," she told David.

"Colm said something about that." David frowned, trying to remember. "He found a notation of her death in 1824."

Ellie made a vague sound of regret. "Then we are trying to find a connection between an anonymous patient, an orphan adopted by a Scottish sea captain, and the French lady's letters."

The massive grandfather clock above them struck four, and David looked up in surprise. "Look at the time. I've forgotten my manners entirely." Raising his voice, he called for Mrs. Peterson, who appeared at the door with her boots on and a scarf over her head.

"Where are you off to?" he growled.

"Home," Mrs. Peterson answered with a lift of her ample chin. "You don't need three women fawning over you."

"If it isn't too much trouble," David said with obvious sarcasm, "could we have tea before you take yourself off?"

"It's all prepared," she replied bluntly. "One of your ladies can carry it in when you're ready."

"I'll do it," Mercedes offered, forestalling the acid comment evident from David's expression. "If you'll show me the kitchen, Mrs. Peterson."

She went off with the housekeeper, who said as they traversed a long, dark-paneled passageway, "It does no good to spoil him, y'know. He'll just get more demanding if you do for him too much."

The kitchen was brick, with gleaming pots and pans hung within arm's reach of whatever their most frequent use might be.

On a butcher-block island in the center sat a silver tray on which were three cups, cream and sugar bowls, spoons, and a plate of something covered with a crisply ironed white napkin. On the stove a kettle hummed, and beside it an earthenware pot sat next to a tin filled with fragrant loose tea. Peeking under the cloth, Mercedes found an assortment of quick breads and cookies. Biscuits, Mrs. Peterson would have said.

"You've been baking."

"It isn't much." The stout housekeeper's voice revealed pride nonetheless. "If you'd said you were coming, I'd have done more." She looked at Mercedes with grudging approval. "You're good for him, you know. Get him out of his shell a bit."

"I got him shot," she answered, remembering the dangers she, Colm, and David had faced together.

The housekeeper smiled with unaccustomed humor. "That part wasn't such an advantage, but he's begun seeing people again, become interested in things. He'll never be a social sort, but he's gone to the theater once or twice with one of his nephews. He even joined a committee that's working on historic preservation in the town."

"That's good to hear. Life isn't meant to be lived so alone."

"I'm too old to be doing for him," Mrs. Peterson said gruffly. "I'd never leave him without, but I'm of an age that wants to spend time with the grandchildren."

Mercedes hadn't imagined Mrs. Peterson with anyone of her own, and she glanced at her pudding face with new interest. "I see."

Embarrassed to have revealed such personal information, Mrs. Peterson turned abruptly and picked up a heavy wool sweater from a chair. Gesturing at the teapot, now steaming energetically on the gas range, she asked, "Do you know how to make tea properly?"

"Actually, no, but Ellie will. She never uses teabags."

Mrs. Peterson's face had darkened at the mention of Ellie, but her brows shot upward. "Imagine that. And her an American too." She scooped up her purse, conveniently positioned next to the door, and left, pulling the heavy piece of solid oak into its frame with a decisive thud.

When Mercedes returned to the den with the tray of tea things, she found two gray heads almost touching as they peered at the pages of Charlie Dickens' papers.

Seeing her in the doorway, Eleanor asked, "David, do you mind if I pour, since you're temporarily incapacitated?"

"Please," David replied, and an old-fashioned ritual began that the two of them seemed perfectly attuned to. Mercedes watched in awe. It was as if *Masterpiece Theatre* had come alive before her eyes. With grace and a faint formality, Ellie spooned a measured amount of loose tea into the pot, poured hot water over it and monitored the brewing process. David watched appreciatively.

"What else can you tell us about Colm's discoveries?" Mercedes asked as they waited.

"I've tried to remember exactly what he said," David replied. "He'd found a primary source in a town on the Firth of Foray, just north of Glasgow. Something ending in -*burgh*, I think."

His eyes went to a shelf, and Mercedes jumped up to get the atlas he sought. In moments he stabbed a spot with his finger. "There, that's it. Colm went to Coleburgh. A woman there had done a family history that included your sea captain. He said she was very helpful."

"Coleburgh?" Mercedes responded to the name but couldn't think where she'd heard it recently.

"Captain MacPherson sailed from there," Ellie said. Judging the tea ready at that point, she handed out steaming cups to her companions and uncovered the plate of food, setting it near David so he could reach it easily. He helped himself to a piece of spice bread, deftly balancing it on his saucer as he took the first sip of tea.

After a brief search on her iPad, Mercedes reported, "There's a partial MacPherson family history on line, the work of a woman named Emily Brown. It's evidently still in progress, since she asks for anyone who has information to contribute." Reading on she added, "She's making a book."

"Should be wildly successful," David commented. "Everyone wants to be Scottish these days, whether they are or not."

Mercedes gave him a look before returning to the screen. "Here's a bit from the time we're interested in. Lewis MacPherson, whose father was a brother to Mrs. Brown's great-great grandfather, was a sailing captain. He retired from the sea to take care of his father Andrew after the old man suffered a paralyzing stroke."

"Lewis was a good son," Ellie said approvingly.

"That's not the best part," Mercedes said, holding up a finger. "Andrew had a second stroke and died in 1824. Soon afterward a Frenchman with a grievous facial injury showed up in the village, asking questions about Lewis. Being a wary group, the villagers shrugged and scratched their heads as if they knew nothing. By the time the Frenchman learned that Lewis' home was some distance outside Coleburgh, MacPherson had been warned of the man's arrival. He was gone, and no one there ever heard from him again."

"Did the Frenchman give up and return to France?"

Mercedes set the device aside and stood up. "It doesn't say. I suppose the writer was concerned only with the disappearance of her cousin. In a small town like that, such things become legend."

"Not many apparently honest businessmen disappear in the middle of the night," Eleanor agreed.

"Do you mind if I print this stuff?" Mercedes asked David.

He nodded absently, his mind on the information he'd been given. "I wonder who the Frenchman was."

A leather-bound book lay in his lap, and he began paging through it. Ellie said, "David has a book on the French Revolution."

"David has a book on everything," Mercedes answered with a sweeping gesture at the bookshelves that surrounded them. Connecting her iPad to David's printer, she added the story of Lewis MacPherson's flight from Scotland to the others, making a copy for each of them.

As their host skimmed the pages of his book and Ellie replenished their tea, Mercedes stared at the MacPherson history she'd printed. In her mind, she adjusted her itinerary for tomorrow, but she didn't mention it aloud, since that would only cause another argument. Coleburgh was a lot farther north than Birmingham, but she needed to learn what Colm had found out that wasn't in the story before her. She guessed he'd found a clue to where Lewis MacPherson went when he left Coleburgh.

"Both Louise de Jarjayes and Marie-Claudine Bonet are mentioned here," David informed them. "Louise was one of Marie's oldest friends, and Claudine really did stand in for the queen at events she didn't want to attend."

Mercedes helped herself to a biscuit. "With the paint, wigs, and clothes they wore, who'd know the difference unless she was required to speak?"

"According to this," David said, "some of the other courtiers thought Claudine a bit too dedicated to the queen. A bit of a fanatic."

"That sounds like the Invalid the doctor describes, always lecturing on loyalty to the rightful rulers," Ellie put in. "She believed in Divine Right up to the moment she died."

"That sort of devotion might well irritate more moderate factions who tried to counsel Marie and Louis to listen to the people's demands."

"It's tough when someone makes you look bad for wanting to stay in one piece. I wouldn't lose my head for a queen as flighty as

Marie Antoinette."

"Don't be hasty, Mercedes," David chided. "Yes, there are stories about how selfish and greedy Marie was, but people forget she came to France very young. The Marie of 1789 was not the spoiled child she'd been at fifteen."

Ellie, who'd been looking at a book titled simply *Marie Antoinette*, took up the argument. "The queen had her faults, but this says once she had children she tried to be a good mother and act with decorum for their sakes."

"Too little, too late."

David grinned at Eleanor. "The young are so intolerant of the foibles of others."

Rather than rallying to her cousin's defense, Ellie smiled agreement at David. Mercedes could have commented on the intolerance of certain Englishmen for most everyone and a certain lady's unusual attitude of late, but she decided to be amused rather than irritated at this new alliance.

As they shared another cup of perfect tea (at least that's what David termed it) and refreshments, their host turned to present events.

"While all this is intriguing, I fail to see why it merits murder."

"What's worse," Ellie put in, "is that Colm seems to be the only person left alive who can shed light on the subject."

"We hope he's alive," Mercedes said gloomily. "No one's seen him in a week." Except the woman on the phone. She refused to think about that.

"He might be tracking down more clues," David suggested.

"Or staying ahead of whoever killed Dickens," Mercedes countered. "If Colm found out something important, they might well be after him."

Ellie's expression was worried. "If that's true you're in danger as well."

"I watched in the rear view as we drove. No one followed us."

Eleanor gathered herself in a way that indicated she had something important to say. "There was a woman at the hotel in London who made me nervous. I saw her several times in the lobby, lurking, one might say."

"You never mentioned that."

"I wasn't certain she was anything but an innocent stranger, but I did think it wise to be cautious. I made a point of asking the clerk which roads we should take to get to Chatham. I mentioned the Dickens Bed and Breakfast."

"I don't know it."

Eleanor laughed. "I made it up, though there's very likely to be one there, given the town's history."

David chuckled dryly. "Not only lovely but clever, like your cousin." Bowing gallantly, he said, "Eleanor, I am pleased to know you."

"Why thank you, David. You're very sweet."

Mercedes stared at her two companions, forcing herself not to shake her head. Of all the possibilities she'd considered for the first meeting between the two, flirting was one that had never come to mind.

Chapter Fourteen

Toronto, Canada 1842

"Please continue your story, if you are willing," Dickens told his host after Jacques had refreshed their drinks. "I am anxious to hear the rest."

The old man nodded and again took up the tale of his escape. "The ride to Calais was a horror. I had been so many times torn from those I loved that it seemed this last one would break my heart. The giant who carried me so easily must have sensed my grasp on life was fading, for once we were out of the city he stopped briefly and spoke to me. 'You must be strong,' he told me. 'Your poor papa is dead, as you know, but your mother did not die by Dr. Guillotin's machine. I myself put her on a ship, and soon you and I will board one very like it. Together, God willing, we shall find where she has gone.'

"After those heartening words he once again wrapped his cloak around us and started off. I hardly felt the cruel jouncing I received. New courage flooded my veins. My mother was alive, and I would be taken to her. For the first time in years, life was worth the effort it took for me to breathe."

Something in his tone told Dickens the happy ending he'd hoped for had not come to be. "You never found your mother."

"No." It was hard to imagine a single word so filled with despair. "When my rescuer died there was no way to know what the plan for me had been."

The thought of the story's hero dying stopped Dickens short and he frowned. "How were you betrayed?"

The old man's face furrowed. "For many years I tried to guess at the answer to that, but I was so ill, so confused by months of captivity and deprivation. I have only momentary impressions of that night."

"I understand."

"We stopped on the way. The big man put me on the ground and told me to rest, and I think I fell unconscious. Upon awakening I heard voices. 'Will he live?' a man asked and my rescuer replied, 'He is very weak.'

"Someone came to my side and bent down, peering at my face. It was dark. I sensed the man was young and eager to judge for himself if I would live out the night. The other came and stood beside him, and as they regarded me the newcomer asked, 'Do you have the item?'

"'I do,' my protector replied. 'With the money it brings and an heir to rally the people, we may yet succeed in stopping this madness.'

"A few moments later I opened my eyes again and saw the purpose of the meeting had been to supply us with a fresh horse. The smaller man left us, leading the spent horse that had brought us that far.

"When he was sure the other had gone, my protector took a leather bag from inside his tunic. Glancing around once more to be certain no one observed, he opened the drawstring and slid into his hand a magnificent diamond necklace. I remember how the stones caught the moonlight and sparkled like cold fire."

Dickens made an involuntary sound, and the old man started, as if returning from the past to see his guest beside him. "It meant nothing to me at that moment, but later, when I recovered my health and my senses, the image returned. Then I understood what I saw that night."

"Jewels belonging to the royal family," Dickens guessed.

"I had never seen the piece before, though I knew their treasures well," MacPherson replied. "I believe it was the infamous necklace that contributed so greatly to the queen's downfall."

Dickens made the connection and leaned forward in his excitement. "The affair of the diamond necklace!"

"You know the story?"

"Marie Antoinette supposedly commissioned a necklace so expensive that it caused a wave of protest. The people starved while she spent money on trinkets."

Anger rang in the old man's voice when he replied, though he tried to control it. "The whole matter was a cheat perpetrated on gullible people. Thieves convinced a Paris jeweler that Marie wanted such a necklace. When it was finished, the jeweler delivered it to a woman he thought was the queen, but she was an impostor. Those who hated the queen insisted, even after the thieves were caught and punished, that she'd spent money on jewelry that should have fed the children of France."

"Creating the belief that Marie was unsympathetic to their poverty."

"Yes. The necklace became a symbol of wastefulness, despite the fact that Marie and Louis were more modest than most monarchs of the day, and despite the fact they had no idea the piece had been commissioned." MacPherson pointed a gnarled finger at Dickens. "They were innocent!"

The author had contrary thoughts about the innocence of the French monarchy, which had been the epitome of terrible government, but he chose not to argue that question with a French royalist. Instead he went back to the story. "If what you saw as a boy was indeed that necklace, how did it come to be in the hands of your rescuers?"

"I can't say," MacPherson answered. "Though the people responsible for the deceit were caught, the necklace itself was never recovered." His right brow rose. "Your question should be what happened to it after that night?"

Dickens raised his eyebrows. "You don't know?"

"No. Somehow we were followed from Paris. My companion was shot, but he escaped pursuit and located the ship that awaited us. He died soon after we boarded, and I never learned what happened to the necklace."

"Did you not wonder about it?"

MacPherson smiled grimly. "At the time I was beyond being concerned. My adopted father never mentioned it, but I can assure you, he was not a man who'd have profited from something like that for himself."

"An interesting puzzle," Dickens commented. "You never pursued it?"

MacPherson's gaze returned to the fire. "I want nothing to do with such things."

Dickens dropped the subject of the diamond necklace, though it was an intriguing one. "You never found those responsible for your rescue?"

"No. The captain waited on the dock at Dover for many days, but no one came for me."

"Perhaps your protector planned to take you inland himself."

Dark eyes met Charles' own. "They would have kept the number of people who knew of my escape as small as possible. Robespierre and his ilk would have paid a great deal to know I was alive and free." His voice turned bitter. "And they would have risked much to assure I did not continue so."

"And your mother?"

"I ceased hoping that what the giant had told me was true. Captain MacPherson assured me, as gently as he could, that there was no evidence of her escape and no way she could have eluded the guillotine. I suppose I became resigned to it too easily, since I'd accepted her death once before.

"Over several months' time, as my body fought its way free of the illnesses that had plagued me for years, my mind learned to

117

accept that there was kindness in the world. MacPherson was a true father, and he helped me understand that madness can come upon a nation, just as it comes upon some men, changing normality into fiendishness."

Dickens had to agree. "The English, too, beheaded a king no worse than those before him, probably no more deserving of such a death."

"It is the way of things." MacPherson stared into the fire. "The sea became my home, for it treats all men equally. No one there dies because he was born to a certain father, and no one is raised up because he can find the words to whip the waves into a lather. Affairs in France continued unsettled for many years, but to me it was no more than gossip."

"But then you heard of the old woman at Crewe."

"Yes. The doctor said she often wept for her son, and she wore a locket with a portrait of him as a boy. He said jokingly that it could have been me except the boy was pale, not sunbaked." MacPherson wiped moisture from the corner of one eye. "I went to find this woman and discover the truth."

That part of the story Dickens knew well. "When you arrived at Crewe she was dead."

A sigh preceded his response. "She had suffered much, so I could not regret her passing." His expression turned triumphant. "Nevertheless, I found my answer. As I hid in the trees, waiting for you to bring me food and word of her condition, a formidable woman came striding down the beach, as bold as a gull. She called out to me, saying we must talk." He chuckled. "Even as hardened as I was to fear by then, she was a little frightening. I had to answer pointed questions to her satisfaction before I was allowed to ask my own."

Dickens smiled at the memory of his grandmother in her fiercer moods, and MacPherson went on. "Once she believed I had come in an earnest desire for truth and that I might indeed be the son Tante Claudine had mourned all those years, she told me she was dead. Before we parted, she gave me a box containing things the Invalid had cherished. One was the portrait she'd been wearing when rescued."

"Yes," Dickens interrupted in his excitement. "I remember it was painted on ivory. She often showed it to me."

MacPherson nodded. "The portrait was my childhood likeness. It proved the woman you knew as Tante Claudine was indeed my beloved mother."

"Who was one of the queen's inner circle," Dicken guessed. "I recall she spoke of the court as if intimately acquainted with it."

The old man regarded his guest with amusement. "Well she might," he said proudly. "For my mother was Marie Antoinette herself."

***

SALISBURY

"There has to be more to the story than this." Mercedes waved at the papers before them. It was late in the evening, and she was eager for tomorrow, to begin her search for Lonnie, and if that turned out well, then Colm. "Two events of minor interest: a woman escaped the Terror and found sanctuary at Crewe Hall, and a sailing captain made an orphaned émigré his heir."

"What if Alex von Fersen engaged a cousin in Scotland to help escaping émigrés?" Ellie asked.

Mercedes acknowledged the possibility with a nod. "There was plenty of sympathy for the French nobility in Scotland."

"But who did von Fersen concentrate his efforts on?" David looked up with sudden inspiration. "He's no Scarlet Pimpernel, saving random nobles from the National Barber. He was focused solely on the royal family."

Mercedes stared at her friend as the light dawned. "Are you saying the boy the *Thistle* rescued was Marie's son?"

119

"Once she was dead, what more could von Fersen do for his beloved Marie than save her child?"

"He was the prisoner of fanatics for a long time." Ellie looked for a spot in some documents she'd printed off. "'Great effort was made to reeducate the boy. His jailers made Louis praise the Revolution and call everyone *Citizen*.'"

Mercedes sighed. "It would be nice to think von Fersen succeeded with Louis where he failed with his parents."

Ellie's face lit with excitement. "The dauphin's name was Louis-Charles. The *Thistle* was eventually registered to Lewis Charles MacPherson."

"Exactly what I was getting at." David sat back with a smug expression.

"But Louis died. His tuberculosis couldn't be halted."

"What was called tuberculosis in those days could have been a number of lesser lung ailments," Ellie argued. "Serious childhood allergies sometimes fade with fresh air and exercise."

"Like sailing."

"If the boy was removed from smoky palaces and germy cities, he might have flourished." Smiling, she said, "Remember the line 'returned to life' from *A Tale of Two Cities*? I'm beginning to think Dickens knew far more than he ever told about the secrets of the French Revolution."

Mercedes' mind was on the captain's story. "Then the man who brought the boy to the ship was an escort, not a family member."

"We're guessing again," Ellie cautioned, "but it explains why no one met the ship in England." She patted the book she'd consulted. "According to this, even the king's sister had been guillotined by then."

"If anyone in France discovered the heir was alive," David mused, "it would have caused a furor among the various groups vying for power."

"The revolutionary council would have wanted him back desperately."

"To a life of captivity," Mercedes said grimly, "and probably death from lung problems."

"And if they couldn't control him, they'd have wanted him dead." David took up the book Ellie had set aside, scanning the page for references to the dauphin. After a while he made a harrumph of disgust. "The revolutionaries subjected the child to the worst abuses, making him sing their songs and admit to horrible things like an incestuous relationship with his mother." He paused with his finger on the spot he'd been reading from. "If Louis-Charles did escape, he'd probably have been near death from shabby treatment and close to insanity from psychological torture."

"MacPherson knew the only way to save Louis was to give him a completely new life."

"Louis-Charles, heir to the French throne, became Lewis Charles MacPherson, seaman. He thrived and even took over the business when his adopted father retired."

"It's hard to believe the son of a king lived his life as a trading ship captain." Mercedes ate the last biscuit, wiping the crumbs on her napkin.

David poured himself more tea. "After what he'd been through, one can only hope he found a measure of peace."

Ellie agreed. "Lewis Charles probably lived a much happier life than he could have as Louis Charles, caught up in the power struggles of the time."

Mercedes began stacking their cups and trash on the tray. "Accepting for a moment that this is all possible, who'd have known the dauphin escaped?"

"Those who arranged it," David guessed. "That would have

been kept to a small number after so many previous failures."

"Some probably died in the Terror. It's possible the knowledge was lost."

"But Andrew MacPherson didn't take any chances," Eleanor said. "He stopped trading with France altogether."

"Even when the revolution ended, there'd have been danger there for the boy," David mused. "The Bourbon relatives were schemers of the worst sort."

"They didn't mend their ways after a revolution decimated the family?"

"Decidedly not." David went into lecture mode. "Monsieur, one of Louis' brothers, had worked tirelessly his whole life to discredit the king and queen, hoping he'd be asked to take over if they were rejected. He and his friends were responsible for some of the worst rumors about Marie."

"Creep!" Ellie commented.

Instead of looking irritated, as Mercedes expected, David smiled at her almost fondly. "You know, of course, that Marie never played at being a milkmaid. She never said, 'Let them eat cake' when told that her people had no bread. There was a malicious, planned campaign to make the people hate her, and Monsieur was at its head."

"Did he ever get his wish?"

David's lips twitched in disapproval. "Twice, actually. He was made king when Napoleon was defeated, had to run away when Napoleon returned, and eventually ruled as Louis XVIII."

"Then it wouldn't have been in his interest for Louis XVII to reappear."

"If there was a whisper the child was alive, no doubt they'd have sent spies out looking for him," Ellie said disapprovingly. "A boy who'd already been through hell had to spend the rest of his life looking over his shoulder."

"But not so much so in Scotland," David commented. "In those days a man could remain anonymous fairly easily."

His comment struck Mercedes. If a man wanted to get lost, was Scotland still the place to do it? If Colm was hiding from someone, wouldn't he have gone north, to familiar territory? Without mentioning it to her two companions, she solidified tomorrow's itinerary in her mind: first Birmingham, then Coleburgh, Scotland.

She spent a restless night in one of David's spare rooms, despite fresh sheets on the bed and a vase of cheerful snapdragons snipped from the garden's last blooms on the stand beside it. It seemed Mrs. Peterson had a second sense about such things, and Mercedes wondered as she stared at the ceiling if breakfast was already planned.

CHAPTER FIFTEEN

CHATHAM, ENGLAND

Carrie called Scylla after two hours' search in Chatham. "They aren't here. They must have changed their plans."

"Or they sent you off on a chase," Scylla said archly. "Maybe you aren't as invisible as you imagine, Charybdis."

Though angered by the tone of the comment and use of her full name, which she hated, Carrie also suspected the old woman had misled her. The gawky old thing had spoken loudly when asking for directions to Chatham. Carrie assumed she was hard of hearing, but now she realized she'd meant to be overheard. *Damn!*

"I'll find them."

"Of course you will. It isn't hard to predict where they'll go next."

"Coleburgh, of course. They'll want to see where Lewis MacPherson lived. And they'll want to talk to Emily."

"See that Emily doesn't talk to them, will you?" The sweet tone turned sour. "And don't screw it up this time."

Carrie didn't bother to answer until she'd replaced the phone in its cradle. "My pleasure, Sis," she muttered.

***

SALISBURY

Mercedes was up early the next morning, but David and Ellie were already downstairs. When she entered the dining room, he spoke as if their conversation the night before was continuing. "I had an idea concerning Eleanor's photos."

Mercedes took a plate and approached the sideboard, where there was bacon, scrambled eggs, toast, and hash browns. "Is Mrs. Peterson here already?"

"I did breakfast." Ellie smiled shyly. "When I came downstairs to find David already up, I thought food might be in order."

David sat rather crookedly at the table due to his extended leg, with an empty plate before him. Ellie rose and set various dishes near so he could take a second helping. When he finished, she whisked them away to the warming table. She also refilled his teacup before taking her seat again. Mercedes watched in awe, wondering how her bluestocking cousin had become Hannah Housewife overnight.

"The photos, Mercedes," David prompted. "I might have something."

"What's that?"

He passed a sheet of paper to her, an enlarged photo of Dickens' shop, where he'd circled in ink a group of figurines that sat in a tight row on the counter. "Look at that cluster. Does it seem random to you?"

Mercedes tilted her head, studying the photo as she bit into a crispy slice of bacon. "Not really, now that you mention it."

Like a stern professor David asked, "Why do you say that?"

"They're oddly mixed and set too close. If it was meant to be a display, they'd be placed apart. And I see three Artful Dodgers mixed with characters from completely different books."

"Just as we said." David sounded triumphant.

"But what does it mean?"

"We've no idea." Ellie sipped at her tea. "But it could be a message."

"From—?"

"Mr. Dickens, I suppose, but we don't know that, either."

Mercedes noticed that David and Ellie were now "we," but she was more concerned with the possibilities of the figurines sending a message."

"It could be from Colm. He might have tried to tell us something."

"If it's a code," David said, "It's likely to be a very simple one. Names of the characters, perhaps."

"First or last?"

He shrugged. "Neither works well." He glanced at a napkin where he'd taken notes. First names get us *DABAJLA*. Last names make it *CDSDJLMD*."

"There's a space," Mercedes commented. "Maybe whoever set it up couldn't find a character to represent a letter."

"Perhaps time was limited. He used what he could, sending a mixed message, some first names, some last."

"I'll do the permutations this morning," David promised. "Call when you reach Birmingham and I'll tell you what I've figured out."

Ellie planned to confirm or deny their theory that Louis-Charles, Dauphin of France, and Lewis Charles MacPherson, Scottish sea captain, were the same person. Though hard to accept, the conclusion explained the importance of the documents. Dickens had evidently collected whatever he could in an attempt to prove the dauphin escaped France.

"It happens all the time," David had said at breakfast. "A cataclysmic upheaval removes a ruling family, and for years afterward there are those who claim to be a surviving member."

"Anastasia of Russia," Eleanor supplied.

"And a dozen others, all claiming to be rightful heirs to some throne. Dickens would have wanted proof before he supported any such claim."

"But if he knew the Invalid at Crewe—"

"A half-mad shipwreck survivor. Who's to say she was what she claimed?"

Mercedes tried to imagine how events might have progressed. "If Dickens met the son, the story might have caught his interest."

"Unlikely," David said. "With the shipwreck and the death of his escort, Lewis would have had no way to find his mother again."

"I only hope all this speculation gives us a clue where Colm might be."

"Yes," David agreed. "Finding him must be our first priority."

As she navigated the minimal traffic northward, Mercedes considered what the importance of the Dickens papers might be. Someone wanted them badly enough to kill for them, which meant wealth in some form was to be had. If Louis-Charles had escaped, perhaps his protector took something of value along. Many emigres had brought jewelry, since it was easily hidden in clothing and readily converted into cash. If something valuable had come with Louis-Charles, where had it gone? There'd been no change in the captain's lifestyle, no bigger ship or lavish retirement lifestyle.

The drive to Birmingham and back would take Mercedes all day, but it was necessary. Lonnie was odd in many ways, one of which was that he didn't believe in owning a telephone. "Why would a bloke want some stranger to be able to find 'im wherever he goes?" Colm reported him saying. When Lonnie had reason to be in touch with the world, he temporarily saddled himself with a track phone supplied with prepaid minutes. Otherwise, he conferred only with those who visited in person. "For him it's not a bad way to live," Colm commented. "Outside the people he sees every day, there aren't many who'd contact Lonnie for anything he's interested in hearing about."

Colm had described the procedure for contacting Lonnie in a sort of comic monologue, and she followed the route he'd described. On the southern outskirts of the city, she located a pub called Geordie's Joint. The place was set slightly apart from a group of elderly factories, its exterior fading into obscurity, its sign chipped and peeling. She climbed several steps to a door plastered with ads for a variety of local events: a darts tournament, a harvest supper, and an upcoming charity football match between the Bedworth Blighters and the Coleshill Cavaliers.

Inside, the place was dark as a fun-house, though it was eleven in the morning. An odd collection of items added to the carnival feeling. Along the walls and over the long, battered bar, rows of Halloween masks hung from a crossbar: grinning, antic faces in garish colors and tattered finery. They'd been there a long time, and some of their glory had faded, but they drew her eye momentarily. When she looked away from the masks, every other eye in the place was on her.

The patrons were all men, all dressed for hard labor. Their expressions ran a gamut: some were appreciative of the attractive woman before them, others appeared unhappy about a female in their midst, and still others seemed discomfited by the presence of someone who might judge them for having a pint with their lunch. Possibly instead of lunch.

Moving to the bar, Mercedes spoke to a woman who slouched there, her back against an ancient cash register that dwarfed her. "I'm looking for a friend, Lonnie Beeks."

The woman took a deep drag off her bitter-smelling cigarette. "You're after Lonnie?"

"He helped me once." In the silence that followed she offered, "Maybe he's mentioned Mercedes?"

That sent the innkeeper's eyebrows almost to her hairline. "You're Miss Maxwell?" At the name, expressions all over the pub changed. Interest replaced distrust and lust, and a couple of the men moved closer to the bar, not exactly toward her, but into better listening range.

"Lonnie's told us about you," a bearded, bald, and very black-skinned giant informed her. "Said he helped with that Shakespeare business. We didn't know whether to believe him."

"He did," Mercedes stated firmly. "And I need him again."

"I'll get him." The skinny man who spoke could have been Lonnie's older brother: same frame, similar features, though his hair was more Adam Ant than punk; his face was older than Lonnie's and free of metal decoration. "I shall recur shortly." Without waiting for a response, he hurried out a door at the back, and they heard footsteps going down an unseen set of stairs.

"He'll be right back," the woman behind the bar said. "He's bought himself a thesaurus, and sometimes it makes him hard to follow, yeah?" Nodding, Mercedes suppressed the smile that threatened.

"I'd be proud to stand you to a drink," said the large man, who hadn't stopped staring. His gaze seemed benign rather than disconcerting, and she found him un-scary despite his notable size. "Give Miss Maxwell a Guinness, would yow, Shirley, me bab?"

She had to take a beat while her mind translated the local dialect, Brummie, into something comprehensible. Since she'd had practice with Lonnie, it wasn't too difficult.

Sensing that politeness required acceptance, Mercedes thanked him and sipped at the bitter drink the barmaid set before her. It seemed to please the group, though she'd have preferred a soda. They were trying to be nice, and she was stuck as they all waited for the start of the next scene in this interesting departure from normalcy.

What conversation the bar's patrons could muster was stilted and artificial. Mercedes could tell they wanted her to like them, but they were also uncomfortable with strangers. Though she tried to appear down-to-earth, perceptions are much stronger than reality. She'd been reported in major newspapers. They were unknown in the world and expected to continue to be. None of them could think of anything to say that was important enough, in their own minds, to interest a celebrity.

"Did you come over from the States then?" a chunky fellow asked.

"Yes. We got in on Tuesday."

"How was the flight?" said another, not to be left out.

Mercedes answered in the polite cliché. "Long, but what

are you going to do?" They all nodded as if she'd said something wise.

"Lonnie's on about you all the time." The speaker had a James Dean hairstyle and spoke without removing the cigarette from between his lips. "He says your boyfriend almost beat the–beat him when first you met."

"We didn't know Lonnie then." She smiled mischievously. "But I might do it myself if he keeps me waiting too long." As she'd hoped, her humorous threat caused general laughter. Flights from Detroit were outside their experience, but a woman who'd threaten their pal Lonnie was relatable.

Footsteps up the back stairs brought an end to the conversation. The door opened and the skinny man stepped through, gesturing like a magician. "Here he is!" Behind him came a sleepy-looking Lonnie, his expression confused. Mercedes glanced at her watch and stifled a smile. Lonnie still lived like a teenager, up till all hours and sleeping until noon.

When he recognized her, Lonnie's face broke into a huge smile. "Miss Maxwell! It really is you then! I thought Sharkey was having me on."

"It's me," she replied. "How are you, Lonnie?" With every face in the bar turned toward them, they hugged rather self-consciously. A murmur went through the crowd. One of their own knew someone famous, and that someone had come in search of him. It was the biggest news of the year, outside of football championships.

Lonnie introduced Mercedes all over again, and she had to greet Shirley, the bar maid; Ike, the smiling giant; and Sharkey, the thin man who turned out to indeed be a relative. "Me cousin," Lonnie told her, "but he's a mate too." He named the others in the bar, who smiled or waved or tipped their caps.

Mercedes waved vaguely in their direction, overwhelmed by numbers.

Sensing the need for privacy, Lonnie suggested they take a booth in the corner. "You've been very kind," Mercedes told the pub in general as she followed Lonnie, her drink in hand. Sharkey would have liked to join them, but Lonnie nixed that idea with a shake of his head.

When they were settled Lonnie asked, "What's gone wrong then?"

Mercedes felt embarrassed that Lonnie instinctively understood she wouldn't be here if she didn't need him badly.

"Do you know where Colm is?"

Lonnie's face darkened. "No."

"When did you hear from him last?"

"Three, maybe four days ago." From his manner there was more he could have said.

"Did he act funny when you saw him?"

Lonnie drummed nervously on the table. "I didn't see him. He phoned and left a message with Shirley. Short and sweet: 'Tell Lonnie I can't help him after all. He's not to call again.' That's it: 'Don't call me and I won't call you.'"

"What was he going to help you with?"

"A job." Lonnie settled back in the booth. "See, Colm got me a stint with that lot he was touring with, the Bard's Company. It was only gofer stuff, but I got interested in lighting and picked up quite a bit from the techs. They said I'm a natural for it. Colm was going to talk to someone he knew at a year-round theater about taking me on now the tour's over."

"That was nice of him."

132

"He seemed real keen on it, you know? Said he was sure I'd get in. Then suddenly he can't be bothered to make the introductions. In fact, he can't be bothered to even talk to me about it." Lonnie's voice reflected his hurt. "I didn't think he was like that."

"He's not." She wasn't the only one Colm had let down in the past week. He'd neglected promises to David and Lonnie as well. More certain than ever that he was in trouble, she told Lonnie about Colm's canceled trip to Detroit. She mentioned his investigation of Charlie Dickens' documents but left out the French Revolution. That could come later if necessary.

"Dickens is dead?" Lonnie ran his tongue stud over chapped lips. "Poor bloke! He was a good sort, for all his prices were something awful."

"How did you come to meet Mr. Dickens?"

"Like I said, I was gofer for the Bard's Company. Before they went on summer tour, they rehearsed at a hall on the West End. For one of the shows, *Romeo and Juliet* it was, they'd changed the setting to Victorian England. They asked me to find some special props, so I combed the shops for genuine-looking items, you know?"

"Very conscientious on your part."

"This theater stuff gets into your head, it really does. Some of the chaps say, 'It's just a play, Lon,' but I like to see it done right, you know?"

"I know." She was pleased that he'd found something to care about in life. After only a few minutes she noticed he was more alert than when she'd first met him, less jittery. Maybe he'd stopped bombarding his brain with chemicals. She hoped Colm had had a part in that.

"Anyway, I found Dickens' shop and picked up a few things. In passing I mentioned knowing you and Colm."

Mercedes guessed that mention of his famous friends was a regular part of Lonnie's introductory remarks these days. "Did he show you the papers?"

He sipped at the stout Shirley had set before him. "No, but he told me about wanting to sell them. Charlie hoped they were worth something, but I didn't see it. People think they've got valuable stuff lying about 'cause of those programs on the telly where blokes find lost paintings or golden statues in their attic. I bet most of 'em don't end up living on no yacht." Frowning, he asked, "You think Colm might be in trouble over those papers?"

"I'm afraid so. I was hoping you might have some idea where he is."

"Well, I don't, and that's a fact, Miss Maxwell. I'm sorry."

She sighed. "I don't even know where he was when he called me." Emotion caught her and she added, "I'm afraid for him, Lonnie."

He set down the empty glass. "What do you think we should do?"

Mercedes considered. Lonnie did seem more together than he'd been a year ago, and she knew she could trust him. She glanced at her watch: almost noon. Four hours to Coleburgh, maybe five. She could see Emily Brown today and head back to David's in the morning. "You said *we*. Does that mean you're free to help me look for Colm?"

Lonnie grinned. "Hey, the bloke owes me a job, don't he? I'll be happy to help you track 'im down."

Chapter Sixteen

Somewhere Outside London

"Are you certain they'll connect the corpse in Chelsea to Dickens' death?" Scylla asked when her sister called.

"She's wearing the coat she described so nicely to the police inspector in London. I put the cell phone I used to call Maxwell in her purse, with her prints on it. And I put the inspector's card in her pocket. That way the London police will be contacted."

"What if the inspector goes to Chelsea and recognizes her as the girl who came to tattle on Colm?"

"In the first place, I had my minder smash up her face a bit, so she hardly looks like herself. Second, the inspector in London doesn't know he's ever seen the dead woman before, so there's no reason for him to drive to Chelsea. By the time the cops look for their prostitute witness, none of this will matter."

"That sounds right."

"Gee, thanks, Sis. Now how is our Colm doing with his research?"

"He's figured out where MacPherson went when he left Scotland, and he thinks he took the item we want with him."

"So we know where to look?"

"Not precisely. He says it takes time to sift through everything."

Carrie made an impatient sound. "I hope your Scot isn't dragging his feet."

"I'll see to the Scot. Just worry about your part of things."

A snicker. "You're quite willing to let Mr. Kennedy have his way."

"Not true," Scylla replied. Though Kennedy appealed to her, she'd never admit it to Carrie.

"Just remind him we can hurt people he cares about if he doesn't stay focused." In a dreamy tone she added, "Watching the whore die was a bit of a kick. Now I know what it feels like, I wouldn't mind doing it again."

***

BIRMINGHAM

While Lonnie caught his friends up on the news, Mercedes called David's house to report in. She told Eleanor about Lonnie's experience, ending with, "He has no idea where Colm is." Desperation made her voice waver, though she tried to control it.

Ellie was sympathetic but not encouraging. "We've had bad news here. A Police Inspector Blaine called. He's very interested in Colm's whereabouts."

"The police have concluded he's missing?"

"Yes, but they think they know why. He's the main suspect in the murder of Charles W. Dickens."

"That's impossible!"

"David told the inspector that, but he says they have a good case. A witness saw Colm and a woman go into the shop. His fingerprints are on the glass counter where the documents were kept. Mr. Dickens had apparently cleaned it shortly before they arrived, so there was just the one set."

"But that doesn't mean Colm killed him. Someone else may have come along afterward."

"There was no forced entry. It looks as though the two visitors came in near closing time and possibly locked the door behind them. At some point they shot Dickens and took the papers from the display case. They left by a back door, which locked behind them."

136

"Only Colm's fingerprints at the scene?"

"Yes." Ellie tried to sound positive. "Even the figurines on the counter. David says Colm arranged them, whatever good that does us."

"He hasn't figured out what they mean?"

"Not yet, but he will." Ellie paused. "There's something else."

"What's that?"

"A murder victim found last night in Chelsea is possibly the woman who was with Colm that night. Her coat, an unusual shade of green with distinctive buttons and belt, matches the witness' description. And Mercedes?"

She felt dread settle in her stomach. "Yes?"

"The woman had a cell phone in her purse. She'd made a call a short while before she died."

"And?"

"She called you."

Mercedes had no idea what to say. Sensing her discomfort, Ellie covered by telling how David had grudgingly allowed her to help him move from his chair to the couch for a nap. "He's tired out from all this excitement, but he's anxious to speak with you when you return."

"Ellie, I'm not coming back today. I'm going to drive up into Scotland and find Emily Burns, the woman who's writing the MacPherson family history."

Now it was Ellie who seemed at a loss for words. "Do you think it's wise to go off on your own, Mercedes? You hardly have the resources to locate Colm on your own."

"Lonnie's going to help."

Eleanor didn't comment on how pitiful adding one out-of-work drifter with no visible assets to their number was. "Colm needs to turn himself in," she said. "The police should hear his side of things. It's the right way to go forward."

Ellie was correct. Going off to Scotland was a little like shooting an arrow into the darkness. Still, if she knew what Colm had learned about the Dickens documents, she might get a clue where he'd gone.

"I'll tell Colm that when I find him, but Ellie, I have to do this. Lonnie and I will be fine."

She was glad Eleanor couldn't see what she was looking at, for Lonnie at that moment would hardly have inspired confidence. He was balancing a spoon on the end of his nose, much to his mates' delight. Their muted but appreciative laughter came through the glass doors.

"Please be careful. And if you find out where Colm is, let the police handle it. David agrees." Ellie spoke as if they were a couple of long standing and she could speak for him.

Mercedes wondered if David really felt that way. Ellie might well doubt Colm's integrity, since she didn't know him. If the police said he was guilty of two murders, she was half convinced. But Mercedes wasn't convinced at all, and she doubted David was either. His objections to her going on alone were based on other concerns, and he was probably right.

"How is David's leg?"

"There's some swelling around the incision. We're going to drive over to the clinic this afternoon and let the doctor take a look." There was concern in Ellie's voice, but not for the reason Mercedes expected. "I hope I do well driving on the wrong side of the road."

"Don't let David hear you say it that way," she warned. "It's English, so it can't be the wrong side of anything."

Chuckling, Ellie brought up a new subject. "I've done some digging to discover what these people might be after. There is something of value associated with the French Revolution that was never accounted for."

"What's that?"

"Have you heard of the Affair of the Diamond Necklace?"

Mercedes' mind worked quickly to recover what she knew of Marie Antoinette's scandal. "The piece of jewelry the queen ordered that made the people so angry with her?"

"Yes, except she had no idea it existed. Only when the bill arrived did Marie and Louis learn of the very expensive necklace."

"Was it never found?"

"No. Most think it was broken up and sold, diamond by diamond."

She made a guess from Ellie's tone. "But that can't be proven."

"No."

"You're saying the necklace might still exist?"

Now Ellie's voice betrayed excitement. "The plotters were caught and punished, but the scandal damaged Marie's reputation badly. From then on, nothing she said was believed."

"And revolutionary furor grew."

"Louis and Marie must have felt the danger closing in on them. If the necklace was recovered, they might have kept it a secret. It would have been comforting to know they had diamonds for financial security."

"But when they were arrested, everything was taken."

"True." Ellie hesitated, perhaps building tension. "But Axel von Fersen was never arrested. Marie trusted him, and he was able to move about freely."

"A diplomat from a foreign country."

"Exactly. With his help and the diamond necklace, they could literally have broken off chunks to bribe their way out of the country."

"Then why didn't they?"

"I think they believed the people of France would come to their senses. Remember, they considered themselves God's chosen representatives on earth."

"Then Louis died at the guillotine."

"Yes. They waited too long, hoping the revolution would end or that rulers from other nations would step in and rescue him."

"When that didn't happen, Axel must have become desperate."

"Yes. If they could kill Louis, would they not kill Marie, who was more hated than the king ever was? Again he tried to arrange an escape."

"But he failed."

"Yes. On October 16, 1793, Marie went to the guillotine, despite her friends' plans and an appeal to her brother in Austria to save her."

"How awful." With the reading she'd done, Mercedes had become more sympathetic to the murdered queen. Though frivolous as a young woman, she'd been brave at the end and concerned above all for her children.

"When Axel couldn't save Marie, he might have turned his efforts to saving her son," Ellie finished triumphantly. "If he was successful in that, he might have sent the necklace with the boy to assure he was provided for."

Mercedes glanced at Lonnie, who was now engaged in a game of darts. "Captain MacPherson never mentioned an item of value."

"We're talking about a canny Scot, Mercedes. Say he found the necklace on the body of the boy's guardian. It's worth a fortune. I think it's likely he'd keep it a secret."

"And sell it later to fund the boy's future?"

"David says that would have meant danger to the child. If MacPherson knew Louis was Dauphin of France, he'd have done everything in his power to hide him from the world."

Mercedes saw the logic of it. "Make him into a good Scottish lad."

"Exactly. They grew close, and eventually the captain gave him the shipping business."

"If there's a trace of that necklace to be found," Mercedes said, "it will be in Coleburgh. Something Colm learned there changed all his plans."

"It well may be what got him into the mess he's in now." Ellie added in a worried tone, "And it also got Charlie Dickens killed."

CHAPTER SEVENTEEN

TORONTO, 1842

Dickens and Charles Fersen parted at midnight, shaking hands warmly. Though they were unlikely to meet again, Dickens felt close to the bogeyman from his childhood who'd become a compelling character in light of his revelations.

As he followed Jacques to the door, Dickens thought on the life of Louis-Lewis, royal heir, cabin boy, hunted man, and prosperous Canadian businessman. It was an amazing story. How would he choose to tell it when the time came? He'd have to find proof, of course. The world wouldn't accept the word of one man that he was Marie and Louis' son. He'd ask his publisher to make inquiries, or perhaps hire an investigator. Surely with a little money and some encouragement, there were people who could contribute to the story through journals or letters or tales told over the generations.

When they reached the foyer, Jacques hesitated before opening the door. "He told you most of it," he said, resting his hand on the door handle. "Perhaps you would like to hear the rest."

Dickens turned to look at the old man. His ruined face flickered in the candlelight, but in his eyes was a plea. Like Lewis Fersen, Jacques wanted to unburden the secrets of his soul. Dickens nodded. "I am most interested."

"Will you sit, sir?" He indicated a stool against the wall, and gathering the tails of his coat, Dickens sat on it. Jacques stood, there being no other chair in the entryway. Being a servant, he was no doubt used to standing and would have been uncomfortable seated in the presence of a guest.

The foyer was much colder than Fersen's study, but the story made Dickens forget the chill, the darkness, and the lateness of the hour. He heard Charles Fersen's story from the opposite side.

"I grew up in Paris," Jacques began. "My widowed mother had six children and no money, so I learned to fight for every scrap of food. As we played in the muddy streets, we looked up to see the nobles passing in their coaches, accompanied by servants who seemed to us blessed, since they wore fine livery and ate well. The sight of them was hard to take when your belly was empty and your skin chafed from the cold." He stared into a dark corner. "When I was five, a fine carriage came speeding down the street. My younger brother was playing in a puddle." He stopped, and his head bent almost to his chest. "The wheels struck him." His voice sounded choked for a moment but he went on. "He died the next day. The driver did not even slow down."

"I'm sorry."

Taking a moment to recover his poise, Jacques went on. "I tell you this only because you need to understand how much I hated the aristos. My disgust covered each and every one, and I had no concept of good among them. In the way of much of mankind, I lumped all who were not like me into one lot." Taking a step, he set the oil lamp into an alcove where its light cast shadows on the hollow in his face. "When the revolution began, I did whatever I could to help bring down the aristos. In my mind they deserved whatever horrible things happened, all of them.

"Though my part in building a new France was not large, I was trusted to do certain things. I was quick, fearless, and able to hold my tongue and listen. When a rumor circulated there was a plot to steal the dauphin from his cell, I was sent to spy on those suspected of the crime. I gained their confidence to the point that on the night of the escape, I was ordered to meet one Phillippe, a giant of a man, at a certain spot on the road and provide him with a fresh horse.

"My superior among the revolutionaries, a man named Durand, told me there were two prizes at stake, the boy and a fabulous necklace set with diamonds. Since Durand wanted all the credit, he chose to keep the details of the escape a secret between himself and me. I told him where I was to deliver the horse. He would follow them, kill the escort, and recover the boy and the necklace."

Dickens had heard of Marie Antoinette's necklace, and his interest quickened. He said nothing, allowing Jacques to tell his tale.

"I met Phillippe as ordered, and we switched horses. The boy was very sick, but I felt nothing for him. He had had the good things in life while I had nothing. It didn't matter to me if he died.

"I never saw Durand again. His friends found him dead beside the road, but no one except me knew what he'd been doing there. I realized the giant Phillippe had killed Durand and escaped. I did not know then that he had suffered a mortal wound as well.

"Furious that the pampered boy had escaped our justice, I decided to make it my mission to hunt Philippe and the boy down. I would return the necklace and the dauphin to France." Jacques gave Dickens a self-deprecating smile. "As you can see, I was a true son of the Revolution."

Dickens pictured the unhappy young man's need to feel important and his desire to get revenge on those he blamed for everything that had happened in his life. It was possible, Dickens thought, that he might have turned out that way himself, given a different personality. He'd chosen to fight the evil in the world with words, which he believed was a better way.

Clearing his throat, Jacques went on. "It took me several weeks to learn the name of a ship that might have carried the dauphin away. It took much longer to find it, since it traded at many ports. When I finally found the *Thistle*, the captain claimed he had no knowledge of the escape. No one remembered seeing Phillippe at any of the ports the ship had visited. After a year, I returned to France, but my failure rankled. I never forgot it."

Jacques unconsciously straightened his posture. "I became a soldier, for France's enemies were gathering around us. I joined the ranks, and in time Napoleon came to lead us to victory after victory." His eyes grew sad as he went on. "My heart broke when the General was defeated, but the army was all I knew by then. I was there when he returned from Elba, and I nearly burst with pride when my comrades, rather than arresting him, joined his last campaign, making the royalists tremble and run away."

His smile was brief. "But he was defeated a second time, and the Bourbons ruled again." Jacques touched the depression in his jaw absently. "I was badly wounded in that last battle, and for some time my world was reduced to a cot and a sea of pain."

"When I recovered, the royals were busy undoing most of the good the revolution and the General had accomplished. Those who had supported Napoleon were targets of reprisal, and with my unique face, I was easily recognizable. When several of my former comrades in arms were killed, I left France forever and settled in England."

"Why there?" Dickens asked.

Jacques' smile was crooked due to his disfigurement. "I had some familiarity with it due to my search for the dauphin all those years before. I spoke the language; I knew the docks." After a pause he added, "And when the wind is right at Dover, a man can smell the air of France."

Dickens nodded. "You never went back?"

He made a swatting gesture. "To what? The royals had regained their power, and I could not bear to see commemorations of the glorious Louis XVI and his martyred queen, Marie Antoinette." The crooked smile flashed again briefly. "I was still a firebrand then, furious the ultras got their way after so many of my friends had spilt blood to stop them."

"How did you come to Canada?"

Jacques nodded once, as if admitting it was time to set aside politics and get on with the story. "I worked on the docks at Dover, loading and unloading cargo. In a tavern one night, I met a Scotsman who'd sailed with Andrew MacPherson. When he

145

learned I was French, he told a story—one that had gained him free drinks on many nights. He said the *Thistle* left France one night during the revolution with two secret passengers: a giant of a man who died along the way, and a boy who seemed likely to die but did not."

Jacques' face lit with the memory. "The tale brought everything back: Phillippe, the sickly boy, and Durand's contention that a diamond necklace left France with them. My old passions were inflamed. What wonders could be accomplished if I proved what I suspected! Finding the dauphin would throw the French royalist government into chaos. Locating Marie Antoinette's fabulous necklace would make me a rich man. Best of all, I would be a hero to those who supported the ideals of liberty, equality, and brotherhood." "But you had to find the dauphin first."

"The Scotsman said MacPherson lived in a town called Coleburgh. I took the next available ship north and made my way there. Andrew MacPherson was dead, but his son, Lewis, lived outside of town. I remembered the boy from the day I had questioned MacPherson, many years before. It seemed impossible that he was Louis of the Bourbons, but when I asked in the village about MacPherson's wife, I learned he'd never married. I knew then what had happened.

"I was too insistent with my questions, and the villagers turned distrustful and quiet. No one would say exactly where MacPherson lived. I pretended it didn't matter, and after a time found a child too young to understand he shouldn't point the way." Jacques smiled his crooked smile. "When I got to the place, Lewis MacPherson was gone. I knew for certain then that he was Louis-Charles, heir to the throne of France. I resolved to follow him and avenge myself on the aristos once and for all."

***

BIRMINGHAM

When Mercedes returned to the taproom, Lonnie and the two chums she'd met earlier were talking at a table in the corner.

"I didn't blab to the whole crowd," Lonnie told her, "but Ike and Sharkey know Colm might be in trouble."

"It's worse than I thought," Mercedes said bleakly. "The police think he killed Charlie Dickens and another person as well." She didn't say that the woman was the one who'd claimed to be Colm's lover. That part was still too painful to say out loud.

"Colm? He would never!" Lonnie was incredulous.

"He's been in here a few times," Ike said. "Kennedy ain't the killer type."

"Well, he might kill someone that merited castigation," Sharkey opined. At a look he got from Lonnie he defended his statement. "I mean, a man'll do what he's got to, won't he? And if he had to, Mr. Kennedy is a man, ain't he? I don't say he did. I just said he could. If he had to. That's what I meant."

"Pay him no mind," Ike told Mercedes earnestly. "He goes on."

"So what are you going to do now?" Lonnie asked.

"There's a town in Scotland where Colm interviewed a woman about all this. I'm going to see if she'll talk to me as well."

Lonnie stood. "I'll get me kit."

Ike put an extra-large hand on Lonnie's arm. "If people are getting killed, it's not safe for the two of you to drive around alone. We'll come along."

Mercedes looked at him in shock. "Come along?"

He grinned shyly. "I'm pretty handy in a fight, Miss."

Not to be outdone, Sharkey spoke up. "I'm no gargantuan like Ike here, but I can handle meself. Played football in school. That anneals a man."

"When you was at school, the balls were pig bladders!" Lonnie jeered.

"Look, guys, I appreciate the offer, but I'm driving a very small car. There's hardly enough room for Lonnie and me."

Sharkey's face lit up at her statement. "No worries. We'll take mine. It's quite commodious."

Mercedes spent several minutes trying to talk her way out of taking Lonnie's mates along. Lonnie at first took her part but in the end switched sides. "It might be a good thing, Miss Maxwell. If anyone is out to hunt you down and hurt you, they won't be expecting a crowd, and they'd never expect to find you in Sharkey's car."

"But I'm in a hurry."

"Then you'll like the Streak," Sharkey said. "We done some work on her, and she precipitates down the road. The ride's a bit rough in first and second, but in third it smooths out real nice." He made hand gestures to indicate bumpy and then smooth and fast. "And the interior is—"

"Roomy, like he said," Ike interrupted. "If we find Mr. Kennedy somewhere and he needs to come with us, he'll fit." He slapped Lonnie so hard that his thin frame shuddered. "Course we could always leave this worthless bloke behind in Scotland. Serve him right."

"Whose bit is this anyway?" Lonnie asked resentfully.

In the end they wore her down, like ten-year-olds intent on a camping trip. She told herself it was only for one night. Tomorrow she'd head back to David's. How bad could it be?

Part of that question was answered when she saw the Streak, a hearse that had been re-outfitted, remodeled, and retooled. It was apparently a joint project between the three men, though Sharkey owned the vehicle and insisted on doing all of the driving. The first hour on the road was dedicated to listing the car's delights, with the occasional warning to "mind the island, Shark," (roundabout) or "Look out for the mother with her babby!" from Lonnie. Mercedes soon felt like she was back in high school, on one of those first dates that never progresses to a second. Luckily, all she had to do was grunt appreciatively when one of them stopped long enough to allow comment. Then they were off again: same subject, different mechanical system.

Chapter Eighteen

Coleburgh, Scotland

Coleburgh was known for expensive real estate and lovely views. Like much of Scotland, the city was aslant, its edges along the waters where the River Clyde became the Firth of Clyde. It was picturesque, and from the looks of it, efforts had been made in the last few decades to appeal to tourists since Glasgow, just a few miles south, was attempting to emerge from its industrial cloud to become a cultural attraction.

"How do we unearth this Emily What's-Her-Name?" Sharkey asked for the third time. "I mean all we got's a name, right? No address, and the name was common, right? I don't recall it, but it was a pedestrian name."

Lonnie patiently explained once more that they'd play it by ear. Sharkey nodded, but his eyes betrayed uncertainty. Mercedes wondered if he'd ever been this far from Birmingham before. If he had, it hadn't been often.

"The logical place to begin is at a museum," she said. "If they have one."

Coleburgh had no museum as such, but there were two possibilities for historical information. Hill House, owned by the National Trust, had come too late in the town's history to be helpful. That left the Lomond Tapestry Center, a cozy storefront with a cheery green awning proclaiming its existence.

"Someone here will point us in a direction," Mercedes told the others. Once Sharkey located a parking spot large enough for his pride and joy, there was some argument about who'd escort her inside. All three men agreed she needed company, but none of them was keen on tapestry.

"I'll go myself and be back in two minutes," Mercedes insisted. "One of you can wait on the sidewalk, one in the car, and the third can scout out a place to have dinner after we've seen Mrs. Brown." They'd snacked on the way north, but the growls of Sharkey's stomach indicated that hadn't been sufficient. "I'll buy."

She was back in almost the time she'd predicted. The woman inside had recognized Emily Brown's name immediately. "She's a sort of icon," Mercedes was told. "Related to everyone and never forgets anything. She lives on the hill, looking over the Clyde. Bannon Street."

"Will she mind a visitor?"

"Not at all. Emily loves company, since she doesn't get out much anymore. You'll find her house easily enough. It's painted purple." She saw that Mercedes didn't get it and added, "For the thistle, y'know."

It wasn't difficult to find Bannon Street, which intersected MacGillivray near the crest of the hill. Once there, they drove until they saw a house the shade of thistle-flower, with green accents and mullioned windows.

"Looks a veritable carnival," Sharkey commented.

"Park on the street, and I'll go in alone," Mercedes ordered. "It might frighten an elderly lady to have three strange men appear at her front door."

She'd just stepped onto the porch when a voice made her start. "Hullo there!" It came from her left, and looking around, she saw a woman sitting near a window that had been cranked open to let in the afternoon sun. Though barely visible in the shadows of the interior, her voice sounded cheerful and younger than Mercedes guessed she actually was.

"Emily Brown?"

"Aye."

"I'm Mercedes Maxwell. I've come in hopes that you spoke

with a friend of mine recently, Colm Kennedy."

"Oh, yes, Colm! A lovely, lovely man." Mercedes felt relief at the affectionate tone. "You'll have to let yourself in, dear. It's hard for me to get up and down these days. Turn left when you get inside, and you'll find me."

Mercedes waved toward Sharkey's car to let her companions know she'd made contact. The car pulled away, as they'd discussed, so the neighbors' suspicions weren't aroused by an unfamiliar (and unconventional) vehicle "lurking" (Sharkey's term) outside the woman's house. Their plan was to find Sharkey some crisps to tide him over then return in a half hour.

Stepping onto the brick porch, Mercedes pushed open the heavy wooden door. Inside was a dark passageway littered with boxes filled with a variety of objects, some of which she had no name for. A doorway on the left led to a sunlit room, and she turned into it to find Miss Emily Brown seated in a wheelchair and smiling a welcome.

Emily was so tiny she seemed likely to be crushed by normal human contact. Her eyes, two bright spots almost lost in a raisin face, were alive with interest and kindness. She wore a jogging suit that had been washed until its original color was lost. Her hair was thin, and her scalp shone through, but efforts had been made to arrange it attractively. Despite the fact she hadn't expected company, she'd added bright red lipstick and clip-on earrings the size of half-dollars.

"Hullo." The old woman offered a hand so light it seemed Mercedes touched only air. "You're Colm's friend?"

Mercedes went directly to her purpose. "I'm worried about him, Mrs. Brown. After he visited you he made phone calls, but no one has seen him."

Emily's expression reflected concern. "I hope he hasn't had an accident."

"If he had, we'd have heard by now. It's something else. That's

152

why I wondered what he came here for."

The wrinkled face showed surprise. "He was interested in my family history." She seemed pleased that someone was. "Colm was doing research for a man from London who wanted to know about one of the MacPhersons. Since my mother was a MacPherson, I have many of the family's documents."

"And you're trying to make sense of them," Mercedes commented. "Very commendable."

Emily's head twitched in a minor gesture of pride. "My niece helped me, and we made a little pamphlet. She plans to publish it on Amazon and update it every year or so. No matter where in the world they go, the Coleburgh MacPhersons will be able to find their heritage." Reaching into a basket beside her chair, she took out a small booklet bound with plastic wire, cheaply made but colorful. She handed it to Mercedes.

"I know Colm was interested in Lewis Charles MacPherson."

"A relative from several generations back," Emily said with a nod. "I told what I know, but we have no idea what became of him after he left Coleburgh."

"Can you tell me what you told Colm?"

"Certainly." The lady set her hands in her lap. Her face became animated as she spoke, telling part of the story she loved and had preserved. "The MacPhersons have been in Coleburgh for centuries, and they are often men of the sea. Andrew MacPherson was a bachelor, but one year he returned from his travels with a boy, Lewis."

"That was 1795." The woman nodded, but Mercedes chided herself for the interruption. Detailed questions could come later. Right now she should let Emily tell the story her own way.

"At first the boy's presence was considered odd. People were distrustful of foreigners, even children. Ian MacPherson, who is my direct ancestor, mentioned the child in his journals in a rather disapproving way. Lewis didn't speak. He was sickly. He was afraid of everyone but Andrew. Over time he became used to the townspeople and they to him. His health improved, he began to speak, smile, and even laugh. Eventually he gained a good reputation: kind and gentle with everyone, and completely devoted to Andrew. When Lewis took over the *Thistle*, he was as successful as Andrew had been."

"Did Lewis have any other family?"

Emily shook her head. "He never married, though Ian's journal says there were girls in the town who'd have been pleased to have him ask. He used the profits from their shipping business to help those who suffered ill fortune but refused recognition for his good deeds. He always said he'd done no more than anyone should for his fellow men."

"He sounds like a true philanthropist."

"Lewis claimed Andrew taught him that kindness is its own reward." She raised an arthritic finger. "Of course, only the two of them knew what sort of life Andrew saved the boy from." After a momentary pause to consider what that might have been, Emily went on. "When Andrew had a stroke, Lewis quit the sea to care for him."

"And how did he make his living then?"

"He sold the *Thistle* but kept a share in the profits from her voyages, which brought in enough money for his needs, since they were simple ones." Emily fingered the fabric of her sweater. "Andrew never fully recovered from the stroke. He died when a second one struck a year or so afterward."

"And Lewis left Coleburgh after that?"

The bright eyes lit with the chance to make her story intriguing. "Not voluntarily. You see, shortly after Andrew's funeral, a man came to town asking about Lewis—a Frenchman." She emphasized the word to show how shocking the man's appearance in town must have been. "He was cruelly disfigured, they say, probably a musket ball to the jaw." She rubbed her own jaw in sympathy. "First the stranger sought out Ian MacPherson with questions about Andrew and his adopted son." She tilted her head to eye Mercedes coyly. "Of course, Ian told him nothing. Nor did anyone else in Coleburgh. Why would they tell a stranger about one of their own?"

"Why indeed?" They chuckled in recognition that Emily was doing exactly that at the moment.

"It's long past and can't hurt anyone now," Emily defended herself. Mercedes hoped she spoke the truth.

"The Frenchman's manner was hard, and the villagers took a dislike to him and avoided answering his questions. He took a room at the local inn, saying he intended to stay until he found the man. Someone hurried out to the MacPherson home to warn Lewis." She slapped her knee as if all this had happened yesterday. "The next thing anyone knew, Lewis was gone from Coleburgh."

"Gone?"

"Without telling a soul where he was going." The old lady raised her hands like a magician finishing a trick.

"Didn't he have friends he might have told or written to later?"

"Apparently not. Eventually Ian MacPherson took over the house, but he found nothing in it to explain Lewis' departure."

"And the Frenchman?"

"After a week or so, he left too."

"Where did he go?"

Emily raised skimpy eyebrows. "That's no concern of ours."

"Is there anything else about Lewis MacPherson? Anything Colm asked you about?"

"Not that I can recall." Emily tilted her head like a parakeet. "Colm thought Lewis had been rescued from the French Revolution as a boy."

"Yes," Mercedes said. "We think he was a child of the French nobility."

"Ian mentions his odd accent, but as far as I can tell, Ian MacPherson never left Coleburgh. I doubt he was aware of the troubles in France." She sighed. "There was a time when events outside a certain radius meant little to people like us. Now the news makes a body mad with reports of death and despair everywhere one looks."

"I agree. Twenty-four-hour news will be the death of society."

Emily gestured at the booklet Mercedes held in her lap. "There's something I couldn't offer Colm when he visited. Those were still at the printer, but they arrived yesterday. I'm happy to give you that one if it helps your purpose."

"*The MacPhersons of Coleburgh*," Mercedes read. "This is wonderful, Mrs. Brown. May I pay you, at least for the printing costs?"

Emily waved a hand. "I'm thrilled someone has interest in our family. Colm will want to see it, I think, when you find him. When you've both finished with it, you might donate it to some library."

"How about the one at the University at Glasgow? Colm's uncle teaches there, and he'd be delighted to have access to another bit of Scots history."

"Perfect!" Mrs. Brown's face lit with another thought. "Colm wanted to look at my original sources, so I let him go upstairs and get Ian MacPherson's journal. He was very excited to see it, and I let him copy some of the pages." She glanced at the boxes in the hall and shrugged ruefully. "I used to have a scanner, but it's packed away now. Colm was particularly taken with Lewis' drawing of his favorite toy."

"Do you have the journal now?"

The old woman's face showed regret as she gestured toward the crowded hallway. "I'm afraid it's gone. As you might have guessed from the obstacle course in the hallway, I'm getting ready to relocate." Her eyes dimmed somewhat as she spoke, but she kept a determined smile. "I'll be moving to a place where my health can be monitored, one of those places they used to call nursing homes but now are called Pleasant Valley or Autumn Memories."

Her tone indicated she wasn't happy about leaving her home. "My family worries about me being here alone." She glanced out the window for a moment, and Mercedes felt a stab of pity. It would be hard to give up this pleasant house with its pretty front garden.

After a moment Emily continued briskly. "Anyhow, I'm downsizing. I think that's the term. I gave all my historical papers to the niece who printed and bound the booklet you have there." A twist of her head indicated she'd remembered something. "I did find a sheet Colm must have lost when he put the copies into his portfolio. It was on the floor in the hallway after he left."

"Do you still have it?"

"Oh, I don't think so, dear. They've nearly cleaned the place out." When she saw Mercedes' disappointment Emily said, "It was the entry in Ian's journal where he described the Frenchman, and in the margin he'd written a single word: *Toronto*. Ian might have heard that's where Lewis went, I suppose, but he never clarified it."

He might have heard that's where the Frenchman had gone, Mercedes thought.

When she left Emily Brown, Mercedes found the car parked a short distance away. She showed the booklet to Ike, Sharkey, and Lonnie, explaining that she was now fairly certain Lewis MacPherson had actually been Louis-Charles, Dauphin of France. "He left Coleburgh when a Frenchman came looking for hm. The revolution was long over, but the French monarchy wouldn't want him to reappear and throw everything into chaos."

"Sounds right," Lonnie agreed.

"He'd probably dreaded something like that his whole life."

She wondered if it was time to mention that Lewis might have taken with him a fabulous diamond necklace. Not yet, she decided. The necklace was still theoretical.

Lonnie asked. "How does this help us find Colm?"

Mercedes was perusing the book. "I don't know."

The pages were neatly laid out, and each generation was a chapter. The genealogy went back so far that she commented, "Americans are lucky if they know their great-grandparents' names. You people speak of Stone Age relatives as if you just had them over for tea and crumpets."

"That's because most of our houses are older than your whole country," Ike commented wryly.

Leafing through the book Mercedes observed, "She even included pictures. Look, here's Ian MacPherson. Now is that a typical Scot or what?"

"They all look alike," Sharkey opined.

"What's that, then?" Lonnie leaned over into the back seat in order to get a look at the booklet.

Mercedes read the caption. "Drawings in charcoal found in the MacPherson home. I wonder if Lewis made them as a boy."

"I suppose his disappearance is the only bit of mystery the MacPhersons have," Lonnie leaned even further over the seat.

Unwilling to be left out, Sharkey turned to see the pictures as well, taking his eyes off the road. "Family history stuff is quite ennuious. The old lady prolly played it up a bit, using every photo and scrap of info."

"If you want to look, Shark, pull over somewhere," Ike ordered. "You're making me nervous."

Sharkey obeyed, turning into the parking area of a grocery. "There's a wooden horse, a sailing ship, and a toy that looks like one of those dancing men," he said as if the others couldn't see what was before them.

"They have those at fairs," Lonnie said. "Carvers make 'em and sell 'em."

"Me grandad had one." Sharkey said. "There's strings running through the arms and legs, and when you move a lever, the man dances. Grandad used to whistle a tune and make it go in time to the music. Great fun, but he never let us touch it for fear we'd break the strings or tangle them." He stared at the picture fondly. "Ours was a gypsy man."

"This one's a sailor," Lonnie said redundantly.

Ike pulled the booklet close. "There are letters at the bottom, but I can't see what it says."

Lonnie peeled Sharkey's glasses off, causing him to yelp in protest. "Use these to magnify. They're an inch thick."

"They are not," the outraged Sharkey responded, but when Lonnie put one lens over the page, Mercedes was able to make out letters.

"There's an *L* at the beginning and an *S* at the end."

"Lewis." Lonnie sank back in his seat. "I'd bet on it."

"The toy belonged to the guy you're after?" Ike asked.

"Probably."

He nodded wisely. "When Lewis disappeared, someone found these drawings and kept them to remember him by."

"And Emily put them in her book. Maybe she knows more about them."

"We might speak to the niece as well," Ike said. "See if we can get a look at the original journal. Shall we go back?"

Mercedes considered. "Mrs. Brown is pretty frail, and she's being moved to a care facility. Let's make a list of questions we need answered, so we don't keep bugging her when she's got so much on her mind."

"We could procure something to eat while we think," Sharkey

suggested. "I'm half starved."

"You always are," Lonnie teased. "We'll get you some mushy peas; how'd that be?"

CHAPTER NINETEEN

COLEBURGH

Along with mushy peas, Sharkey downed a stunning amount of other food, including anything on his companions' plates that they didn't want or couldn't finish. Mercedes marveled at his capacity, since she judged his weight to be around one fifty. As they ate she read from the pamphlet's chapters on Andrew and Lewis MacPherson's generations, carefully keeping the booklet away from chip grease and spilled vinegar. In the end their questions for Emily Brown mainly pertained to her sources.

They didn't all have to go back to Emily's home, but the three men insisted they'd ride along, having nothing better to do. Ike and Sharkey seemed glad to be away from uninspiring jobs and time spent hanging out at Geordie's. As Sharkey put it, "We approbate living there, but it's the same all the time, isn't it? So even though it's stuff we like, and it's all the time the same, it gets to be all the same stuff, you know?"

When they neared the house, things were no longer quiet. In the drive sat an ambulance and two police cars. Ike turned to Mercedes. "Shall I see what's going on?"

"I don't know" Mercedes began doubtfully, but he was already rummaging in the open area behind the back seat, which looked like it might serve as Sharkey's home at times. Taking up an empty cardboard box, he tucked its flaps in neatly so it appeared to be sealed. Another search produced a cap with the letters AIM emblazoned across the front. Ike put it on and pulled the bill low over his eyes. With a wink to Mercedes he said, "Back in a sec."

Sharkey pulled away then stopped the car again farther down the hill. Heads turned backward at awkward angles, they watched as Ike approached the house with the hurried gait of someone on a schedule. A policeman met him halfway up the drive, his manner peremptory. Ike spoke quickly, as if harried and frustrated. The other made gestures indicating he was giving directions. Ike nodded, asked another question, and the cop pointed again. With a final nod, Ike started away, the box still under his arm.

As if on impulse, he turned back to the officer and spoke again, gesturing at the purple house. The policeman answered succinctly, and Ike's posture stiffened in surprise. He asked something else, and the man gave one additional, terse comment. Shaking his head Ike moved off, away from them and up the street. Understanding the plan without observable communication, Sharkey went around the block and met Ike well out of sight of the Brown home. Climbing into the back seat, Ike tossed his prop back onto the jumble behind him.

"She's dead," he reported. "Fell down the stairs."

"What?" It was a group response.

"She couldn't climb stairs," Mercedes objected. "She was in a wheelchair."

"Must have, the cop says. Her niece came and found her at the bottom."

They looked at each other, aware that things had taken a dire turn. "Let's get out of here," Mercedes suggested, and Sharkey responded with alacrity, heading down the hill to the town center. A delivery van pulled out behind them, and Mercedes glanced at it uneasily. Someone was bound to have noticed Sharkey's unique vehicle had been in Emily Brown's neighborhood twice on the day she died. She hoped the men in that van weren't dialing the local police at this moment.

"It wasn't an accident," she said when they were back in the grocer's parking lot. "That poor woman was murdered."

"How would we explain that to the police?" Lonnie asked. "Other than them that killed her, you were the last person to see Mrs. Brown alive."

Sharkey turned to look at her from the front seat. "Maybe we should progress back to England." With a sniff he added, "To keep you safe."

"I should tell the police what I know," Mercedes insisted. "The person who killed Emily Brown was the same one who killed Charlie Dickens."

"Which they'll think is Colm," Lonnie argued. "He visited them both to ask about some old papers, and then they died." He tilted his head at Mercedes. "They might even decide you have something to do with it as well."

She wasn't convinced, though Lonnie had more experience in dealing with the police than she did. "Trust me," he said earnestly. "If they consider the poor old thing's death suspicious, they'll look for the easiest answer. You are a stranger. You were there this morning, so—"

"Bob's your uncle," Sharkey supplied.

"But if I tell them the truth, they'll know to look for someone else."

"And what's the truth?" Ike's tone was gentle. "That an old lady was killed because her ancestor adopted the king of France two hundred years back?"

Mercedes bit her lip. "If we leave Coleburgh without telling what we know, we're impeding a police investigation."

"Not like we haven't done that before," Sharkey mumbled.

She was too distracted to take note. "Mrs. Brown said Colm had visited the local library. Maybe someone there will recall what he asked to see."

"You can't go walking around now that we know there's killers in this place," Lonnie objected.

"It's a library," she told him. "Killers seldom haunt the stacks."

In the end they decided to split up. Ike and Mercedes would visit the library while Lonnie and Sharkey found them a place to spend the night. She wasn't looking forward to the call she'd have to make, telling her cousin she wasn't coming back quite yet. She'd worry about that later.

"We need to incognito Miss Maxwell, in case someone saw her go in that house," Sharkey insisted. He found an odd-looking cap and a wildly-colored scarf in the car's treasures, and Lonnie loaned her his wraparound sunglasses. Mercedes thought she looked like an escapee from a seventies spy film.

Their entry at the library caused a stir. Though there weren't many people there, the reaction to a black, bearded giant was palpable. A young mother scooted her daughter's chair closer to her, and a woman took up her pile of books and stepped quickly away from the reception desk as they approached.

"Hello," Mercedes said to the woman behind the desk. "I'm wondering who might have spoken to a man who was here a few days ago looking for original sources of Coleburgh's history."

"That would be Will," the woman said. "He's in the Special Collections area." She pointed toward the back of the building.

Will was a bespectacled young man with the attitude of a spoiled rock star. "I'm sure I can't recall what every person who comes in here looks at," he told them in an irritated tone.

She wondered how many outsiders set foot inside the Coleburgh library, much less in Special Collections. "I thought perhaps you'd remember a stranger interested in the MacPhersons."

"I can't say that I do. I have my own work, so I don't pay attention to every smooth-voiced chap who wants to satisfy his curiosity about something."

"Smooth-voiced" told her the man had spoken to Colm but was being perverse. While she tried to think of a way to charm the information out of him, Ike lost patience. Taking a step forward, he laid a hand on the man's shoulder. It was gentle. It wasn't the least bit threatening. It was almost as if Ike offered friendship and reassurance to a troubled soul. "What'd he look at?"

The librarian seemed frozen for a moment. Then he swallowed once and spoke, haltingly at first but with greater assurance as Ike stepped back. He addressed Mercedes, avoiding eye contact with Ike. "He was interested in passengers leaving Coleburgh for America in the early 1800s. I helped him bring up the manifests, and he spent some time searching them, one by one. When he didn't find what he wanted, he began again. He looked for *MacPherson*, but when that didn't work, he tried something German—von Something."

"Von Fersen?"

He shrugged. "That sounds right."

"And did he find it?"

"He did." The librarian went to the computer and typed until he found what he was looking for. "Charles von Fersen left on May 20th, 1825. Destination was Nova Scotia." Glancing at Ike he asked, "Does that help?"

"It does," Mercedes replied. "It really does."

Sharkey and Lonnie had taken rooms at a run-down B&B, claiming they were a Celtic band headed for a festival at Loch Lomond.

"The only suspicious thing about that," Ike commented with a grin, "is most of that lot would only take one room. Savin' a bit o' cash, you know."

In her room Mercedes paced for a while, unable to forget the amiable Mrs. Brown and worried she might have been partly responsible for her death. She hoped against hope it had been an accident, but in her heart she believed it had not. After she'd passed the same spider huddled in a corner at least twenty times, Mercedes' thoughts were interrupted by the ring of the telephone that sat on the nightstand in her room.

"Miss," a nasal voice said, "there's a woman here to see you.

Says she's a relative, but we don't give out guests' room numbers."

"Ellie?"

"I've forgotten her name, but she's tall and maybe seventy. Talks American, like you."

"That's her."

"She had a little trouble coming north. Hit a sheep, she says. She's having a look at the damage to her car."

"Was she hurt?"

"Nothing serious, she says. She bumped her knee quite badly, and she thinks the car might be leaking fluid."

"That's not good."

"I told her to park in the back because there's better light there. If you want to help her, you can take the exit to your right as you come down the stairs."

"Thank you."

Wondering how Ellie had come there and why, Mercedes made her way down the hall and stairs. The exit door was slightly sticky, and she had to push to get it open. As a result she was off balance when a hand grabbed her wrist and pulled her forward. Instead of a garden, she found herself at the back of the building, in a narrow alley with several trash bins lined against a board fence. Two men flanked the door, and the smaller one closed it behind her while the other pulled her forward, spinning her around. In an instant she was clamped against him, her arm pinned against her body. The man's other hand covered her mouth before she could take breath to scream. With one easy move her attacker lifted her off the ground and carried her toward a beige van.

Mercedes fought with everything she had, kicking and flailing her free arm. When they reached the bland vehicle her abductor set her down, turned her so she faced him, and struck her once across the face, dazing her. Between them the men lifted her and tossed her into the back. She landed hard on a thin carpet that smelled vaguely of dog. The door slid shut, closing out the fading daylight.

Around her there was nothing. At the front, a metal grate separated the driver's seat from the cargo area. Mercedes rolled onto hands and knees and then gasped in pain. Somewhere in the last few seconds her already damaged knee had registered another hit, probably on the edge of the door frame. Despite that she crawled to the door and felt frantically along its edge. There was no handle on the inside. She was trapped in a moving cage. The two men got in the front, and the van was away within seconds. She'd hardly had time to be afraid, but there was plenty of time for it now.

Mercedes thought back to the call she'd received. The caller hadn't said Ellie's name, which she hoped meant her captors didn't know who Eleanor was or where she was. Still, they'd guessed she would come to Coleburgh to see Emily Brown. They'd killed the old woman and then followed them, waiting for the chance to get Mercedes alone.

Why me? she thought, but the answer was obvious. Silencing her—and Colm, she thought with a sense of panic—was key to keeping the story of Lewis MacPherson quiet. Lonnie and his friends might go to the police, but they had no proof and a distinct lack of credibility and were therefore likely to be dismissed. She was the one the police might listen to, the one who could tie several recent deaths to a centuries-old mystery. She'd been careless, too quick to believe the voice on the phone. Now she was in trouble.

They drove north, at least that's what she judged from glimpses of water on her left. Soon the houses were behind them, and the countryside turned to hills dotted with grazing sheep and cattle. Day had turned to night, and the water was visible only as shimmering reflections of moonlight sweeping its surface.

"Where are you taking me?" she demanded, but neither man answered. When she asked again, the man in the passenger seat turned and said clearly, as if to a naughty child, "Shut up." He was the one who'd struck her, and there was enough threat in those two words to keep Mercedes quiet.

After a time she began to shiver. The van's heater seemed unable to heat more than the cab, and her bare arms prickled with goose bumps. She tried to endure it, but as the minutes ticked by, she could no longer stop her teeth from chattering. "It's freezing back here!" she shouted. She felt like a baby, but the cold interfered with thought, and she was determined to stay alert.

The man in the passenger seat looked back dispassionately, unmoved by her condition, but the driver responded. "There's an extra jacket behind the seat," he told his companion. "Shove it under the grating."

The jacket smelled of old tobacco and motor oil, but she put it on, pulling her hands up into the sleeves and zipping it close at the neckline. The men went back to ignoring her, and she settled at the front, as near the ineffective heater as she could get. Pulling her icy feet up under her body, she waited to see what would happen next.

It was too dark to see when they turned onto a tertiary road, but Mercedes could tell by the bumps that it wasn't well maintained. The van slowed as it encountered rocks and pits that signaled infrequent use. As they crested a rise, the van's lights shone upward briefly then dropped to earth again. After at least two miles, she saw an old farmhouse in the distance, dimly outlined in the headlights. They drove toward it, passing outbuildings and pieces of farm equipment, some modern, some positively historical. The van rolled up to the door, and the passenger went inside for a few moments. He returned with a key and a receipt. "The bunkhouse is farther down," he said, "on the far side of the larger barn."

They motored slowly onward until they came to their destination. A security light over the door illuminated a sign that said *Fish Heaven*. "Nice choice, Carl," the driver said. "We can't be seen from the main house."

"My dad brought me here a long time ago," Carl replied. "We're meant to be fishing."

"Fishing, eh? I've drowned a few worms in my day."

"We won't be here long enough for it," Carl explained. "We leave for Canada soon, maybe even tomorrow." He raised his voice to speak to Mercedes. "You ready for a plane ride, little lady?"

She cringed at the thought, but the other man chuckled as he pulled up next to the stone building, long and low, with a thatched roof and wide wooden doors on either end. What would happen when they got inside?

They left her in the van. "We gotta customize your room before you see it," Carl commented. From behind the seat the driver took a bag of tools and a roll of chicken wire.

As soon as they were gone, Mercedes checked the van for escape possibilities. The floor was solid, the grate at the front firmly attached, and the door mechanism, though she could feel through the hole where the handle had been, was too stiff for her to move with her fingers.

Giving up, she sat limply against the opposite wall. Her only hope was that both men didn't come for her when they'd readied the room. She doubted that would happen, since they seemed used to working as a team. Bracing herself against the wall, she plotted a desperate move. When the door slid open she would fling herself out, surprising her captors and perhaps disconcerting their efforts long enough that she could escape in the darkness.

And then? She was miles from anywhere and totally lost. Still, anything was better than waiting to see what those two intended. She searched the van one more time, looking for something she could use as a weapon. There was nothing. She put her hands into the pockets of the jacket she'd been given, trying to warm them. In the left pocket there was nothing. In the right-hand one was a piece of paper. No help at all.

Hearing a noise at the door she tensed, ready to spring. As she gathered her courage, she heard a low rumble. "Miss Maxwell, are you there?"

"Ike!"

The door slid open and she saw the flash of white teeth in the dimness. "Come on now, quickly."

She climbed out, her sore knee protesting as her foot touched the ground. "How did you find me?"

"I was having a cig up in me room, and I looked out the window and saw them take you. I was too late to stop it, so I took Sharkey's car and followed." Ike's voice took on a different tone. "Had to hot wire it. He won't like that."

Just then the door to the bunkhouse opened. "Go!" Ike gave her a push in the opposite direction. Forgetting her damaged knee, Mercedes took off with Ike right behind her. Rounding the van they crossed the driveway and ducked behind some machinery. Carl called, "Max! Get a torch!" The van door opened and closed. A light strafed the darkness, sweeping in arcs and stopping at anything that looked out of place.

"Can you get to the farmhouse?" Ike said in Mercedes' ear.

"I think so."

"Go then."

"But—"

A hand on her shoulder stopped the argument, and Mercedes moved away, running a twisted course so the balers, rakes, and combines hid her from view. The light continued for a few moments, but then there was a muffled groan, and it went out.

"Carl?" A voice called softly. "Carl?"

He didn't answer, and the other man said no more. Mercedes hobbled along, but she hadn't yet reached the house when someone came up behind her. She froze in fear, but Ike said, "It's only me. They're out of it, but we have to decide what to do next."

"Call the police?" she asked tentatively.

"That's an option," Ike allowed. "We've got them for abduction. But the plodders will want to chat with you, and that'll hold you up for some time."

"You're saying we should leave?"

"It's up to you. My guess is these guys are just soldiers, doing what they're told. They probably can't tell us much."

"What did you do to them?"

"Nothing permanent." His tone was casual. "They wouldna hurt you."

"How do you know?"

"If whoever sent them wanted you dead, they'd have killed you at the inn. If they meant to torture you for information, they'd have sent somebody smarter." There was a hint of humor in his voice. "I'd guess they planned to use you for leverage."

"Against Colm?"

"Makes sense, yeah?"

Ike's casual approach to the whole situation amazed her, but she realized his advice was good. If she stuck around to press charges against the two men, she'd delay her chance to find Colm.

"You're right, Ike," she said. "We've got more important things to do."

CHAPTER TWENTY

NEAR TORONTO, CANADA

The small jet roared along. Through breaks in the clouds around them, Colm saw a dark mass, possibly Newfoundland. Scylla was again on the phone, speaking to her sister. When she hung up she stood to stretch her legs, a pleasure denied her companion.

"Your friend Mercedes Maxwell's in Coleburgh. Are you sure she doesn't know what's involved here?" Scylla regarded Colm with eyes that glittered with resentment. "She's awfully keen to unravel this puzzle."

Colm shook his head. "Mercedes needs to make things come out right."

Her smile was arch. "I think your little American doesn't want to give up on you, darling. We can't let her get too close."

"She's going at it from a different direction, so it will take much longer," Colm assured her. "Mercedes is no danger to your plans."

Scylla's face puckered with concentration. "It's not that I don't believe you, love, but you're hardly an objective observer." She met Colm's eyes directly. "You have two days once we land in Toronto. If in that time you haven't found my diamonds, your Ms. Maxwell dies."

Colm's face hardened, but he spoke casually. "I'll soon know if I'm right. If I am, you'll have your prize."

She bent to caress his face. "And if you're wrong, I'll still have you."

Scylla walked away, graceful as a leopard. Colm watched as she moved toward the pilot's cabin. As soon as the door closed he went to work, looking for a way to release the handcuffs that anchored him to the seat. It took only a few minutes to realize it was no use.

He'd have to look for a chance to escape once they got on the ground.

***

COLEBURGH, SCOTLAND

Mercedes and Ike found their two companions almost frantic when they returned to the B&B. Once they'd assured Lonnie and Sharkey they were unharmed, they turned to the matter of avoiding further encounters with what Sharkey termed "bad criminals." In Mercedes' world the adjective wasn't necessary, but she'd suspected her new friends operated with a slightly different set of rules.

"None of this makes sense," Sharkey commented. "This bloke Charlie's papers languished around in his shop for years, supposeably worthless. Now they're causing kidnapping and murder. What changed?"

"Someone had a piece of the puzzle we didn't have," Mercedes said. Since these men had taken her so completely into their care, she decided it was time to trust them with all that she knew. She told them about the diamond necklace and the possibility it had come to Scotland with MacPherson.

Though she guessed her listeners had all stepped outside the law at some point, she had no fear that Lonnie, Ike, and Sharkey would be blinded by lust for the fabulous diamond necklace. These men lived by a code, and while it wasn't exactly Society's ideal, none of them would cheat or steal from someone they called friend. Mercedes was their friend, and Ike had risked his life for her. In fact she was pretty sure he'd have died to save her. Such courage was rare, and it made her feel slightly better about the dangers of her present situation.

***

1793 PARIS

"Widow Capet. It is time." Her jailor, a man chosen both for his

173

dour disposition and his hatred of the monarchy, directed a grim smile at her.

Marie Antoinette had no way to make herself presentable, but it no longer mattered. Her maid fluttered about, tears coursing down her cheeks as she combed her mistress' lank hair with her fingers and wiped dirt from her face with a wet finger. It was useless: she was so emaciated, so aged by sorrow, that the woman who'd been queen of France was unrecognizable in the face of the woman who today would be beheaded at the guillotine.

The thought of the mob seeing her this way, unkempt and haggard, no longer had the power to upset Marie. They'd taken everything from her. Louis was dead. Axel had been unable to arrange her release or convince anyone outside France to help. She hadn't seen her beloved Louis-Charles in...She didn't know how long. The days had begun to meld together.

They took him in July, saying the king was henceforth theirs. She'd held them off until they threatened to kill her daughter if she didn't give up her son. A month after that she lost contact with the rest of her family. Transferred to the Conciergerie Prison with only the maid as companion, she became Antoinette Capet, or more often, Prisoner Number Two Hundred-eighty.

There'd been a trial of sorts, but the outcome was known before it began. Two days ago she'd been sentenced to death. Writing a final letter to her sister-in-law Elisabeth, she'd asked her to give the children her love and tell them not to seek revenge. After that, it was a matter of waiting.

"What is the day, citizen?" She'd learned that if she didn't address the jailor in this way, she received no answer.

"It is October sixteenth, the morning of your death," he responded in a hard tone. "We will see if you have the courage to face it well."

Usually she tried not to respond to his stupid cruelty, but an answer came out before she could stop herself. "Courage? I have shown it for years. Think you I shall lose it at the moment when my sufferings are to end?"

His answer was a snort of disbelief, and she wondered if she could indeed be brave. The guillotine was designed to be quick, but when she stood before it, would she faint from fear? She hoped she could die calmly, as Louis had. But the horror of the grinning crowds, the shouted insults, and the blood of all those who had gone before might combine to defeat her.

A guard came with scissors and cut her hair with rough snips, the better to sever her neck. This was almost a kindness, since she'd heard stories of botched executions where the subject didn't die with the first blow. Still, her head felt light without the weight of her hair, her neck chilly in the dank air.

More guards met her at the door of her cell, silent and unsmiling. One of them bound her hands in front. *As if I have the strength to fight my way free,* she thought.

No one spoke, but they moved to surround her as she stepped out of confinement for the first time in two months. Her confessor was waiting, and he took his place behind her, already mouthing prayers for her soul. He whispered something in her ear, apparently a comforting scripture, and then fell back, his head low. Her heart raced, but she gave no outward sign.

Outside the prison, she clutched her stomach and fell to the ground, retching. "I am sick. Please!"

One of the guards said something both cruel and disgusting, but another barked a command. "Over there." He gestured toward the wall, and she staggered away, still crouched. It was known that her body had reacted to the stresses of her imprisonment, and none of the guards wanted to be near when noxious substances were emitted.

The priest, followed, apparently dutiful. Several of Marie's friends waited by the wall, and they took the opportunity to do final service to their queen. Using their bodies, they shielded her from the eyes of the guards so that her agony was somewhat private. One man shouted a jeering comment. "Your guts are telling you they will soon be missing your head!'

In the cluster of women, Marie felt the rope that held her hands fall away. Her cap was snatched from her head and a scarf of thick wool replaced it. She was pulled to her feet, and Louise de Jarjaye spoke quickly in her ear. "Be quiet, my dear, and keep your head down. Behave as if you cannot bear to see the poor queen die, and I will lead you away."

"But what—?"

"Hush, now! There's no time. Do as I say." Marie had never heard such forcefulness from Louise, but her months of captivity served her well. She did as she was told without further question.

When the group of women parted a prisoner emerged, weak and staggering. The priest stepped in to help as she returned to the guards, still bent over in pain. The tumbril sat at the gateway, and the woman was assisted into it, none too gently. Her ride through the streets would take an hour, and the crowds would scream all manner of hateful things at her. She would sit bravely through it all, her back straight and her face expressionless. At the end, when she knelt to place her head under the blade of the guillotine, she was afraid, but also exultant. For Marie Claudine, friend of the Queen of France, had accomplished her purpose. She'd saved Marie from death. She regarded it as an honor to take her place, fooling the fools who thought they were good enough to rule France.

***

COLEBURGH

They moved to a different B&B, hiding the car at the back and counting on the number of such establishments in the area to make it impossible for their pursuers to find them.

The next morning Mercedes rose early and sat in her tiny

bedroom until she could no longer stand it. She'd tried to sleep in the few hours of darkness left of the night, but images of being trapped in the back of the old van, fearful of what would happen to her, had made that impossible. At six she went downstairs to find the three men already there, heads together in quiet conference. "Ike persuaded the host to start breakfast a little early," Lonnie reported, and Mercedes smiled despite her exhaustion. Any suggestion the big man made seemed likely to be treated as if it were a command.

The sun was still a gray ghost on the horizon, and the inn's corners were cold, so Mercedes still wore the jacket she'd been given by her captors. "Sorry if I smell like cigarette smoke, but it's warm."

"No worries, but we should get you something decent to wear," Lonnie said. "When the shops open up—"

"We'll be long gone," Ike broke in. "We need to get Miss Maxwell somewhere safe."

"But something Colm found out here gave him the answers he was looking for," she objected. "We just don't know what it was."

"We know MacPherson left here and went to Canada," Lonnie said. "I'd say Colm has gone to wherever MacPherson ended up."

"Right. His family might have the necklace and don't know what it is." Sharkey seemed fascinated by the possibility of discovering historical secrets. "They might think it's just paste, but it would be worth a very emphatic amount of money today. I mean, diamonds is always worth a lot, but old diamonds what's been worn by queens and all would be worth even more, right?"

"So what's the old lady at Crewe got to do with MacPherson?" Lonnie asked as they tucked into eggs, sausages, and tea. "Why did Dickens keep all that stuff about her?"

"We think Charles met her when he was a child. She might have told him things that got him interested in the story of Lewis MacPherson."

"Maybe she brought the necklace from France," Sharkey proposed, "and kept it for the royal family."

"I don't think she could have. Tante Claudine was shipwrecked and found half-dead on the English shore. If she'd had anything of value, those who rescued her would have found it. If the necklace does exist, it had to have come across the Channel with the boy."

Lonnie thought about that. "The bodyguard died, you said."

"Which would have left Captain MacPherson in charge of Louis and the necklace."

Lonnie seemed to be trying to picture the situation in his mind's eye. "As they're crossing the channel, he finds out he's got a very important kid and a diamond necklace. Could have been a big payoff for him."

"MacPherson was a straight arrow," Mercedes said. "If he thought the necklace put the boy in danger, I think he'd have hidden it."

"You say he was religious," Ike said. "He might have believed what Scripture says about money being the root of all evil."

"It's the *love* of money," Sharkey put in, and they all looked at him in wonder. "Well, it is. Me gran' was a great one for quoting the Bible, trying to make me into a better bloke. Some of it just adhered to me, dayn't it?"

They all chuckled at that, but Mercedes went on building a scenario. "MacPherson probably intended to give the necklace to Louis eventually, but the family history says he had a stroke and was unable to communicate in the last months of his life." She shook her head. "Imagine his frustration. He couldn't let his adopted son know he possessed a fortune in diamonds."

Lonnie screwed up his face in the way Mercedes recognized meant deep thought. "So when the old man's dead, Lewis finds out somebody that knows his real identity is on his trail. He leaves Coleburgh, maybe headed for Canada. Where did he end up? And

178

did the necklace go with him?"

Ike wiped his mouth with his napkin. "My theory is that's what whoever has Colm is trying to find out."

Sharkey nodded. "Colm had Charlie Dickens' papers, so they grabbed him. Now they're afraid Miss Maxwell might find the necklace first."

"They could have it if I could be sure Colm's okay." Mercedes bit at a fingernail. "What happens when they get what they want from him? If they've killed for the information already, what's to stop them—" She broke off, unable to finish the thought.

"Colm isn't stupid," Lonnie said in a valiant effort to reassure her. "He'll figure out ways to make sure they need him."

"Right," Ike put in. "He'll feed them the information in bits."

"Or give them disinformation," Sharkey corrected, laying a finger alongside his nose.

"Maybe we do need the police." Lonnie looked to Mercedes, but she recalled Ike's earlier assessment. "What would we tell them?"

"We can't prove Colm's a prisoner," Ike said. "Why should they believe us? Because we have some little old lady's book of family ancestry?"

Sharkey pointed with his fork. "Mercedes was kidnapped, wasn't she?"

"And what evidence do you think there'll be of that?" Ike pushed his empty plate aside. "Once those guys get free, they'll erase any trace of their presence." He picked up his teacup, which looked miniature in his hand. "We've got nothing."

As they spoke, Mercedes had put her hand into the pocket of the jacket provided by her captors. "Look at this."

She showed them the piece of paper. In a hurried, careless scrawl was a number followed by *Br. A T-O-R. 9:35.*"

Mercedes handed the paper around. "They were supposed to

call someone when they had you secure," Ike surmised. "What's *Tor* then?"

"Torrenham!" Sharkey suggested. "I got a cousin there."

"That makes it a sure bet, then," Lonnie scoffed. "If Benny's there, it's the center of criminal activity in England."

"Think Canada," Mercedes prompted.

Lonnie's eyes rounded. "It's Toronto! They're going to Toronto."

"If they've taken Colm there, dealing with the police here will slow me down. I can't risk it."

"Right," Ike said. "We can always look up a Mountie when we get there."

Mercedes' eyes widened. "You're going with me?"

Lonnie grinned. "I've always wanted to see the Great White North. Do they live in igloos, like on the cartoons, or have they got huts and all nowadays?"

***

COLEBURGH

Mercedes called David as Sharkey drove to Birmingham in a sulk. The only one of the three who didn't have a passport, he would not be making the trip to Canada. He wasn't at all pleased at the prospect of being left behind.

"You have passports?" Mercedes had asked doubtfully at breakfast.

"Yeah, sure." Lonnie was cheerful. "Me and Ike had a band for a while, the Brummie Ghouls. We wore black and drew skulls over our faces in white paint. It looked cool."

Considering the shiny blackness of Ike's skin, Mercedes had trouble imagining it, but she murmured, "Right."

"We got passports last year 'cause we hooked up with this

180

other group, Purple Magenta, who was going on world tour. They was going to have us open for them in Bahrain."

"But the Purps got arrested for trafficking," Sharkey put in gleefully. "They didn't go nowhere except to a penal institution."

"*We* never went to jail," Lonnie said with a sniff. "We was released for lack of evidence."

Mercedes chose not to ask if lack of evidence translated to lack of guilt. Instead she tried to dissuade Ike and Lonnie, arguing their presence was unnecessary. Neither would consider for a moment letting her go alone.

"If your Mr. Kennedy's in trouble, you're going to need us," Ike argued.

"But it should look like I'm alone, like I'm giving up and going home."

"We can blend," Lonnie insisted. "I'll get a cap and dress like a toff, wear stuff that covers me body art. I'll even take out the studs."

She regarded Ike, hard to miss due to his massive size and deep black skin. Still, judging from his performance last night, he was well able to handle himself.

Though they contended they could pay their own way, Mercedes put the tickets on her credit card. She told herself that at least if anyone was looking for her, they'd be seeking one or two lone females, not a mixed party of three.

The next step was to call Ellie and David and explain her altered travel plans. She chose to explain it to Ellie, fearing David's pointed questions. When she'd covered the basics, leaving out her recent kidnapping, she ended with her intention to travel to Toronto. "You can stay where you are, and I'll meet you somewhere in a few days."

Ellie had ideas of her own. "I'll meet you in Toronto," she said firmly. "You might need my help."

Mercedes thought she had all the help she could cope with at the moment, but she heard David's voice and guessed he was listening in. "Of course she'll meet you."

"David needs you," Mercedes tried, but he spoke again.

"For pity's sake! I'm not some hothouse plant that needs tending."

Giving up, she spoke to David directly. "Judging from your mood, I'd say you're in some discomfort."

"And I will get over it. How do you women think I've functioned for seventy-four years without you? Eleanor will lend credence to your case, being a citizen of the country, having some maturity, and—" He alluded to Lonnie, "—lacking exotic personal adornment. You may keep me informed of your progress, and I'll do what I can from here."

"I suppose you're right."

"Of course I am," David spoke more calmly once he'd won. "I shall continue to study your Dickens papers carefully. Mrs. Peterson will get my medicine and see to my needs."

Mercedes knew that was true. Weary of her job or no, Mrs. Peterson cared about her employer and would see to his care.

"All right," she conceded. "You can probably get a connecting flight from Salisbury. I'll be at the Royal York by midnight tonight, I hope."

"Eleanor did come up with something that makes sense in light of what you've told us," David said. "We tried for some time to decode the figurines left on the counter in Dickens' shop. I had decided they meant nothing, but she kept putting the letters together this way and that." He paused. "Eleanor, will you tell her?"

Ellie's voice came through again. "Well, one of the combinations I made fits with Toronto. There was no sense to be made from all letters of the characters' first names nor their last names. But if you mix them, one possibility comes out—at least I think so."

Sensing she was hesitant to say what she'd found, Mercedes encouraged her. "What might the figurines' names spell out, Ellie?"

"Well, there's David Copperfield, which gives us a *C*, and the Artful Dodger, which we can use for a vowel. That's *C-A*. Then there's Bill Sikes, from Oliver Twist. We'll take the *S*. Then a second Artful Dodger, another *A*. Next is Jarvis Lorry; we'll use the *L*, then a space. I'm guessing whoever set the figurines up simply couldn't find a character to signify the letter he wanted. After that is Luci Manette, which gives us an *M*, and yet another Artful Dodger, a final *A*."

Mercedes had been picturing the letters in her mind as Ellie named them. "*C-A-S-A-L*-something-*M-A*."

"You know it, don't you?" Ellie asked. "Casa Loma is one of the big tourist attractions in Toronto. You've figured out the country and the city. Could it be that Colm was trying to tell you where he expected to end up?"

CHAPTER TWENTY-ONE

BIRMINGHAM

Birmingham's airport was crowded with the usual mix of travelers. Business people strode confidently forward, dragging wheeled suitcases that seemed part of them. Bewildered children were clutched, carried, and wheeled by parents whose eyes focused upward, scanning signs for the correct destination. Uniformed staff performed their tasks with practiced precision and barely concealed boredom.

"What's this?" the baggage checker asked suspiciously.

"Lip gloss," Mercedes replied, feeling silly at the need to pronounce so obvious a fact.

"What's this?"

"Hand lotion." The man's expression never changed, never relaxed, but he did thrust the plastic bucket at her and turn away, signaling she was free to go. She stepped forward and stopped to wait for Lonnie and Ike, who were behind her in line. Lonnie gave her a cheerful grin then grimaced to signal impatience. As his knapsack went through the scanner, Mercedes saw the woman behind the machine frown, lean in for a better look, and then glance at him in disbelief.

Lonnie looked almost normal, having done all he'd promised to make himself less conspicuous. He wasn't bad looking "dressed down" to near normality, and his appearance shouldn't have called the attention of the screeners. "Step over here if you will, sir." The order was polite but firm.

Glancing at Mercedes, Lonnie obeyed. She craned her neck as unobtrusively as possible to get a look at what had caused the security worker's concern. The officer pulled something from

Lonnie's knapsack and then opened his hand to show it. Lonnie's face froze at the sight. A bullet!

Mercedes looked over to the next line, where Ike had just passed through the metal detector. Watching the officer's expression as Ike's bag went through the machine, she caught a similar look of recognition. "Here," the man called, and a burly officer stepped up.

"This way, sir," he said to Ike, pulling the bag from the conveyer. He waited, stone-faced, for Ike to do as ordered. As he moved to comply Ike looked at Mercedes, his expression conveying an understanding Lonnie's had not. *Go on,* his eyes signaled, and she nodded. They'd been set up. She could stay with them and miss the plane or leave them to sort things out and follow later. Ike was giving her permission to go. She went, glad no one realized they'd been traveling together. Still, she had to be extra cautious. It seemed her pursuers knew everything they did.

While waiting for boarding, Mercedes called Ellie. "Can you tell me exactly what the woman in the hotel that first night looked like? The one you fed the false story to?" Of course she had to explain why she wanted to know, and she gave an abridged version of the last day's events, ending with, "Someone is keeping tabs."

Ellie wasted no further effort trying to change her plans. "I'd say she was in her late twenties, about your height with dark hair and eyes. She was thin, and pretty in a rather plastic way. That's all I remember except that she had very small ears."

"Small ears?"

"Yes, I notice ears for some reason, and this woman's were almost miniature. Her hair was pulled up that day. I don't suppose you'd see them in most circumstances."

"Thanks, Ellie."

"Be extra careful," Ellie warned. "I'm glad you have a couple of men along to protect you."

"Mmm. I'd better go. See you soon."

As she waited for the boarding call, Mercedes found herself examining every attractive woman in the vicinity. There were two that fit Ellie's description. One had her hair down, so her ears were invisible, and the other, who'd clipped her dark hair back from her face with barrettes, had ears of normal size—at least as far as Mercedes had ever considered the dimensions of those appendages. Both women were absorbed in reading and paid no obvious attention to her, even when she moved around the waiting area.

A bored worker spoke into the microphone, informing passengers that their flight was over-booked. The airline was looking for a passenger with a flexible schedule who'd be willing to accept a free future flight in return for taking a later one today. Acting on a sudden impulse, Mercedes approached the counter and smiled at the woman who'd made the announcement. "I have a request that may sound strange."

One eyebrow quirked doubtfully. She'd heard all the stories, it implied, and disapproved of most.

"I write romance novels. You might know my pen name, Jerilyn Savage?" She shook her head, but a spark of interest showed, and she checked Mercedes out more closely. Novelists apparently looked just like everyone else.

"My books do well in the States," she explained, "but they're just starting to spread to Europe. My heroine is a time-traveler who becomes one of Genghis Khan's wives."

"I see." The woman's gaze unfocused momentarily as she pictured that scenario.

"I'm hoping you might be able to help me. There's a woman who's a huge fan of my work, and that was flattering at first. Lately she's become kind of...obsessed."

"A stalker?"

"I hate to put it that way, but yes. She shows up at my appearances, follows me to restaurants, stays in the same hotels, and even takes the same flights as I do. She thinks we're friends, which makes things awkward for me."

"How does she know where you are?"

Mercedes grimaced helplessly. "I don't know. It's like she has my phone tapped or something."

The employee pursed her lips. "She's got into your computer, I bet. She can see your reservations and such."

"That's very possible," Mercedes said, making a mental note to no longer use her tablet for such things. "Right now I'd just like to get back home without her harassing me on the plane." She leaned toward the woman. "On the way over, she asked the man in the seat next to me if he'd mind switching with her so we could 'confer'. Honestly, she'd be pitiful if she weren't so invasive."

"There's all kinds in the world," the woman opined. "Some aren't easy to deal with."

"I won't ask you to do anything that's against policy, but if a dark-haired woman of about my age comes up after I walk away and asks, could you kind of imply that I took the offer of a later flight? I'll leave the area for a while, and maybe she'll think I changed my itinerary. I'll return just in time to board."

Her newest friend turned stern. "You should seek legal means to stop her from following you."

"You're right," Mercedes agreed. "I'll do that as soon as I get home."

The clerk nodded, her eyes passing over the waiting area in search of the woman Mercedes had described. "If she asks what flight you took, I should put her on that one?"

"I don't think you'll have to lie. You can just tell her the next available flight to Toronto is at—"

"Ten-thirty this evening," the woman supplied.

"That would be great. Thank you." Mercedes put her boarding pass on the counter. Taking the hint the clerk picked it up, typed some random strokes into her computer, made an apparent notation, and handed it back.

"You've got fifteen minutes." Now her smile was conspiratorial. "Can you stay out of sight for that long?"

"I think so. And thank you very much." Mercedes retreated down the concourse, hoping she appeared bound for somewhere else. If she'd looked back, she'd have seen the woman with long dark hair get up and approach the airline desk. The flight attendant suppressed a smile as she explained the terms of the reward for passengers with flexible schedules.

***

TORONTO

"What now?" Scylla demanded as they left the plane of a private airstrip. A rental car waited, and she took the driver's seat as Colm was guided to the front and his right hand cuffed to the armrest. The man who accompanied them—Scylla called him Rick—pocketed his gun and climbed into the back, his manner turning from intimidating to passive like a cyborg going into rest mode.

Rick was on the high end of average in height, but his shoulders and arms were oversized. He focused all his energy on Colm, treating him neither gently nor abusively. He was simply efficient. Colm guessed he was hired muscle, since he and Scylla didn't seem to know each other well. Rick had seemed familiar with the private jet while Scylla wasn't, which meant the jet and the muscle belonged to someone else.

Though he'd been watchful since his capture, there'd been no opportunity to escape. Rick was a professional, and Scylla was naturally suspicious. She flirted and teased, but she never let down her guard. It wasn't surprising that Scylla drove, leaving Rick free to handle any escape Colm might attempt. He tried not to let himself think ahead to the logical result of their careful but emotionless planning.

188

"The boss arranged private lodging," Rick said as she started the car. "Just follow the directions on the screen."

Scylla nodded then turned to Colm. "On the way you can tell me why we're in Toronto and where we'll be going now that we're here."

Colm had been parceling out the information as slowly as possible, prolonging his life and hoping for a chance at escape or rescue. First he'd insisted he needed time to do more research, though actually he'd known since his visit to Coleburgh that Toronto was his best chance of finding Lewis MacPherson's trail. Now that they were at their final destination, Scylla would demand he take her to the diamond necklace Lewis probably never knew he owned. The British police could no longer find him, and the Canadian police had no idea he was in their country. Once again, he told his captor as much as he had to and no more.

"Lewis MacPherson arrived in Canada in 1825. His entry papers list his ultimate destination as Toronto."

"Then the necklace is here?"

"It's not a certainty," Colm warned. "We're putting together bits of cloth with holes in it and trying to make a blanket. We don't even know the necklace wasn't broken and sold in pieces."

She shook her head. "Records I found in France indicate the king's agents tracked the piece down. They kept it a secret because of the scandal, but it was rumored Louis entrusted it to his great friend, Axel von Fersen."

"Who couldn't save Louis but managed to spirit the queen away while Claudine died in her place." Even the sardonic Scylla seemed impressed.

"Axel probably planned to bring the necklace and join her in England."

"A widow with a fortune in jewels. How romantic."

"She must have begged him to save her son as well, and Axel

189

couldn't say no to Marie."

"He arranged that too. Why didn't the three of them live happily ever after in Dover?"

"The ship meant to take Marie to England wrecked in a storm. Axel thought she was drowned."

"But with the boy and the necklace, he might still save the monarchy."

"I'm sure that was his thought. Either by bribery or trickery, they got the boy out of the prison and left a dead child in his place."

"How do you know that?"

He shrugged. "I don't know it, but if you read MacPherson's log, you'd know."

Scylla rolled her eyes. "You're the boy who's brilliant at this." When he didn't comment she went on. "So von Fersen sent the necklace with the escort, to provide for the boy when he reached England."

"Axel himself was beginning to come under scrutiny due to his loyalty to the royal family." Colm shifted in the seat and his handcuffs made a metallic sound. "Someone discovered their plan. Though he got the dauphin to the *Thistle*, the escort died, leaving the boy a mystery and the necklace a secret."

"The ship captain felt sorry for the kid and adopted him. I know all that."

Colm continued as if she had not interrupted. "MacPherson must have found the necklace on the chaperone's corpse, but he was more interested in protecting the boy's identity than he was in being rich."

"To each his own," Scylla opined. To encourage Colm to go on she prompted, "He hid the necklace."

"Yes, which became a problem. Andrew's brother records in his journal that he was completely paralyzed by a stroke in the last months of his life."

"He couldn't speak or write." Scylla chewed at her lip, picturing the frustration that must have caused the captain. "No way to tell Lewis about the treasure he'd hidden away for him."

"Ian MacPherson mentions Andrew's agitation. They thought he had something to tell, but no one could comprehend it. Lewis noticed his father would often stare at a toy Lewis had received as a boy."

Scylla made a turn ordered by the GPS, but her mind was on Colm's account. "A toy?"

"Andrew would become very excited when the toy was in his range of vision. He'd make strangled sounds and glare at it as if angry, the way stroke patients often do. They concluded he was living in the past, when Lewis was young and enjoyed playing with it."

"What was this toy?"

"A dancing puppet, a jointed wooden figure with wires run through the limbs. It was set onto a block of teak from an old ship's timber, and the dancer, painted in bright colors, was a sailor who jigged madly when a lever was moved. It was cleverly done, and the boy loved it."

"So why was old MacPherson so focused on it?"

"That's the interesting part." Colm almost forgot he was being forced to reveal information. "Sometime after Lewis left Scotland, Ian MacPherson encountered an old sailor in the tavern. The man, who'd sailed many times with Andrew MacPherson, mentioned a special toy he'd once made for the captain's son, one with a hidden compartment."

Scylla turned to look at Colm, eyes wide. "Watch it!" Rick said from the back seat, and she sped up as the light above them turned from amber to red.

Colm wished for a moment his revelation had caused a fender-bender. How would they explain having a man chained to the armrest? Watchful for a second opportunity, he went on with the story. "The woodcarver made a secret compartment in the base, a box about six by four by three inches. MacPherson swore him to secrecy, but the sailor saw no harm in mentioning it once the captain was dead. He claimed he'd made the cover so tight no one would ever guess it could be removed."

"You think the necklace is inside the toy."

"There was a drawing of it in MacPherson's house. Emily Brown included it in her book on the family."

"So you've known all along where the necklace is. You lied to me, Colm."

Caught out, he equivocated. "Knowing where the necklace was hidden isn't the same as knowing where the toy might be now. I can't say if Lewis stayed in Toronto. I can't even say if he brought the toy to Canada with him."

"Any evidence point to an answer for either of those questions?"

Colm pushed back his hair with his free hand. "A man calling himself Charles Fersen bought a home in Toronto in 1826. And since there's no mention of finding the dancing sailor in his house in Scotland, I think it's likely he brought the toy along, perhaps as a memento of his father."

Scylla drove on for a while. "What happened to the toy when he died?"

"Having no living heirs, Charles Fersen left his entire estate to charity. His will ordered the contents of the house be sold at auction and the proceeds given to charity as well."

"Again, what happened to the toy?"

Colm grimaced. "This is the most tenuous part of the theory, but records indicate a man named Pellatt bought a great deal of MacPherson's estate. Pellatt was a successful businessman who loved unique things, and he had a collection of handmade toys. I think he'd have liked the dancing sailor."

Scylla sighed. "I'm hearing lots more theory than fact, here, lover."

"That's what I've been doing the last week, checking and re-checking." Licking his lips, Colm went on. "Pellatt's estate passed to his son at his death. The son is remembered in Toronto as the man who built for himself one of the grandest homes in North America, the 'castle on a hill,' Casa Loma."

"I've heard of that." Suddenly her voice vibrated with excitement.

"The story of Sir Henry's building, maintaining, and eventually losing Casa Loma is told and retold to tourists daily, with interesting little tidbits thrown in. For example, local farmers were paid one dollar for each large stone they brought for the building of the wall surrounding the estate. That was a large reward in 1913, and the guides claim that crops around Toronto went unharvested that year because men could make more money selling unwanted rocks from their fields to Henry Pellatt."

"How droll, but get back to business. You think Pellatt had the sailor toy?"

"If the toy still exists, the only place I know to look for it is at Casa Loma." Trying to project both confidence and caution, Colm raised a finger. "I warn you, the castle's been through a lot of changes since Sir Henry built it. He lost his fortune, and everything he had was sold at auction."

In a tone Colm found both funny and frightening, she asked, "What if someone bought our little sailor? We might never find him!"

"I looked at the auction listing, which is part of the tour guides' patter. It lists the sale of the huge pipe organ and the magnificent chandeliers, but there's no record of a sailor toy being sold."

"So the necklace is still there!"

Colm didn't mention the other possibility: that the toy had been sold in a lot, seen as not worth an individual listing. "We'll find out, I suppose."

"Soon," she said. "I have a few things to arrange, but we'll visit this castle of yours tomorrow afternoon." Putting a hand on Colm's arm she dug her nails into the skin. "If your theory turns out to be wrong, darling, you won't have to worry about me much longer." At a command from the GPS, Scylla turned into a driveway. "And if your girlfriend shows up here, my sister's friend Robert will handle her. He's not much in the looks department, but Robert knows how to tie up loose ends."

Any way this turns out, I'm a loose end. Colm had no expectation he'd be allowed to live, whether they found the necklace at Casa Loma or not.

CHAPTER TWENTY-TWO

TORONTO: 1842

Night had turned to morning, but Charles Dickens sat transfixed by the story Jacques told. "You followed Lewis MacPherson to Canada?"

He nodded. "The trail was fresh, and he had few choices, being in a great hurry. I learned that a man of his description calling himself von Fersen was on his way to Nova Scotia. I was a few weeks behind him, since I had to wait for a ship, but I was determined not to lose him this time. In Halifax I learned he'd gone west, so I did the same. When I arrived here, I found no word of *von* Fersen, but someone recalled there was a Charles Fersen staying at a local hotel.

"I waited outside the place the next morning. When he left his room after breakfast I recognized him, even after so many years. He had the Bourbon nose and his mother's grace of movement. He left on foot, heading out of the city. I followed, lagging back so he would not notice me.

"Fersen walked a long way. Though I did not know it at the time, he was coming here, to a property he'd bought a few days before. The house at that time was much more modest, but it was already furnished, an advantage to one who'd brought almost nothing with him from Scotland. Charles planned to move into the house that day.

"The land outside Toronto was fairly empty then, and I followed him along a mere cart path, past fields of grain and animal pastures." Jacques' eyes met Dickens', hinting this was an important part. "When he skirted a fenced area and disappeared into some trees ahead, I thought I could make up time by jumping the fence and cutting across the field. There was a lone animal there, but he was far away and busy grazing." He made his crooked smile again. "I was a city boy, Monsieur. I knew nothing of bulls and their territorial ways."

Though he told the story lightly, Dickens realized the next part had been deadly serious. "I was only halfway across when a bull charged, angry as only a bull can be at an interloper in what he considers his territory. He ran at me full tilt, caught me on his horns, and tossed me into the air like a rag doll. I felt myself rise and then fall, and I heard a sickening crunch in my leg as I landed. I must have cried out; I don't remember. The bull didn't stop his attack but ran at me several times, head low and snorting. Once he ran directly over me. I felt his hooves catch at my clothing."

"What did you do?"

"The only thing I could do. I covered my head with my arms and waited to die." Jacques paused, as a good storyteller does when he's come to a place where the listener needs time to imagine the horror of the moment.

"Suddenly I heard a voice shouting commands. I peeked out to see Fersen approaching the bull with a stout stick in his hands. He shouted over and over, drawing the animal's attention to him. Confused, the bull left me and turned at him. Fersen danced out of the way like a matador, whacking the bull soundly on the nose as he did. The bull charged again, but he twirled out of the way. After the bull passed he scooped up a fist-sized rock and threw it, hitting the bull on the neck. Another rock followed, and another. The bull tossed its head angrily. Fersen shouted at it, insulting its mother and its lack of courage. His aim was true, and the bull suffered several direct hits to tender places on its anatomy." Jacques chuckled. "In the end the creature ceded defeat and trotted off."

"Leaving you hurt."

Jacques shrugged. "Badly hurt. Fersen bent over me, his stick still in hand in case the animal returned. 'Can you walk?' he asked. 'If you will support me, I think I can.' I replied. I saw in his eyes a reaction at my French accent and ruined face, which I'm sure had been described to him by his friends in Coleburgh. Still, he slung my arm around his shoulders and helped me to the fence. It was a trial to get over it, but we managed. Fersen left me on a grassy spot well out of the bull's range of vision. In time he returned with a two-wheeled cart, which he helped me into. Acting as a draft animal, he then pulled it the short distance to his house.

"Inside, he put me in the only bed and went to fetch a doctor. The man shook his head at the beating my poor leg had taken, but he set it and splinted it tightly. He said if I could stay off it for several weeks, the leg would heal."

Jacques pressed his lips together for a moment. "I was sure Fersen knew who I was. There were of course many Frenchmen in Canada at that time, but who would have followed him out into the country except the man who meant to harm him? Knowing he would want me gone as soon as possible, I asked the doctor if there was somewhere I might stay while I recovered. Before he could answer Charles said, 'You must stay here. My home isn't quite in condition for a guest, but you are welcome.'"

The old man stared at a spot beyond Dickens, somewhere in the past. After a few moments, the author spoke. "Because of his kindness, you became his friend."

He thought about it for some time. "Friends? Perhaps. Brothers, more like, joined by a past that might have killed us but did not."

"Did you ever speak of your reason for searching him out?"

"No." Jacques spread his hands. "There was no reason, you see. We knew each other's hearts from the first. His hatred for those who hurt him had died long before, and following his example, I was able to let mine go as well. If he could forgive me for the death of his father, the persecution of his mother, and the years of dread and fear I had inflicted on him, I could forget that he was anyone other than Charles Fersen, Toronto businessman." Jacques folded his hands as if ending a prayer. "That is what I did."

***

TORONTO

Mercedes' plane touched down in Toronto at 9:00 pm, and she located a shuttle marked *City Centre* with no difficulty. At just after 11:00, she opened the door to her room at the Royal York, an elegant holdover from Victorian days that maintained a high standard of service in the heart of Toronto.

She'd made the reservation from a pay phone and withdrawn enough cash from an ATM to pay expenses without leaving a trail of credit card receipts. Though she wasn't sure how her movements were being tracked, she didn't intend to make it easy.

If the figurines had been arranged as a message from Colm, she'd find something at Casa Loma. It wasn't much to go on, but she guessed the mental steps Colm must have made: Lewis left Scotland for Toronto, bringing the sailor toy, which must have been left to someone who donated it to Casa Loma. There were gaps, but she didn't have time to try to fill them in.

Mercedes spent some time re-familiarizing herself with Toronto's transit system, streets, and landmarks. She'd visited several times as a tourist, but this trip was different. Knowledge of the city's layout could be crucial.

As she studied, David phoned. "Eleanor is on her way. Mrs. Peterson took her to the airport in her Mini-Cooper."

Mercedes didn't know whether to be happy about that or not. She was hesitant to put her cousin in danger, but she felt very much alone in an unfamiliar city with no idea what her next move should be. "I'll text her the hotel and her room number." She'd gotten Ellie her own room as a safety precaution. No sense setting her up for danger.

"What do you plan to do?"

Trying to sound confident, she said, "I'll visit Casa Loma in the morning."

"Take your two sturdy friends along," David ordered. "They can provide protection in case someone is there waiting for you to show." She didn't tell him she'd lost Lonnie and Ike. Were they on their way, or were they under arrest? David was on his own mind track. "Tell me about this castle in Canada."

"It's the work of Henry Pellatt, a millionaire who was quite the spendthrift. It came long after MacPherson, or Dickens for that matter."

"If Lewis took the necklace to Canada, perhaps he sold it to this Pellatt."

Mercedes paced as they spoke. "If he did no one else knew of it, and everything Pellatt owned eventually went up for auction." She rubbed at the tense spot between her eyes. "David, I have to find that necklace before whoever has Colm does and use it to make them set him free."

"You can't be sure it's in that place."

"No." Her tone was grim. "But it's the only chance I have."

Assuring David she'd be even more careful than before and do nothing even the slightest bit foolish, Mercedes ended the call and tried to organize her thoughts. What did she know for certain? Not everything, but a plausible story was taking shape. She believed Andrew MacPherson had died in possession of a secret he longed to tell and could not. Had Lewis finished his life in Canada, an emigrant from Scotland like so many others in the 1800s? Had he built a new life, unaware that he possessed a priceless bit of history?

She shook her head in frustration at so many unanswered questions, some of which were forever unanswerable. Might the toy still exist, with the necklace hidden inside and unsuspected all these years? If so, what had come to light recently that stirred interest in finding it? Whatever it was had led Colm into danger. Judging from his casual acceptance of the assignment, he hadn't begun expecting either possible wealth or danger. Yet she was certain that what he'd learned had brought him to the attention of people so eager to find the necklace that they'd taken him prisoner, perhaps even—No, she wouldn't let her mind go there.

Concentrate on finding the necklace. Colm thought the toy could be at Casa Loma. That meant his captors would go there and try to steal it. She had to stop them, because once it was theirs, what good would Colm be to them?

None at all. They'd set the whole thing up to look as if Colm were the treasure seeker. His prints on the case in Dickens' shop. The murder of the woman seen with him in Charlie's shop. That made Mercedes stop for a moment. If they were framing Colm for the crimes, it was likely he would appear at the castle, so they could frame him for theft as well as murder.

Casa Loma. That was where Mercedes would find Colm and somehow help him escape. She recalled the dread she'd once felt as a prisoner aware that her death was imminent. It had taken months to get over the nightmares, the flashbacks, the feeling someone waited in the shadows to attack her.

Fighting back those memories, she forced herself to think. She had to find the toy as soon as possible. She glanced at the clock. Seven hours until the doors of Casa Loma opened to the public for the day. Seven hours until she could do anything. She studied what was available on the Internet about the place, but there wasn't much in terms of what she needed to know. Nowhere was there a notation saying: *This is where we store antique toys and such.*

Chapter Twenty-three

Toronto

The next morning Mercedes entered the boutique nearest her hotel as soon as it opened. A woman spending the day at Casa Loma alone might be unusual enough to draw some attention, so she intended to appear as an art student. Having drawn her dark hair up in a casual ponytail, she bought, a loose, off-shoulder shirt, leggings with holes in the thighs, and flat slipper-type shoes, not practical for climbing around an old structure but suited to her disguise. At Canadian Tire, which offered much more than tires, she bought a large tote bag, a sketch pad and colored pencils. In a shop near Union Station she picked up a couple of sandwiches and two bottles of water. If she seemed to be making drawings of the castle's rooms, the employees should become used to her presence over the course of the day.

Going back to her hotel room, she changed her clothes and packed the tote. Her hands shook with nervousness as she removed the film from the paper and roughed up the pencils so they didn't look brand new. She had to search the castle without getting caught, find the toy, and get it out of the building undetected. Having no practice in breaking rules or thievery, Mercedes didn't relish the day ahead.

As she crossed the elegant lobby of the hotel, a man stepped up and took her arm. She didn't recognize his new look until he grinned and said, "We made it, luv."

"Lonnie!" Mercedes hugged him in joy. "How did—"

"We insisted it was a prank from a mate. Since there wasn't a gun or nothing in our gear, they eventually believed us and let us on a later flight." He glanced around. "Were you followed here?"

"I don't think so. I lost a woman who was shadowing me at the airport in Scotland."

Lonnie sniffed. "I'd like to meet up with that one again! Slippin' things into a bloke's luggage!" Returning to the moment, he pointed. "Come on. Ike's watching the other side so we'd be sure to see you."

They found Ike leaning against a pillar, his large frame downplayed by the casual pose and his air of patience, very like a husband whose wife was taking a long time to appear. "Where were you headed?" Lonnie asked.

"I'll tell you on the way." Mercedes was suddenly more confident with the reappearance of the two men.

"Half a mo," Ike ordered. He took a cell phone out of his pocket and handed it to Mercedes. "Track phone," he said succinctly. "No records." He produced a second phone exactly like the first and punched in a number. "We've found her. Can you meet us in the lobby?"

Ike listened, ended the call, and gave Mercedes a grin. "We sent your cousin to her room to get some rest. We thought the old sweetheart could use it after the long flight."

"Eleanor's here too?"

"I think your friend David pulled some strings," Lonnie said admiringly. "We arrived to find her asking for your room number."

"So we introduced ourselves and talked things over with her. She's quite a girl, your Eleanor."

"That's for sure," Mercedes agreed.

Eleanor joined them shortly, looked composed and fresh, as usual. She kissed Mercedes' cheek, murmuring, "You look awful!" To the group as a whole she said, "What's next?"

Though the delay was worrisome, Mercedes brought them up to date on her plan. To her relief, no one tried to change her mind.

"You've done it right," Ike said. "The police will only complicate things."

"They always do," Lonnie volunteered, but a look from Ike warned him off pontificating on police in general.

"I think we'll have a better chance of finding this toy as a group," Eleanor put in. "You can be the student doing drawings of the rooms, I like that. Lonnie and I will play the young man taking his gram to see the castle."

"Mother," Lonnie said gallantly. "My gran looks way older than you."

"Very kind," Eleanor replied. "Now Ichabod—"

"Ike," he corrected her hastily. With an embarrassed look at Mercedes he added, "To prove we were who we said, we showed her our passports. She says Ichabod is a perfectly good name."

"It is," Eleanor insisted. "Just because one literary Ichabod was a bit of a sissy doesn't mean you should be ashamed of it."

"Yeah," Lonnie put in with an ironic grin, "just because the other Ichabod was scrawny and cowardly and—" At a look from Ike, he composed his features into a more respectful expression. "So what's our plan for knocking off this castle then?"

An hour later, two people left the DuPont station, the northernmost stop on the city's Spadina subway line. A woman with an oversized bag emblazoned with *Seneca College* stepped quickly forward, intent on the short walk uphill to Casa Loma. The formidable black man paid her no mind, but he stopped several times along the way to take pictures of the castle with a digital camera that looked much too small for his hands.

The castle was indeed a spectacle. Situated on the rise that gave it its name, Casa Loma was a huge stone mansion, in its time the largest private home in America. It was complete with towers, a 5-acre garden, amazing stables reached by an underground, 800-foot tunnel, and room after room of elegant design. When its owner, Henry Pellatt, went broke in the 1930's, the city had taken over the building and eventually, with the cooperation of the local Kiwanis organization, opened it as a tourist attraction. It had been a very wise move on their part.

As Mercedes and Ike made their way from the subway to the Castle, a step-on tour bus passed them and swung into the narrow gateway in the low outer wall. From it descended a man who turned to help an older woman down the steps. They made their way to the entrance where he ushered her through the door and then stopped to pay their entry fee.

"Where would you like to start?" he asked.

The woman considered briefly. "I'd like to see the stables first."

Consulting the diagram he'd been given at the kiosk, he pointed to a set of stairs. "Lower level, then. It looks like quite a hike, but we've got all day."

They disappeared just as the student entered the central room, which boasted a huge marble staircase and a balcony that ran almost completely around the hall below it. After looking around critically, the woman turned right and headed up to the second level. She stood at the railing for a while, observing the flow of people below and around her, consulting the floor plan on her pamphlet.

The castle staff was relaxed but observant. Mercedes doubted they had much trouble here aside from rowdy kids and the occasional graffiti artist. No one seemed to pay her any special attention, but she opened her sketch pad and made a quick drawing of the scene below to justify her presence.

It was an impressive view. The castle's main floor boasted the Great Hall, Library, Dining Room, Conservatory, Serving Room, Peacock Alley, Sir Henry's Study, Smoking Room, Billiards Room, and Oak Room. Visitors moved below her, pointing out furnishings and commenting on the place's grandeur.

Once Mercedes had completed the first sketch, she moved down the hallway, peering into doorways as she passed. A door about halfway down was marked *Staff Only*. Waiting until no one was looking, she tried the handle. Locked. Frustrated, she went on, apparently observing the various displays. In fact she was wondering why she'd ever thought she could pull this off.

An odd sound startled her until she realized it was the phone Ike had given her. Frowns from those around her signaled displeasure at the interruption, and she backed out of the room and found an alcove where she answered.

"Miss Maxwell?"

"Ike, where are you?"

"I'm in the attic. I think this is the main storage area." He gave directions, and Mercedes quickly located the correct stairway. Narrower and less attractive than those in the more public areas, these stairs allowed those with a sense of adventure and a strong pair of lungs to climb to the highest points of the castle, the turrets. She'd done it on her first visit several years ago, and deemed the view of the city below well worth the effort. This time she didn't take the last set of stairs but waited while a trio of teen girls descended. When they'd giggled on their way, she looked for the door Ike had described. It was back a bit and under the stairs, with a sign that said *No Admittance*. Ike's face appeared in a narrow slit, and he opened the door fully. "This way."

The room they entered was dark and smelled of old dust. Ike waited by the door for a few moments as the sound of footsteps ascended then pounded along the corridor above. When it was quiet, he moved a large box in front of the door. "It won't keep anyone out, but it will give us a heads up," he said with a wink.

"How did you get in here? The storage room I found was locked."

"I don't think they'll miss these for a while." Ike held up a ring of keys. "In places like this they often leave a set or two in plain view in the staff room, so guys can use them if they need to get in somewhere." With a grin he finished, "When your assets are mostly furniture, there's no great danger some bloke's going to walk off with it during the day."

"You're amazing." Secretly Mercedes wondered how Ike knew so much about security—or security flaws—in public buildings. Better not to know.

He pulled a slim flashlight from his pocket, and Mercedes rummaged in her bag for the one she'd brought. Before them was a long, narrow room with only roof timbers above. Plank shelves lined one whole wall, and on them were boxes of various sizes and conditions. Some were very old and bore hand-lettered labels. Newer boxes had computer-made tags with better information: date of storage, contents, and some sort of numbering system.

Mercedes ignored the newer boxes and moved to one of the older ones, made of wood slats and very dusty. Across the front was printed *Old Christmas* in block letters. With Ike's help she pried up the lid. Inside were tree decorations, bedraggled and very plain. She moved on. Ike went in the opposite direction. They checked the boxes one by one, opening some that looked likely but ignoring those with labels like *Garden Tools*. They found none that seemed likely to have a toy inside such as the one in the drawing.

A noise at the door froze them for a second. "There's something in the way," a muffled voice said, and another urged, "Can you push it aside? Here, I'll help." The box skidded over the rough floor, first in short bursts, then in a smooth slide. Ike grabbed Mercedes' hand and pulled her to the back of the room. At the end there was a small space between the shelving and the wall, and he pushed her behind a large box just as a dim light went on overhead. Mercedes kept her head down, but she heard surprised voices exclaim at the sight of Ike standing in the castle storeroom.

"Hey, what are you doing in here?" a man demanded.

"Just having a look at what's not on display," he replied calmly.

"Well, I'm afraid you can't do that." The voice was tentative, no doubt in deference to Ike's size. If he resisted, they'd have a hard time removing him.

"No problem. I'll be on my way." Ike moved to the front, and Mercedes peeked cautiously from her hiding place. Whatever the two young men had come for was forgotten as they followed Ike out and closed the door, probably following to assure he left the property.

Mercedes turned her flash on as their steps receded. Its light gave little comfort: Ike might be arrested. Should she go after them and try to explain?

Yeah, right. Explain that we came here to steal an item to exchange for the life of a man no one believes is in danger?

As she stood considering her options, the word her tiny flashlight illuminated finally penetrated her consciousness: *Toys.* She slipped from behind the box, stifling a cough from the thick layer of dust she'd stirred up. She suspected she had only minutes before the two men returned for whatever they'd been looking for earlier.

The box had a hinged lid fastened with metal buckles. Inside were partitioned spaces of different sizes that accommodated an array of old-fashioned toys. Lying atop the contents was a booklet titled, *Canada Plays.* The first page explained the box's contents were part of a traveling exhibit sent out to elementary schools: hands-on exhibits that introduced toys of the past to children of the present.

Quickly but with great anticipation, Mercedes began removing items from the box. A porcelain-faced baby doll, a pair of old-fashioned ice skates, a top, and a Raggedy Ann and Andy formed the top layer. Setting those aside, she pulled out a thin plywood spacer. There, in the center of the second level, was the sailor. His paint was faded and some of his strings were almost worn through, but he was whole, with hair made of hemp and tiny nail heads serving as buttons on his shirt and shoes.

There was no time to admire him. From the bag she took a towel borrowed from the hotel and wrapped the toy. Laying it in the bottom of the bag, she put her sketch pad on top. Next she replaced the rest of the items in the box and stacked others atop it. With luck it would be some time before the theft was discovered. Shouldering her tote bag, Mercedes made her way to the door and stood for a moment listening for movement outside.

It was quiet, safe for her to leave the storeroom, descend to the main level, and casually exit the building. She grasped the knob and tried to turn it. There was no movement. The men who'd escorted Ike out had locked the door behind them. She was trapped inside.

Chapter Twenty-four

Colm was awakened from the half-sleep he'd imposed upon himself by a noise at the door. Rick entered the room with his usual care, coming only as far in as necessary and allowing no chance for his prisoner to slip past him. He set a bag on the floor.

"Put these on." After a moment, the slightest trace of humor showed as he added, "She says you have to look the part." He left then, and Colm heard the lock click into place.

He sat up. It was late in the day, but he didn't know the exact hour, since they'd taken his watch and phone. In the bag he found an outfit that screamed, "Look at me!" Leather pants with zippers everywhere. Knock-off Jimmy Choo boots. A burgundy blazer accompanied by a white shirt with almost no collar. And to go over it all, a cape. A *cape*. Colm consoled himself with the thought that anyone who knew him wouldn't believe for a moment he'd dress that way voluntarily.

A few minutes later he followed Rick down a hallway and a staircase to the main floor of an almost empty, early 20th century house. Observing its original woodwork and unique, pressed-tin ceiling might have been a pleasure in other circumstances, but not now.

The house was in bad shape, but it was brick, which Colm had discovered made a great prison. The windows were covered with decorative grille that served to keep him in as well as keeping intruders out. The room they'd locked him in faced the blank brick wall of the next house which was empty. No help there.

As she'd led him to the room where he'd been held, Scylla told him the neighborhood was currently undergoing a renaissance. "Old places are being bought and refurbished by people who want to live near the city center," she said. "Robert rented with the option to buy, and the landlord was thrilled. Of course we won't be staying long, but for now we have privacy."

He followed Rick to the living room, where Scylla sat on a lumpy couch, looking at him with eyes that seemed to see right into his brain. "How are you, lover? A bit jet-lagged?"

"Yeah," Colm replied. The fuzzier she thought his mind, the more likely she'd let down her guard. Not that she'd done that so far.

A raised eyebrow indicated her mistrust of his agreement, but she moved to the business at hand. "It's time to find out if your theory is correct. If all goes well, I'll have the toy by midnight and you'll be a free man."

Liar, Colm thought, but he tried to look hopeful. "I've been wondering, Scylla, how did you come to believe the necklace might still exist?"

After some consideration, she reached for her purse. "Rick had to park the car some distance from here, so we have a few minutes to chat." Removing a piece of paper from her bag, she handed it to him. "This is a copy of something I found while doing graduate work in Paris." She smiled at Colm's look of disbelief. "It's true. I have a degree in history, and once upon a time, I planned to become a museum curator." She made a moue of self-deprecation. "I wanted to make my mark on the historical community." She tilted her head to one side. "I think finding Marie Antoinette's necklace will do that. Like your Mercedes, who made a name for herself with the Shakespeare letter."

"Mercedes managed to do it without murdering anyone."

Scylla shrugged. "Good for her."

"If you're a history student, how do you fly around on jets and keep shady characters at your beck and call?"

Now she smiled. "Sister Carrie never wanted an education. She likes money, so she hooked up with Robert Collins." One brow rose. "If you were into studying modern criminals, you'd know the name. He's quite well known."

"He's funding all this?"

She waved a hand. "It isn't like he knows the details. He heard 'diamond necklace' and gave Carrie the go-ahead to do whatever it takes to find it."

"He'll get a cut of the proceeds."

She made a little grimace. "Among other things."

Colm scanned the sheet she'd provided, a translation of a letter. After Colm read the message once, he read it again, this time more carefully. Unless one knew more than was here, it meant little. But to him, it was the missing piece of the puzzle.

Paris

September 14, 1795

Citizen Robespierre,

You will not know my name, but I am a true son of the revolution. I have sworn to kill the dauphin, who did not die but escaped prison, and return to France the queen's diamond necklace, stolen from the people by the aristos. I go to England for liberty, equality, and brotherhood.

Jacques Martin

"Who was Jacques Martin?"

Scylla waved impatiently. "He doesn't matter, since it's obvious he failed. What matters is evidence that Marie Antoinette's diamond necklace went to England in 1795."

"Why did no one take note of this until now?"

"I suppose because there was no further word from Jacques. He sounds like a fanatic, but still, I kept his letter, intrigued by its possibilities. Then one day I read on the Internet that a poncey little shop owner had in his possession an account of a sea captain who picked up a wounded man and a sick boy the night before this letter was written.

"I emailed Mr. Dickens. At first he was very willing to sell the documents, but by the time I got there, he'd turned cagey. He said his friend Colm Kennedy believed the documents were more important than they appeared. Of course he thought it had to do with his illustrious ancestor, but he said you were looking into the matter." She looked at Colm through her lashes. "That's when I called my sister and asked if she and Robert could help me out with a project."

"So you killed Dickens and waited for me to show up. Why didn't you just kill me too and take the documents?"

"I wanted to know what you'd discovered that made you warn Charlie not to sell." Patting Colm's arm, she turned him toward the door. "You're very clever, darling."

Colm snorted a laugh. "Under threat of death to myself and others."

"And now that we know where the diamonds have hidden for more than a century, you're going to help me retrieve them."

"Why me?" he asked, though he thought he knew what the answer was.

"You're famous, love. We'll use your success to open some doors." She touched the garish cape he carried folder over his arm. "You'll put that on. You'll schmooze a bit, playing the egotistical actor. With a little luck we'll find the toy and get it out of there. If we aren't lucky, you'll be arrested." With a nasty smile she added, "If that happens, I'll see that Miss Maxwell pays."

Colm made a gesture of resignation. "I'll do my best."

Scylla handed him a glossy brochure. "Study that. I went to the castle this morning, and the toy isn't in any of the public rooms. I've marked the areas that have *No Entry* signs. If they still have the dancing sailor, he's packed away somewhere."

That "if" was Colm's biggest concern. His best chance of survival was finding the toy. If he could escape Scylla and her loaner muscle with the toy in his possession, it would become a bargaining chip. He wasn't sure he could do it, but in public, they'd have to pretend he was a free man. No handcuffs, no visible weapons. It was the only chance to escape he'd get.

***

CASA LOMA, TORONTO

Mercedes cringed as she heard steps approaching the storeroom. More than one person. Should she hide, try to evade them, or give up and get thrown out, as Ike had done? Though she could do no good locked in, she was reluctant to reveal her presence. Once the staff was aware of her, she'd have a much harder time getting back inside. She knelt behind the box, as before, and hoped whatever they'd come for was near the front.

It was. The two staffers went directly to some boxes at the center of the space, never looking into the dim recesses at the back of the room. They were still discussing Ike, who'd convinced them he was a harmless kook in search of a not-open-to-the-public adventure.

"He was a big one," said one young man. "Good thing he wasn't violent."

"Yeah, I'd like to see you take him on, Gary," the other teased.

Gary huffed disdainfully. "I didn't see you offering to lay hands on him."

"Got more sense than stupid up in my skull," the other asserted. Their voices faded, but she heard, "I can come back up for that last one."

As the door swung to almost closed behind them, Mercedes rose from her hiding place and caught it. Listening until it seemed quiet on the other side, she peeked out. The area was empty for the moment. She was out the door in an instant, and when steps sounded on the floor above and two winded women began to descend the stairs, she waited as if poised to go up.

"The view is worth it, at least I think so," one woman joked as she stopped on the landing to catch her breath. Mercedes smiled and went up, waiting only long enough for the women to get ahead of her a bit before coming back down. Her last and most dangerous task lay ahead: getting out of the castle without anyone finding out she had stolen property in her bag.

Wandering apparently aimlessly, Mercedes considered her options. In the library was a door that led onto the terrace. Going outside, she made her way across the tile expanse, down a set of stairs, and past a fountain to the terrace edge, where there was a seat backed by bushes. Sitting down as if to rest, she set her bag on the low wall behind the bench and waited until no one was looking directly at her. Casually she removed her sketch pad as if getting ready to draw the castle's exterior. With her other hand she took out the towel-wrapped toy and wedged it between the wall and a sturdy branch.

After a few minutes of sketching, she rose and apparently regarded the view from the wall. Before her, slices of Toronto peeped through the tree branches. Looking down, she assured herself that no one would notice the bundle lodged there.

Back inside, Mercedes stopped to reconnoiter. Guests had begun heading for the exits as staff moved them along politely but firmly. Casa Loma was closing for the day. One guard made eye contact with Mercedes, and she understood the implication: *Move along, your time is up.*

As she smiled at him to signal compliance, something

occurred that could only be described as a grand entrance. A man in a long black cape, its right edge thrown back to reveal a green silk lining, strode into the room. He wore a haughty expression as he explained to a reluctant staffer that he wanted to speak to the person in charge. Despite the fact that she'd never seen him in clothes like that or wearing that expression, Mercedes recognized Colm Kennedy. Turning, she hurried up the stairs and watched the performance from the balcony.

With Colm was a striking woman of about Mercedes' age. Her clothes were subdued but perfectly tailored and she wore dark glasses and a scarf wrapped around her hair and neck, à la Audrey Hepburn. Though her eyes were hidden, her attention focused on Colm and never wavered.

A middle-aged woman in a staff jacket appeared. Half glasses lay on her chest, held there by a length of chain. She said something to Colm in a low tone, but his answer was loud enough for all to hear. "Do you know who I am?"

When the woman admitted rather coldly that she did not, he smiled forgivingly. "My name is Colm Kennedy. I've just finished a season at Stratford." He paused then added fatuously, "Yours, of course, not ours." He reached out and took her hand. "And you are—?"

"Mrs. Peyton." Her voice warmed a bit upon learning she addressed an actor. Mercedes imagined her asking herself if he was someone whose name her friends would recognize. "May I ask what shows you were in?"

Colm paused, and she guessed he was wondering which shows she might have seen. "I was Orlando in *As You Like It* and Larry in *A Chorus Line*. Of course I played several minor roles and understudied as well." He touched her arm. "They know how to get their money's worth from a fellow."

The woman liked getting an insider's view. "A busy summer then."

"But very successful." Colm's tone implied he'd garnered all sorts of acclaim. "The problem is, dear lady, that tomorrow I must return to London to begin work on *Les Miz*." He bowed slightly. "I'll be portraying Javert."

That struck a chord, and she laid a hand on her chest. "I love that show."

"As do I," Colm agreed. "I was hoping to do some sightseeing before I leave Toronto, and now I find the place I'm most interested in, Casa Loma, is closing for the day."

The woman looked around her. Most of the tourists had gone, and the staff watched with interest. What would she do with this flamboyant actor? Turn him away? The woman's chin firmed with sudden decision. "I could stay a few minutes and show you around." She frowned at the entourage waiting behind Colm, the woman and two glum-looking men. "I'm afraid I can only escort you and the lady. The others will have to wait outside."

Colm's apparent joy was effusive. "That will be acceptable, and we understand completely. It's kind of you to do this, Ms. Peyton, very kind."

Turning to her staff, Peyton said briskly, "Close everything up except the front door. I'll turn on the alarms and lock up when we're done."

As the workers moved to obey, Mercedes hurried down the stairs. Breathlessly she gushed, "You're Colm Kennedy!"

Colm managed to hide his surprise at her appearance and maintain the persona he'd chosen. "I am."

"I saw you in Edinburgh last winter. You were wonderful!"

"You're too kind," he said with just the right mix of pride and impatience.

"Could I have your autograph, please?" Mercedes thrust a scrap of paper at him, along with a charcoal pencil.

"Of course." As he scrawled his name across the paper,

Mercedes saw his eyes take in the message she'd scribbled. *I have it. By the fountain.* Quickly writing on the paper he said, "And where's your phone? You'll want a photo."

When she got it out, he took the phone from her then leaned in to snap a picture, smiling broadly. Once that was done he slid the phone into her bag and turned away, giving no further sign of interest in the apparently star-struck girl.

Mercedes went out the door, wondering if one of the men leaving ahead of her might be the one who'd tossed her into a van several nights earlier. Taking no chances, she kept her head down and turned in the opposite direction as soon as they exited the building. Behind her Colm's voice boomed as he spoke to Ms. Peyton. "Now, my dear, where shall we begin our tour? You're the expert, and I put myself completely in your care."

CHAPTER TWENTY-FIVE

CASA LOMA

Mercedes was escorted to the main exit by a castle staffer apparently charged with hurrying the slowpokes along. She'd glanced at Colm's supposed signature, which said, *Wait there. Tell no one.* Exiting the gate with the other stragglers, she fell behind then doubled back and hurriedly climbed the low wall. Using buses as cover, she traversed the parking lot and disappeared into the shrubs along the garden edge. It took a while for the staff to leave, but once the gates were locked she made her way to the spot where she'd stashed the toy. Putting it back into her tote bag, she settled in to wait.

Since Colm couldn't know she had Lonnie, Ike, and Ellie with her, Mercedes guessed he hadn't meant them when he said not to tell anyone. She would call them and let them know she'd found Colm.

Except her phone was gone. Going over the last few hours, she realized the only person she'd been close to was Colm. He'd only pretended to return it when he took their photo.

As she crouched in the shadows, Mercedes' traitorous mind tossed out questions she'd didn't want to deal with. Was she absolutely certain Colm was honest? He'd come to the castle with the woman, apparently by choice. They might be working together to find and steal the necklace. On the phone he'd said he was done with her. Was she absolutely certain he wasn't part of this?

She was, she decided. Even with evidence to the contrary, she knew Colm wasn't the kind of person who'd scheme to steal a historic artifact. He wasn't a man who'd kill Charlie Dickens. He hadn't been lying when he claimed he cared for her. He must be lying now only because he had to.

It was after seven when a noise at the doors leading onto the terrace caught her attention. The sky had darkened as much as city skies ever do, and the lights around the estate threw some areas into brightness while spaces outside their reach were dark. Mercedes had begun to shiver in the chilly night air, and she wished she'd brought a jacket. Different shoes would have been nice too, with warm cotton socks. When the noise interrupted her wishing, she leaned forward to peer at the building. The figure who exited was couched and unidentifiable, but the soft whistle she heard confirmed her hopes: the opening notes of "Scotland the Brave."

"Here!" she called, and steps approached.

"Mercedes! I've been frantic."

"How did you get away?"

She couldn't see his face, but Colm's voice betrayed amusement. "Two minutes into the tour, Scylla pushed poor Ms. Peyton into the billiard room and barricaded the door with a chair." Colm enfolded Mercedes in the cloak, warming her until her shivers quieted.

"The poor woman must terrified!"

"But it was a stroke of luck for me. With her safely shut away, I could look after myself alone." Taking Mercedes' hand, he set her phone into it. "Sorry to have stolen this, but I used it to call Scylla. When she turned to answer, I bolted from the room and locked her inside, just as she'd done to Ms. Peyton."

Mercedes glanced at the castle. "If she has a cell phone, she'll call for help. We need to go." Moving cautiously, they circled to the back of the structure, where steep steps led to the street. Crossing at the darkest spot they could find, they avoided the usual route to the subway station by traveling a block over before turning and making their way downhill.

The station was sparsely populated. Standing hunched on the sidewalk, they checked the people milling around inside. None looked like anyone either Mercedes or Colm had seen in the last few days. Colm led the way inside, only to recall he had no money. "She took everything from my pockets."

"I'll pay the fare," she assured him. "You've been through enough."

Once on the train, they relaxed a little. Mercedes opened her bag and pulled the towel back to show Colm the dancing sailor toy. "Do you think it really has a diamond necklace in its base?"

"We'll let the police figure that out," he replied. He touched her face lightly. "I can't tell you how surprised and pleased I was to see you there. Does that mean someone figured out my rudimentary message?"

"My cousin Ellie and David."

"David. Good to know he's well." He touched the tote bag thoughtfully. "I hoped that was here in Toronto, but I had no idea how I'd find it, or if it still existed after all this time."

"But you led those people to the castle. You must have thought it was possible."

"What I was thinking," Colm murmured, "was that I had to stay alive long enough to get away and get back to you. That's all."

"You did brilliantly then." Mercedes' heart warmed, but she knew it wasn't the time to discuss their relationship. It was enough to know how he felt. "I must say, your performance as a pompous actor was inspired."

"Just aping some of the boys I've shared the stage with."

"What do we do now?"

"We take that sailor in your bag to the nearest police station."

Despite the fact she'd have liked to learn the toy's secret herself, Mercedes saw the wisdom of such a course. "I guess it's time we explained ourselves. My reputation is intact, but I'm afraid police in several cities are on the lookout for you by now."

The cell phone in Mercedes' pocket vibrated, and she thought of Lonnie, Ike, and Ellie. They must be worried sick about her by now. Pulling the phone from her pocket, she flipped it open. The number was not one she recognized, and she felt dread returning as she answered.

"Miss Maxwell," a familiar, silky voice came through the line. "I didn't recognize you earlier as the dewy-eyed fan. My mistake."

Mercedes glanced at Colm, whose expression revealed the same dread she felt. "How did you get this number?"

"Blame Colm. He called me from your phone."

"What do you want?"

"I think you know. If you have it, I believe we can make a trade."

"A trade?" A sigh escaped Colm, and Mercedes felt her stomach turn. She tilted the phone so that he could hear what was said.

"There's a lady with me whom you know. Rick found her outside the castle, trying to decide where you might be. To keep her safe from any possible harm, we took her into our care."

Anger took over from fear. "If you hurt her—"

"Let's not start making threats, shall we? Each of us has something the other wants, so it's simply a matter of assuring an even trade. Everyone walks away happy."

Mercedes opened her mouth to argue, but Colm put a hand on hers and shook his head. Reaching into her bag he pulled out a pencil and the sketchbook. *Meeting Place Public.*

"It will have to be somewhere there are people."

"You're going to be reasonable. That's good. Somewhere close, then. I don't want to wait long."

Mercedes recalled the places she'd studied in preparation for this. In the early hours of morning there were few that would be well populated, but she hit on a possibility. "St. Lawrence Market."

Again Colm touched her arm and held up a finger, indicating they needed time. Though she didn't want Ellie in the grasp of criminals any longer than necessary, she realized he was right. "I can be there by eight."

"You *and* Colm. We know he's with you." When Mercedes didn't bother to deny it Scylla went on, "Bring the toy as it is; I want to open it myself. No further clever plans, or your elderly friend is dead." The call ended abruptly.

"That was good," Colm said, "choosing a market. Plenty of people."

"But how do we get Ellie away from them? I don't think they'll let her go."

"Or us either," he said gravely. "Scylla has no intention of leaving anyone alive to tell a tale different than the one she'll spin."

"Why, if she gets the necklace?"

Colm swayed toward Mercedes as the train stopped at King Street. "She wants the diamonds, of course, though I believe her sister Charybdis wants them more. What Scylla craves is credit for uncovering the story of the century: proof that Marie Antoinette and her son survived the Revolution. Once you and I and your cousin are dead, she'll be the expert who solved the riddles of the Dickens Documents. After she got them from the blackguard who killed for them—me."

Mercedes' mind had remained on the names. "Scylla and Charybdis?"

"Their parents couldn't have known how aptly they named their daughters," Colm said. "Twin disasters we somehow must get round, for encountering either one is risking death."

The train was pulling into Union Station, and Colm rose. "We must make a plan. Scylla has a muscle squad behind her, and we have only two."

"I think we can do better than two," Mercedes corrected. "I'm not sure how many are still standing, but it's more than just you and me."

Chapter Twenty-six

St. Lawrence Market, Toronto

At seven a.m., two figures approached the Old Town District of the city, moving down the darker side of Jarvis Street. Typically of modern young couples, they were on their cell phones, ignoring each other as they spoke to someone else.

Mercedes was relieved to have reached Lonnie, who was bruised but ambulatory. "Someone conked me on the head in the loo and shoved a cabinet in front of the door," he told her. "When I was able to stand up again I pushed my way out, but I couldn't find Miss Ellie anywhere."

Ike got on the phone to explain his adventures. Though he managed not to be arrested, he'd been "booted out of their blinkin' castle foreverbloodymore—beg pardon, Miss." Waiting outside the gate, he'd caught a glimpse of Eleanor's frightened face in the window as a dark blue limousine left Casa Loma. "I followed for a block or two," he said apologetically, "but there was no way I could keep up."

"These people are well-organized and ruthless," Mercedes told him. "Lonnie's lucky to be alive, and you saved the situation for me with your quick thinking. We have the toy. Now we're going to use it to get Ellie back." She spoke with more confidence than she felt, but Colm was right. They had to do as he'd suggested and hope things worked out. "Here's what I want you and Lonnie to do."

As they approached the massive, 19th-century brick building, Mercedes silenced her phone and stowed it in her jacket pocket, saying a silent prayer that Colm's perceptions were correct and the situation played out the way he figured it would.

The market was abuzz with activity and awash in smells. Farmers and vendors of amazing variety manned their stalls. There were several dozen meat stands, many run by Mennonites famous for their delicious sausages, fresh beef, and free-range chickens. Often the wives came too, wearing their starched white caps and presenting jams, jellies, breads, and candies. Fruits and vegetables of all kinds sat row upon row, as well as flowers, snack shops, soaps, and homeopathic healing products. Shoppers prowled the crowded aisles, lone women with mesh bags hanging from one arm, couples with strollers, and housewives peering judiciously at apples and pies. Mercedes tried to ignore the cacophony and concentrate on finding a familiar face in the blur of passing humanity.

From earlier visits, Mercedes knew the market had several levels and stretched in multiple directions. Along with the food section where they waited, there were areas for antique vendors and others who sold products from clothing to original artwork. She recalled that part of the market had once been the city jail, and the story was told that the cells often flooded, leaving inmates miserable and even in peril of drowning.

Colm and Mercedes entered the market building on Front Street and made their way to the second level. Here they could look down at the main room and locate Ellie and whoever escorted her as they arrived. Lonnie and Ike would make their entry farther down, to provide warning if the criminals entered at a different point than the one they'd agreed on.

"There." Colm pointed with his chin, and she looked to the doorway. Stopped inside it were four people, Eleanor, the dark-haired woman who'd accompanied Colm to the castle, one of

the men who'd abducted her in Scotland—Carl, she recalled—
and a second man who looked vaguely familiar.

"Is that Scylla?"

Colm nodded. People coming into the market jostled the
trio away from the doorway, and they moved to one side. Scylla
took out her phone and pressed a couple of buttons. Mercedes
was already taking her phone from her pocket when it rang.

"Where are you?" Scylla demanded.

"Look up. About twenty degrees to your right."

Scylla searched the second-floor balcony for a moment,
located them, and smiled as Mercedes held up the tote bag she
carried.

"You have it."

"Yes. But I'm not giving it up until I know Ellie is safely
away from you."

Scylla made a grimace of irritation. "Here's what we'll do.
Your friend will walk toward you while Colm brings the bag to
me. She should reach you about the time he gets here. I'll be
out the door a second later." Her tone hardened as she added,
"Just know this. Carl will be one step behind Miss Millwick. If
the bag doesn't have the toy with its contents intact, he will toss
her over the railing so fast your head will spin." She paused for
effect. "Hers will probably burst on contact with the floor."

That was a mental image Mercedes could have done
without, but tiny beeps coming from the vicinity of Colm's right
hand gave her confidence. Lonnie had given Colm his phone,
and the beeps indicated he was signaling Lonnie and Ike that
Scylla was here. They'd arrive any moment.

"All right. Let her go." With exaggerated slowness
Mercedes handed the tote to Colm, who took it with the same

deliberate speed. They had to give the two men time to get through the crowds and into position to rescue Ellie.

As he set the bag on his shoulder Colm muttered, "Oh-oh."

"What?"

He gestured with his head. "The man moving toward us in the ball cap is Rick, one of her creatures."

Mercedes looked to the left. Only a few booths away from them a man had stopped, apparently looking at merchandise. He was big and seemed to be all muscle. In a way that was both emotionless and challenging, he glanced at Colm and nodded once, encouraging him to do as ordered.

"Lonnie and Ike will be here any second," Colm said. "They'll see to your cousin. I'd best go ahead and do my part." He glanced again at the big man. "If he comes at you, scream as loud as you can and keep screaming." With that he turned left and started away.

As Colm moved toward the stairs, Mercedes looked down at Scylla and raised her chin. They were honoring their part of the bargain. With a scornful smile, Scylla made a gesture at Ellie, who glanced once at Mercedes before walking away. The way her shoulders settled once she was out of Scylla's reach was both heartening and frightening. Ellie thought she was safe, but was she? The man moving behind her indicated she was not.

The scene below unfolded like one of Colm's plays—except the stakes were life and death. Was it possible Scylla would take the toy and let them live? No. Once he was dead and unable to tell his side of the story, Colm would be blamed for all the crimes of the last week. Since she knew the truth, Mercedes was a threat and therefore a second intended victim.

Her gaze focused on a man behind Scylla. He no longer

wore touristy gear, but she realized it was Tim from Wisconsin. In a flash of anger Mercedes realized how Scylla had known where they were. And who had pushed her in front of a van in the rental car lot.

Seeing Tim made Scylla's plan clear in Mercedes' mind. Three men, three victims. As soon as Scylla got her hands on the bag and confirmed that the toy was inside, Carl would toss Ellie over the railing. That would get the attention of everyone in the market. At the same time, the big man would come at Mercedes and kill her quietly, perhaps with a knife. And Tim, whom Colm had never seen before, would do the same to Colm, plunge a knife between his ribs as Scylla hurried out the door with her prize. People in the market would rush to help the poor woman who'd fallen over the balcony rail. No one would see her and Colm die.

Things don't really slow down in a crisis. Mercedes knew that. But it seemed that the next few seconds took forever. Ellie reached the second floor and turned toward Mercedes, her expression a question. As Carl reached the top step, a slight figure pushed through the crowd, crouched low and moving fast. Lonnie collided with Carl while his back foot was off the floor, which meant his momentum carried both men in the same direction. They landed halfway down the steps, sending shoppers screaming, swearing, and stumbling against the railing on either side.

At almost the same time, a noise to her left caught Mercedes' attention. Ike was struggling with the big man, at least at first. Though they were matched in size, Ike's method of combat was methodical and efficient, and in seconds his opponent was dazed and bloody. Ike's grin seemed to say, *No contest.*

Temporarily reassured, Mercedes sought Colm on the main floor. He'd been handing Scylla the bag when Lonnie made his entrance, and they'd both turned to look. Scylla recovered first, grabbing the tote from Colm's shoulder. Tim stepped forward, and Mercedes shouted over the din, "Knife, Colm!"

How he heard she didn't know, but he jumped backward just in time to escape the swipe of the blade. Scylla didn't wait to see what would happen. Shouldering the bag, she disappeared through the exit doors.

Colm had no weapon and nothing to use for defense. All he could do was retreat as his opponent advanced. The crowd was focused either on Lonnie and Carl, who were picking themselves up on the stairs, or on Ike and his opponent, who'd pretty much run out of steam. No one seemed aware that Colm was fighting for his life behind their backs.

"Help him!" Mercedes shouted, pointing. It took several repetitions, but finally a few people turned to see what she was so excited about.

"Hey!" someone called. "Hey, you! Stop that!"

Though no one dared approach a man with a knife, Tim knew he could no longer quietly murder Colm and leave. After a second's pause, he turned and ran out the door. Colm tried to go after him, but people crowded around, asking if he was all right. He said something and gestured toward the door, but Mercedes knew it was too late. Scylla was long gone with the necklace, and Tim would disappear into the crowd on the street.

She was wrong. As Colm looked up to assure himself that she was okay, the door behind him opened and a uniformed policeman stepped in. "Is there someone here named Colm

Kennedy?"

Through the doorway Mercedes saw a small crowd of policemen outside. Four of them held Scylla and Tim by their arms. There was just time to see the furious expression on Scylla's face before the doors closed again.

On her way downstairs Mercedes collected her own little crowd. First Ike joined her, holding his defeated opponent's arm twisted behind his back in a position that looked painful. She and Ike joined Ellie, who stood at the top of the stairs with a slightly bewildered expression. Halfway down they met Lonnie, who held his captive with the help of two heavily tattooed young men. "I told these gents how this bloke stole the lady's purse," he said with a wink.

The crowds parted for them as they joined Colm and his police escort, which had grown to three. The senior officer regarded the two captives, one bloody and the other limping badly. "Can you explain this, Mr. Kennedy?"

"I can," Colm assured him, "but I warn you, it will take some time."

"All right then. Let's let the market get back to its business." Turning to his companions, the officer ordered, "Take these two into custody. Then come back in here and see if you can find someone who saw what went on." As they went to obey, he led the way outside.

Scylla was handcuffed, and a female officer held Mercedes' tote. "What have you done, Colm?" she said bitterly. "What have you done?"

"Called the police, love," he replied. "It's what honest people do when there are criminals about."

Colm told the story once, but the chief officer, whose name

was Driscoll, simply shook his head when he finished. "France, Scotland, museum artifacts. This is a cut or more above my level. I'll have to call someone." Running his tongue over his teeth he added, "I just wish I knew who to call."

As they waited for that to be sorted out, they stood in the car park, surrounded by police cars with lights flashing. Scylla sat in the back of one, looking like a storm cloud. Tim was in another, and though he tried to appear relaxed, Mercedes thought he looked worried. *And well you should be.*

The other two men had been taken away to have their injuries attended to, though neither was badly hurt. Ellie too, was taken to a hospital though she insisted she was perfectly fine. The Toronto PD would not have it said they delayed treatment to anyone, victim or perpetrator.

Lonnie regaled a female officer with the story of his takedown of the dazed and battered Carl. "When I saw him coming after poor Miss Millwick, I knew the only thing to stop him was a crunching rugby tackle. Do they know rugby here in Canada?" When the woman nodded he said, "That's good. In the States they like their American football, but it's nothing compared to rugby. Now that's a sport." He rubbed at his cheekbone, which had smashed against some bony part of his enemy when they hit the stairs together. "Lucky he broke my fall," Lonnie told the officer. "I might have a black eye out of it, though, do you think?"

Ike leaned against a police car, apparently at ease. Again Mercedes wondered about his background. He seemed at times outside the law, yet he didn't fear it. Perhaps when she knew him better, Ike would tell her where he learned to fight so well and why he'd left that life behind.

Driscoll approached, his manner slightly more cheerful.

"I'm to bring the two of you to Ontario Provincial Police headquarters. They'll decide who to call next when they've heard your story." He sounded relieved. "Do not move until I finish here." As he walked away, Driscoll said something to an officer who turned to face Colm and Mercedes, his posture clearly indicating he was on guard duty.

Driscoll went inside the market. It had started to rain, and the policewoman Lonnie had been talking to approached to hand Mercedes an umbrella. "This'll keep off the worst of it," she said. "We've got our hats."

"Thank you."

When she'd walked away Mercedes asked, "What did you tell the police when you called them?"

He recited like a schoolboy. "Due to threats some criminal types made, I had to steal a valuable piece of property from Casa Loma yesterday. They could get it back if they waited outside the market until an attractive woman with a Seneca College tote bag exited." Pushing the wayward lock of hair back from his eyes, he finished, "I must have done a good job selling it. They seem to have been watching every possible exit."

A woman with short blond hair and large black-framed glasses approached the cop who was watching them, a city map in hand. She looked familiar, and Mercedes watched as she asked for directions. In a typical demonstration of Canadian politeness, the man began pointing and explaining. The woman listened closely, but her glance darted briefly to Mercedes and Colm. Dark hair, feline eyes. Who had she seen recently with that same face?

The woman the police had just arrested. How had she gotten away?

Something jabbed into her back, and a voice behind her

said, "Mr. Kennedy, Miss Maxwell, come with me and don't make a fuss. Hurry now, before the officer takes his eyes off my beautiful Carrie."

Colm quickly took in the situation. "You don't need Mercedes. Take me."

"Do what I said. Go past that van and head for the blue car down the row." The man's voice was scratchy and low, and Mercedes got the sense he was used to being obeyed. Colm touched her arm to signal they'd comply, and they went in the direction indicated.

The van shielded them from the cops' view. On the other side was a blue sedan with one back door already open. "Get in," the man ordered. "Kennedy first. If you try anything, I shoot her then you."

Mercedes had very little time to think, but she knew two things: They wouldn't live very long if they let this man take them anywhere, and Colm was at a disadvantage because of the threat to her. She was the one who had to make the first move. Once she did, Colm would act.

In a sudden motion, she swung the umbrella she carried like a golf club. It slapped against the gun, turning it aside. An explosive sound, too close, hurt her ears and made her cringe, but Colm reacted quickly, turning to grab the man's arm. They struggled briefly, but Colm was younger and stronger. He smashed the man's hand against the car until the gun fell to the ground and slid under the van, making a skittering sound. The man punched at Colm, but he ducked, returning a better blow that knocked his opponent backward.

A noise at her right made Mercedes turn, and she saw that the woman had followed them, seen the situation, and bent to reach under the van for the gun. The umbrella she'd used as a weapon was bent and broken, but the handle was intact. Turning it sideways, she used it this time like a softball bat, catching Carrie on her cheekbone. Her head hit the van door, and she fell to the wet pavement.

Now using the battered umbrella as a rake, Mercedes retrieved the gun and ordered, "Stop right now, or I'll shoot you."

Colm's attacker obeyed, and Colm set his hands on his thighs, panting with exertion. "Nice job, Mercedes."

Carrie picked herself up from the ground, her expression dazed, her clothes soaked and grimy. She opened her mouth to say something, but a police officer appeared. "What's going on here?"

Colm grinned. "I think my girlfriend just helped you get a commendation."

Chapter Twenty-seven

There was quite a gathering at the OPP station a few hours later. Mercedes lost track of the officials she was introduced to. Some were law enforcement, and she heard references to Interpol, British, and Canadian police. Others were antiquities experts, hurriedly recruited to give opinions on how to go about dealing with the toy sailor. There was a representative from the Casa Loma board of directors, who seemed confused at the demand for his presence.

There was some speechifying, which was to be expected with such a diverse and politically correct group. Like the monks who once argued how many angels could dance on the head of a pin, they dealt for some time in theories. "If the necklace exists—" "If the piece is inside the toy—"

Finally, when Mercedes wanted to scream it out, someone suggested that the only way to learn the answer was to look. "Since it isn't a particularly valuable piece," a studious-looking young woman said meekly, "there's no harm in opening up the base and looking inside, is there?"

Mercedes had to put her hands behind her back as one of the museum representatives took out a pen knife and began prying at the wooden base of the toy. It took some time, but no one in the room spoke or moved as he worked. The varnish was thick, and he had to slice through it all the way around before he could work at removing the panel at the side. When it finally fell away, a muted sigh went around the room. Tilting the toy, the man put his hand at the opening, and a cloth bag slid into his palm.

A second man, apparently of higher rank than the first, took the bag from his coworker and opened it. He peered inside, grinned up at the little crowd, and emptied the bag into his hand.

The necklace was magnificent, overflowing the hand that held it and catching every ray of light that touched it. Now the sigh was much bigger.

In a gesture worthy of such a prize, the meek woman whipped off her neck scarf and laid it out on the desktop. Reverently the man laid the necklace atop it, arranging it to reveal its glory.

After a moment the ranking police officer said, "Mr. Kennedy, Ms. Maxwell, can you tell us the story of how you came upon this amazing find?"

***

TORONTO

The next few days were busy ones. Mercedes was much in demand for newspaper interviews, but this time she refused them all. "Talk to Colm Kennedy," she told reporters. "He knows all of it." Legal investigations had begun to determine who owned the necklace, Casa Loma or the French government. That would take some time. Colm had received several offers from ghost writers to tell the history-changing story of Lewis MacPherson, rightful heir to the French throne.

"They ain't got a king these days," Lonnie said, "It don't change anything."

"It probably wouldn't have changed things if he'd revealed himself then either," Colm said. "The French had had enough of governmental shifts."

"I wonder why Dickens never revealed what he knew," Mercedes mused. "He must have known who Lewis was, or he wouldn't have saved the papers."

"Maybe they made some sort of deal."

"Like 'Don't tell until after I'm dead?'"

"Something like that."

"But Lewis would have died long before Dickens did."

Colm shrugged, at a loss for an answer. "Maybe Dickens never got notice of Lewis' death. Or perhaps he didn't feel there was enough evidence to prove Lewis' true identity. I guess we'll never know."

"He used bits of it in his books. Remember the woman frozen in time, the one whose home and clothing never changed...?" She stopped, unsure of the character's name.

"Miss Havisham. She was in *Great Expectations*," Colm supplied. "And in *A Tale of Two Cities*, Sydney Carton makes the ultimate sacrifice, going to the guillotine in place of another."

"'It is a far, far better thing I do...'" Mercedes quoted. "More than most of us would do, die for another."

"You came pretty close on my behalf," Colm responded.

"As you've done for me. I guess it's circumstances that make heroes."

Colm chuckled. "Let's avoid those circumstances in future when possible, Miss Maxwell."

"Right-o, Mr. Kennedy. "Right-o."

***

Toronto

Colm's agent sent his passport to Toronto so his presence in Canada became legal. Once matters were settled, Lonnie and Ike returned to Birmingham after securing a promise from Mercedes that she'd come for a real visit soon. "We'll show you the town," Lonnie promised.

"I'll see that he gets a proper phone," Ike promised, "so you'll be able to let him know when you're coming."

Ellie announced that after a brief stop at home she intended to fly back to England. "David needs help getting around, and I'm free to assist for as long as he needs me," she said, her cheeks turning pink.

Recalling Mrs. Peterson's yen for retirement, Mercedes wished her well. "I'm that pleased the two of you get along."

Ellie looked at her in surprise. "Why wouldn't we? We have almost everything in common."

When they'd taken everyone to the proper airport gate and waved their farewells, Colm put an arm around Mercedes' shoulders. "This wasn't quite the way I'd planned to come to America, but it's worked out well."

"It has." She touched his face. "I was so scared when you disappeared."

Typically, he minimized his trials with an airy gesture. "I tried to drop breadcrumbs along the path."

"Mentioning my job and your love of oatmeal."

"And the arrangement of the figurines at poor Charlie's shop. I didn't have long to do it and had to use the tools at hand."

"I'd have missed it entirely, but Ellie noticed."

"She's a great girl, your cousin. Just the match for our friend David."

"I'd never have imagined it, but I believe they have a future together."

Colm's arm dropped to her waist, and he pulled her close. "And now that there's just you and me here in the romantic, cosmopolitan city of Toronto. Mercedes Maxwell, it's time to talk about our future."

****

Dear Reader:

If you enjoyed this book, please consider placing a review somewhere others will see it. Authors rely on word of mouth to spread the news of a new book or series, and no one does that better than happy readers!

Thank you for supporting what we writers love to do!

Peg

Have you read *Shakespeare's Blood?*

Mercedes' first British adventure begins when she agrees to accompany her neighbor on a tour of England and Scotland. She's puzzled when she comes into possession of an old book that claims to have to do with William Shakespeare. When bad things start happening, Mercedes figures out she must solve the book's secrets in order to stay alive. And though there are people who offer to help, who can be trusted with new corpses appearing almost daily?

Other books by Peg Herring

The Simon & Elizabeth Mysteries (Tudor Era Historical)
Her Highness' First Murder
Poison, Your Grace
The Lady Flirts with Death
Her Majesty's Mischief

***

The Loser Mysteries (Contemporary Mystery/Suspense)
Killing Silence
Killing Memories
Killing Despair

***

Clan Macbeth Historical Romance (medieval Scotland)
Macbeth's Niece
Double Toil & Trouble

***

Standalone Mysteries
Somebody Doesn't Like Sarah Leigh (contemporary cozy mystery)
Her Ex-GI P.I. ('60s-era traditional mystery)
Not Dead Yet... ('60s-era paranormal mystery)

***

Writing as Maggie Pill
The Sleuth Sisters Mysteries (cozy Michigan)

If you like lighter mysteries, and if you have sisters, had sisters, or know a little about sisters, you'll love Maggie's series.

The Sleuth Sisters
3 Sleuths, 2 Dogs, 1 Murder
Murder in the Boonies
Sleuthing at Sweet Springs
Eat, Drink, & —Be Wary
Peril, Plots, and Puppies